£2.50

D0335306

A VICAR'S DIARY

A Vicar's Diary

DAVID WILBOURNE

HarperCollins*Publishers*

HarperCollins*Religious*

Part of HarperCollins*Publishers*

77-85 Fulham Palace Road, London w6 8jb

First published in Great Britain in 1998 by HarperCollins*Religious*

1 3 5 7 9 10 8 6 4 2

A catalogue record for this book
is available from the British Library

ISBN 000 628044 7

Printed and bound in Great Britain by
Caledonian International Book Manufacturing Ltd, Glasgow

For Geoffrey Owen Wilbourne
'…unto me a father and a priest.'

ACKNOWLEDGEMENTS

I am grateful to my wife, Rachel, for so painstakingly editing and proof reading the text, to the Archbishop of York for encouraging the venture, to Anne Broadbent and Lynda Sykes who ever patiently offered good advice about word processing, and last but by no means least to the oft-criticized parish priests of the Church of England, whose praises more than deserve to be sung.

PART ONE

✜✜✜✜✜✜✜✜✜✜✜✜✜✜

CHAPTER ONE

The ruddy-faced farmer scratched his head. 'That's go-in' to take some shift-in'!' he pronounced. I was grateful to him for such insight. The two of us stood in a downpour, gazing at a removal van whose rear wheels had sunk to the axle on the lawn of my new home. The lush green grass, sodden from days of relentless rain, was not only wet but also liberally peppered with black specks.

'I see you've been usin' a bit o' coal to gi' wheels some purchase,' he continued. Clearly stating the obvious was this man's trademark, coupled with a ponderous habit of pronouncing every syllable as if it were a word. 'It 'asn't done much good though, 'as it, oth-er than spray it all over t' show?'

I reluctantly agreed with him. Three quarters of the precious contents of my coal shed had got us precisely nowhere; the van, revving loudly, had merely rocked in its ever-deepening tracks, causing me and the two removal men watching to dive for cover as coal flew in all directions. For weeks afterwards I would engage in open-cast mining to try and recover the fuel loss. Looking back to that day after 30 years I can smile; but way back on 28 September 1965 tears loomed very large indeed.

'What I'll do is fetch trac-tor and chain and 'ook it to van's front end. We'll soon 'ave it owt.' Any slowness of speech in my new neighbour was balanced by quickness in action, for within minutes he was back. Cheerfully humming above the engine's roar, he seemed oblivious to the rain which ran relentlessly over his bald head. Whilst his bulky frame seemed disproportionate to the tiny uncabbed tractor on which he awkwardly perched, there was no trace of self-consciousness; rather he was as gleeful as a well-built junior school child sheepishly riding a tiny toddler's trike.

Even so, he was to have his work cut out for him. Having hooked up the chains from the tractor to the removal van, he took up the strain. The engines blasted out at full throttle, exhaust pothering everywhere as, painstakingly slowly, the van inched out of its rut. Mud was scattered along with coal making the landscape look like a pattern concocted by one of those Spirograph toys which had recently taken the market by storm.

However, no sooner had the lorry been hauled out onto drier land than a Morris Minor van splashed up the drive, nosed round it and pulled onto the lawn, stopping in the very spot which we had just cleared. The crunch of the handbrake was accompanied by a loud squelch as the van immediately sank to its axles. Its owner, whom I assumed from the sign writing on the van's side was Ernest Harcourt (Butcher of Distinction), sprang out and treated us to some very undistinguished language. 'Why the hell didn't you stop me parking in this mire?' he complained loudly. 'I've just about had it up to here with this weather.'

'Now then, Ernest, don't take on. There's nowt we can do a-bout it. Per-haps if you had-n't shot up vic-ar-age drive as if you were Don-ald Camp-bell on Con-is-ton Wat-er, you'd 'ave seen it were a bit damp on t' lawn. What are you do-in' up 'ere, any 'ow?'

'I've come to introduce myself to the new vicar before any of the others get to him. Has he arrived yet?'

I felt it was time to show my hand. I was hesitant because, even though I had been a clergyman for four years now, I was still a touch shy about declaring myself. Not that I was ashamed of being a priest. It's just that once people knew, they put on a bit of an act and tried to shield me from reality. And I can't stand that. I gulped and eventually managed to stutter, 'Er, I'm the n–n–new vicar; how can I help you?'

I would have thought it impossible to blush in such torrential rain, but Mr Harcourt proved me wrong, turning a deep shade of crimson. 'Oh I'm so sorry, your Reverence. I didn't realize it was you, or I would have watched my language. You looked so normal, I thought you were one of the removal men.'

His comment simultaneously pleased me and touched a nerve, in that, as a student, I had had a great time working at Martins' Bank in my vacations, enjoying particularly the banter with the staff and the larger-than-life customers. When I let it out of the bag that I was thinking of the Church as a career, my work-mates, when they had stopped laughing, had protested, 'But you can't possibly be a vicar. You're too normal!'

So I wasn't sure whether to thank the butcher for his compliment or to ask how abnormal he expected a clergyman to look. I decided the best course of action was to treat him to one of my silences. The quiet didn't reign for very long, as Mr Harcourt, ever the businessman, pressed home his advantage. 'I wondered if you'd like to buy a bit of meat for your tea? I've got some tasty steak at the back of the van…'

'Are you the butcher who used to deliver regularly to the last vicar?' I asked, somewhat puzzled.

'Oh yes, sir, yes, sir. He always put in a very good order, sir,' he assured me, with a servility which could only grate.

'It's just that I'm sure he mentioned a different name…' Mr Harcourt avoided eye-contact, gazing at his feet, and said nothing. This time I broke the silence. 'Never mind, I'll have half a pound of thick pork sausage for now.' I was determined to resist the steak: curling at the edges, its fat a deep shade of yellow, it had clearly seen better days.

Even then, I ended up with 15 ounces of sausage. 'A good half pound, sir,' Mr Harcourt commented, as if it was him and not me being generous. I could see I would have to watch him if I was going to make ends meet. My salary might have gone up from £400, as assistant curate, to the dizzy heights of £1000 on becoming a vicar, but even then, there was a limit to the number of good half pounds I could afford. Bill Everingham, my farmer neighbour, deepened my suspicions once he had towed the butcher off my lawn and we had seen him drive off in a cloud of spray: 'He's a sly one that Har-court, with-out a doubt. You'd bet-ter watch 'im.'

Never has a prophecy been more quickly fulfilled, because within seconds another van sped up the drive, neatly circum-navigated the parked lorry and plopped into what was now more resembling a water hole than a lawn. On the side of the van was inscribed 'L.C. Hinchcliffe, Butcher of Distinction'.

'That's the name the last vicar recommended to me!' I remarked to Bill, who calmly hooked his tractor to yet another stranded vehicle. So as not to disappoint the good Mr Hinch-cliffe whose praises had been sung by my predecessor, I bought a lamb chop to accompany his rival's sausages. The fact that he was a far more gracious man, neither given to swearing, syco-phancy nor shock at my 'normality', made me resolve that he should be the butcher by appointment to the Vicar. Mr Har-court would be summarily dispatched when he returned for his Friday morning's order.

Harcourt wasn't the only one that day to try it on. Even the affable Bill Everingham's nature seemed to be wearing thin by the end of an afternoon which saw a total of 14 vans opt for the watersplash and tractor-recovery experience. Had I been as gullible as their drivers hoped, I would have concluded that my predecessor was a very well-fed man indeed. For apparently he had not only been fed by butchers Harcourt and Hinchcliffe, but also by three grocers, two fishmen, four breadmen and two milkmen, all of whom assured me with the utmost sincerity, 'Oh yes, sir, the last vicar always placed a regular order with me.' As I learned later, they were somewhat economical with the truth, in that they all had delivered to the vicarage at one time or another, be it the last vicar but one, two or three. Why the culinary excess of all Kirkwith's previous incumbents should have been visited that day upon me, and upon Bill who had to tow them out, seemed bizarre.

The day was bad enough without the tradesmen's intrusion, with the incessant rain soaking carpets and staining furniture. Once the removal men had abandoned me, I sat in my kitchen alone, savouring my chop and sausages to fortify me against the damp chill. Only last night I had been sitting in my cosy flat in East Hull, in the midst of a community which hummed with life, with shops galore just around the corner. Now, a mere 24 hours later, just little old me was rattling around in a sprawling Georgian vicarage, originally built 130 years ago to house a vicar, his wife and dozen children, with half a dozen servants to boot. Even if the rain stopped teeming down and I could peer out, there would hardly be a neighbour to be seen in this rural wilderness. What on earth had possessed me to move here?

I thought of Saint Teresa of Avila, who had travelled through Spain in all weathers on God's business. During one fierce storm her horse threw her into a muddy ditch. As she scrambled out filthy, bruised and at her lowest ebb, she heard a voice from heaven: 'Don't worry, Teresa, this is how I treat my friends.'

'Then I'm not at all surprised, Lord, that you have so few!' Teresa replied, icily. As I shivered in my new home, doors left off their hinges by the decorators, fires unlit because their coal was scattered on my lawn, she had my every sympathy.

One feature of my new home was that its roof had the widest eaves I had ever seen. Bill Everingham, when he wasn't dragging sundry vehicles out of the mud, had waxed lyrical about them. 'Ee, Vic-ar, with an ov-er-hang like that you could teth-er your 'orse by t' front door on a rain-y night and it could sleep and still be dry by t' dawn.' I achieved neither that night, first of all kept awake by the heavy rain drumming on the aforementioned eaves by my bedroom window. When 3am came and I still hadn't slept a wink, my enthusiasm for this architectural novelty was considerably less than Bill's.

Eventually I managed to doze off, only to have my fitful sleep disturbed by a drop of cold water falling onto my head. I convinced myself I had imagined it, and was just drifting off again when another drop hit me straight between the eyes. I jerked awake, staggered out of bed and gingerly felt around the walls for the light switch. I circumnavigated the unfamiliar room three times before my quest was successful, by which time my shins had bruises upon bruises as I bumped into countless packing cases and pieces of furniture, cunningly placed by removal men who clearly had missed their vocation. They should have been obstacle course designers or hurdle-race stewards.

I hobbled back to bed and wrung out my pillow, which was absolutely saturated with dirty water, steadily dripping from the ceiling above my head-board. I shoved my bed to a drier spot, colliding with more strategically placed packing cases and furniture en route. I then padded barefoot down chilly uncarpeted stairs and an even chillier stone-flagged corridor in search of a bucket and a cushion to act as substitute pillow.

At this point my luck changed. Though my search in the living room for a cushion proved elusive, I did discover an aluminium bucket, which the removal men had usefully placed behind the sofa. Even though my brain was sleepy, it had been saturated with enough detective novels to rise to the occasion when presented with an intriguing clue. Miss Marple's eyes narrowed as she announced to the baffled sleuths from Scotland Yard, 'Gentlemen, if the bucket was found in the living room, then the only logical place for the cushions is the washroom sink.' Which was where I was delighted to find them stacked up and, though slightly damp, certainly drier than my pillow. So armed with cushions and bucket I returned thankfully to bed and slept soundly for what remained of the night.

I awoke at 9am to an utter and total silence which I had never previously experienced. It so stunned me that it was several minutes before I placed where I was, with my mind rapidly running a search through my life so far. 'No, you're not in your boyhood home in Thirsk; you'd be hearing the traffic and the hustle and bustle of the market traders by now. Nor are you in Cambridge; bedders and bells were never as quiet as this. Nor are you in Hull; a Hull without gossiping fishwives and ships' hooters and the smell of rotting fish is a contradiction in terms. David, where the hell are you?'

Eventually my brain caught up with itself. 'You're in Kirkwith,' a voice, more reassuring than the first, declared. 'You're the new vicar. You're in charge. You have total responsibility. You're an assistant no longer…'

'Aargh,' I wanted to scream. Instead I steeled myself and had breakfast, with milk galore and a choice of three cereals supplied by yesterday's wave of tradesmen. Since the rain had stopped and the sun was breaking through the cloud, I ventured out into my new domain. Kirkwith was one of the three small villages of which I was to be vicar; that the other two were named Beckwith and Eastwith meant that the whole group were known locally as the Withs, a name which gave a disarming softness to the harsh Yorkshire dialect prevalent in these parts. All three lay to the east of the Derwent, a river which rises in the North York Moors near Scarborough, heads for the sea there but then changes her mind, preferring to bisect Yorkshire by wending her sleepy way for some 50 miles until she reaches the Humber. Only then does she deign to flow into a North Sea which she so resolutely avoided in her infancy.

Weeks of rain meant that the Derwent had burst her banks so that her course was hidden by the Ings, the local name for the lakes formed by the flood water. The graveyard walls of Kirkwith's church, the most easterly point in the village, looked to all intents and purposes like a sea wall as the Ings' water lapped against them.

The sight stopped me in my tracks that first morning: a golden sheet of water reflecting the autumn sun's rays, stretching for miles and miles across the flat Vale of York; geese flying in perfect formation overhead with a call so haunting it wrung my

9

heart; and when the calling stopped, the beating of wings on the still air seemed to mark time for the very world itself. It seemed a good place for a church, teeming as it was with innate holiness.

Not that I was that keen on churches. Inevitably overdosed on them as a vicar's son, I had developed an equally inevitable allergy in my later teenage years, avoiding visiting churches whenever possible. The allergy was now wearing off; thankfully. For whilst the majority of the population might never darken the Church's door, a church-shy vicar would have been quite a novelty. But occasionally the aversion re-emerged and stopped me short, like a former migraine sufferer thinking twice before partaking of the chocolate, cheese or red wine that no longer held any terrors, but had done once.

I felt no such aversion for Kirkwith's church, which attracted me from the outset. The building was early Norman with delightful round dog-tooth arches, pillars askew as their foundations ebbed and flowed with the tide. It was matched well with a squat Tudor tower, defaced with the usual Cyrils and Ednas and Harrys and Elsies, sweethearts and naughty boys of successive generations who had striven to immortalize themselves by engraving the soft limestone.

One piece of graffiti stood out from all the rest. For a start it was written in Latin; not many hooligans in my experience are classical scholars. And the message wasn't the usual obscenity or declaration of undying love, but simply read 'Christopher, son of Robert, pray remember 1536'. As I stood gazing at this a voice startled me:

'Have you come to do some rubbing?'

I swung round to see a little man, black hair greased down by haircream, black moustache waxed to perfection, dressed in black complete with a black gown; he gave me the blackest of looks and seemed to be puffed up with his own importance. Like the Virgin Mary confronted by the angel Gabriel, I wondered what his greeting could possibly mean. I was none the wiser as he gabbled on:

'It's half a crown payable to me for one brass, four shillings for both. And if you get any wax on the brass or stone, you clean it off before you go or you'll have me to answer to.'

I decided that for the second time in 24 hours I wasn't getting the best out of someone and ought to declare myself: 'I'm terribly sorry, but I haven't got the first idea of what you're talking about. I haven't come to do any rubbing, whatever that might mean. I'm the new vicar and I'm simply having a nose around on my first day here.'

Immediately his countenance changed. The black look was suddenly banished and replaced with a beaming smile, a veritable sun breaking through a leaden, gloomy sky. His shoulders relaxed, dissipating the pomp, instantly transforming a formidable foe into a familiar friend.

'Ee, I'm glad to see you. I'm Sam Harsley, and I've been verger here for the last 37 years. Bill Everingham called to see me and me missus last night and said you'd had a right time moving in with all that rain. And believe you me, we've had a right time these last five months without a vicar. Week in week out we never knew who'd be coming to take Morning Prayer. We seem to have had a never-ending stream of retired clergy tottering about, spouting forth on this subject and that subject, sermons going on and on; more Sundays than not my joint was burnt to a cinder before we'd got rid of them. One week the Bishop came and we thought he'd be a breath of fresh air, but he was just as bad as the rest of them with his 'My dear people, let me tell you this,' and 'My dear people, let me tell you that.'

'Really,' I commented, with as much impartiality as I could muster.

'Do you know, that old Mr Simons came from Howden to do a funeral and didn't seem to know one end of the Prayer Book from another. At the graveside he started up with "Dearly beloved brethren, we are gathered here in the sight of God and in the face of this congregation to join together..." I was standing beside him and gave him a sharp dig in the ribs. Perhaps a bit too sharp, since it knocked the prayer book out of his hand. At least it didn't fall into the grave, though. I picked it up for him, found the proper place and he continued as if nothing had gone wrong, "Man that is born of woman hath but a short time to live and is full of misery..." '

As he continued intoning the funeral rite, I feared that if I didn't put a stop to this garrulous little man, ironically so critical of garrulous clergy, then the whole of my first morning here would indeed be full of misery. Like all clergy, I was adept at interrupting people who talked too much, although often I only succeeded in diverting them to another subject rather than stopping them altogether.

'Who's this Christopher, son of Robert, then? And what did he do in 1536 that he needs reminding of?'

The verger halted his funeral recital, took a breath and then launched into the whole complicated story. 'Ee, that'll be Christopher Newt, and Robert, his dad,' began Mr Harsley, speaking with a familiarity as if he had gone to school with them rather than their being dead and buried four centuries ago. 'To cut a long story short, Vicar...' I looked behind me to see who he was addressing and then realized I was the Vicar. I can never quite exorcise a sense of bogusness.

I resumed listening to Mr Harsley. '...in an uprisin' against 'Enry VIII's closin' of the monasteries, the elder squire's son had betrayed the younger, who 'Enry then hanged for treason. Christopher, the elder son, then had qualms. Terrible qualms he had. He felt so sorry for what he had done that he built this tower to try and make amends. It couldn't bring his brother back from the dead, though. And a terrible death it was too, 'anging from Micklegate Bar, with the birds pecking out his innards.' The way the verger told the story made it sound like a gory cross between the Parable of the Prodigal Son and Rolf Harris' 'Two Little Boys'.

As I looked at the crumbling limestone, which would soon need very expensive repair, my mind wandered. It's a fact of life that brothers invariably fall out. I could only be grateful that they didn't all follow Christopher, son of Robert's example in trying to expiate their guilt. Otherwise the number of decaying towers would be greater than the stars in the sky and the Church of England would be crippled trying to maintain them.

And the 'rubbing' which Sam had been so fierce about? Inlaid into the floor of the church's sanctuary were two brass figures of a knight and his lady. Apparently, 'brass rubbings' were all the fashion, with countless devotees trekking to the isolated spot, armed with wax crayons and rolls of paper on which they would take away the knight's imprint. Despite Sam's ministry of 'welcome', they still came in their hordes.

Their kneeling beside the altar for a good hour, scribbling away to produce their own chic decor to show off in living rooms or student pads, struck Sam as supremely poignant. 'Just think, Vicar...' This time I avoided looking over my shoulder. '...in this very same spot as the rubbers kneel, their ancestors knelt. They were probably blind to t' brass and focused on God. This lot are blind to God and focus on t' brass!' As I thought of Christopher, son of Robert, kneeling here whilst plotting his treachery, I was less sure than Sam about the piety of previous generations. Even so, with a few down-to-earth words he had made a good point. Was I wasting my time, trying to get through to this generation, who thought more of its brass than it did of its God?

CHAPTER TWO

Dong; dong; dong; dong: crash! A large lump of plaster fell from the belfry ceiling, fortunately missed me, but hit the Archdeacon a glancing blow on the shoulder. As it did so the whole piece of masonry disintegrated into a cloud of white dust which hid him from our sight. After much coughing and spluttering he re-emerged, with no perceivable ill effects other than that his hair, originally as jet-black as our verger's, had instantly turned snow-white. To judge by the white flakes which suddenly appeared on the shoulders of his black cassock the dramatic change in hair colour was also accompanied by a severe bout of dandruff.

The Archdeacon gave me the sort of withering look which confirmed that I was not exactly impressing my superior. He and the Bishop of Pocklington had turned out on a dark, wet, uninviting October night to install me as Kirkwith's new vicar.

From the start, things had gone wrong. Kirkwith was literally the end of the road, in that the metalled lane gave up a good half mile from the church, which then could only be reached by a muddy farm track. The Archdeacon had bravely, if unwisely, decided to drive over this; the locals, who knew better (as locals are wont), always walked. 'I met him at t' gate to field and told him he'd never get through,' Sam Harsley confided to me later. 'But he'd have none of it. "Open the gate, my good man," he bellowed. "If I could get a tank across the Sahara in the war, getting this car through that field will be child's play." '

The Archdeacon clearly was in a mood which brooked no discussion, so Sam meekly let him through and witnessed the spectacle that followed. 'Ee Vicar, it was a right comical sight. At first he chugged along at a snail's pace, bumping up and down as if he were on safari. But then he startled a cow which was grazing by t' track's side. She stood up to him and kicked at his car door with her hind leg, actually perforatin' t' door's skin. Served him right for taking no notice o' me.'

Sam obviously relished the whole episode. 'And that wasn't the end of it,' he went on, with a gleam in his eye. 'T' Archdeacon pulled up sharp and leapt out to survey t' damage. There was a sickly squelch. His shiny black shoes sank into t' fresh cow sh–' he suddenly remembered himself, '...fresh cow dung that t' frightened animal had left behind, prior to stampeding to t' far side of t' field.'

All this went to explain why when the Archdeacon had staggered through the church door, his temper was as foul as his scent. The cordial greeting of the person giving out the books, 'Good evening, sir, nice weather for ducks!' was met with a curt 'Hmph!' Could this be the same Archdeacon who had written the best-selling *Good Practice for the Pastoral Parson*, containing the immortal advice, 'However hard-pressed you feel, it costs nothing to be civil with those who are oblivious of your troubles'? I suppose his ripe odour meant that those who encountered him weren't oblivious of his troubles for very long.

He certainly didn't allow me to be oblivious of them, giving me a stern lecture in the vestry before the start of the service. The fact that I was highly nervous about what lay ahead that night and beyond, saved me from bursting out laughing as he gave an expurgated account of a heifer using his car door for hoof-target practice. He wagged a stern finger at me: 'What you need here, Wilbourne, is a proper road to the church, with a sturdy fence to stop any wretched cow doing what it did to my car tonight. Otherwise you'll get nobody coming to church and you'll fail before you begin.'

'Oh, I'm so sorry, Archdeacon. I only moved in a couple of days ago, so I haven't quite got round to road-building yet, what with one or two other things on, like repairing leaking roofs and drying out sodden furniture.' His judgemental and insensitive stance had brought out my sarcastic streak.

But my protest fell on deaf ears, simply encouraging a tirade on how wonderful he had been when he first began in a parish. 'Let me tell you,' he hectored, 'On my very first day as a vicar, I swept clean each of my four churches, visited all the church officers, set in motion a new parish magazine and revamped the Sunday school.'

'And I bet you did all that before breakfast?' I interrupted, trying to diffuse his pomp and make him laugh at himself.

All to no avail, although at last the penny dropped and he realized I was being sarcastic. 'Let me tell you, facetiousness in junior clergy will not be tolerated,' he barked, prodding my chest with his finger to drive the point home. The Archdeacon had been a headmaster prior to being ordained; I had the sneaking suspicion that he had carried over just a few traits from his previous career. I could only be grateful that he did not have a cane to hand.

The service duly began. The harmonium wheezed out the first hymn, the Archdeacon walked down the aisle scowling, providing a ripe smell to match well the rural setting. The Bishop of Pocklington was led in by the ever-black Sam Harsley, who walked with a rolling gait, beaming with pride because he had a bishop to pilot into port. You would never guess, from the effusive deference as he bowed the Bishop into his throne, that this was the same person who only yesterday had so vociferously criticized the prelate's preaching. Not that his criticism was without cause. After 20 minutes of 'Good people of Kirkwith, this' and 'Good people of Kirkwith, that,' my eyelids began to droop.

Parishioners from my former haunt in East Hull, who had organized a coach trip for the occasion, shuffled in their pews nonplussed. One of them had stern words with me at the supper which followed: 'David lad, you've let us down. I've timed every sermon you've ever preached and you've never gone over eight minutes. You never warned us that bishops would preach three times that long, and still be spouting on.'

'Well, Mavis,' I quipped. 'Perhaps he's never come across my adage about preaching, "If you don't strike oil in 10 minutes, stop boring!" '

The home team from the Withs had clearly encountered the bishop before and sat staring straight ahead of them like zombies. Bill Everingham, as Kirkwith's august churchwarden, held pride of place on the front pew. He had traded his farm clothes for a suit, very smart but several sizes too small for him, so that he looked ready to burst out of it in several places. Unfortunately he had not quite mastered the very Anglican habit of sleeping with his eyes open; not only were they tightly shut, but his snores became increasingly loud and began to draw the attention of the whole congregation, eager for a diversion after 20-odd minutes of episcopal rambling. A sharp and all too obvious nudge in his ribs from his wife meant he awoke with a loud snort, disappointed to find, no doubt, that the bishop was still in the pulpit and that he hadn't slept through the sermon in its entirety.

Entirety was actually 30 gruelling minutes. This was followed by the legal ceremony to make me vicar, normally pretty routine stuff, but exciting in the extreme compared to the tedium which had preceded it. The fragrant Archdeacon led me by the hand (I resisted the temptation to ask 'Shall we dance?') to various parts of the church which signalled aspects of my new ministry. The symbolism was pretty obvious stuff. The pulpit: preaching God's word; the altar: feeding God's people, and so on. As the impatient Archdeacon dragged me along, I felt a bit like a dog marking his territory: I wanted to pause and take it all in, but my master yanked me on, eager to complete the circuit as quickly as possible. At least I didn't cock my leg at the lectern.

We came unstuck when the service instructions directed us to the font. I hadn't got a clue where the font was, neither had the Archdeacon, so we trotted around the church looking in this corner, that aisle, this porch, that apse, playing a rather novel game of hide and seek. I only hoped the congregation thought it was all part of the ceremony, although as we repeated laps with increasing speed I caught a few eyes twinkling with amusement. As a last resort we peeped behind the curtain screening the tower and found the font lurking there, big enough to bath a sizeable baby in. The appropriate prayer was said by the relieved Archdeacon, at which point we moved on to the bells and further disaster.

Traditionally the number of times you ring your new church bell equals the number of years you intend staying: I resolved to ring a dozen times at the very least until the falling ceiling and whitened Archdeacon brought me to a halt at four. I suppose Christopher, son of Robert, wasn't going to let us easily forget him.

What with dung-splattered roads, flippancy, missing fonts and collapsing towers the Archdeacon wasn't easily going to forget me either. Somewhat unnerved, I went to the bunfight at Kirkwith Hall and made a feeble speech thanking people for their welcome, including a feeble joke about how with so much water around one of tonight's hymns should have been the sailors' traditional hymn, 'Eternal Father, strong to save, whose arm hath bound the restless wave', which raised a feeble laugh. The Archdeacon glowered throughout.

I could only hope that appearances were deceptive. I recalled the story of Edward King, the saintly bishop of Lincoln, inviting a very nervous young man to breakfast to discuss the possibility of ordination. Around the table were several other rather pious and precious looking men who had just completed their training and were about to be ordained. Sensing that his visitor would be intimidated by their holy silence, King leant across and whispered, 'Don't worry, we ain't as good as we look!' I could only hope the Archdeacon wasn't as bad as he looked that fateful night.

As I waved off my fan club from East Hull, I felt as if my umbilical cord had been cut all over again. In many ways it was like saying good-bye to the mum that had nurtured me as a priest. Certainly Hull's society could be thought of as a mother, inevitably matriarchal due to men simply not being around. Even the metalwork smacked of maternity, with countless derricks on the horizon, arching protectively over their cargo on the Humber. I didn't think I would miss that cloying atmosphere.

Nor would I miss the ever-present smell of stale fish, and the sprawling corporation housing estates with children interminably singing, 'When lamps are lighted in town the boats sail out to sea', which belied a dark reality where absent fathers trawled icy waters. But I would miss the camaraderie, the people who initially had been resistant to friendship but had then proved to have hearts of gold. All that I was abandoning, and for what? Still latched onto a childbirth theme, I remembered a quip from my college tutor, 'A new born baby invariably cries because of the sheer terror of existence.' He had been a firmly established bachelor, laughed at by the much married students, who knew better than he that babies cried for more pragmatic reasons. Even so, as I cried inwardly for all the uncertainty that lay ahead, I felt he had a very good point.

Not surprisingly, the morning after the night before I felt distinctly queasy. I guess in part this was due to it suddenly dawning on me what I had taken on: the eternal destiny of every soul in the parish was now my responsibility. The Book of Common Prayer, which was to a priest what a car manual was to a garage mechanic, in outlining the minister's job description offered me little comfort. For it was good enough to remind me not only of the greatness of my fault should any fall from grace because of my negligence, but also of the horrible punishment that would ensue because of the slightest lapse. Little wonder I felt physically sick.

But I also wondered about some of the food I had nibbled at the bunfight. Sandwiches and cakes had been brought from all quarters of the Withs, most made the night before with the result that the slices of bread were curling at the edges and the potted salmon and meat paste they tried to contain had that distinctly dried out and past-it look. They had been transported to Kirkwith Hall in Land-Rovers, farm trucks and even tractors, skimpily covered by tea-towels to protect them from the mud, straw and a hundred and one other unmentionable things that farm vehicles usually contained.

The tea-towels themselves looked as if they had seen better days. One looked so filthy that as the feast was prepared I risked life and limb by very delicately querying its cleanliness with its owner: 'Mrs Weighton, are you sure it's all right to use that tea-towel?'

'Course it is, vicar, don't worry. It's an old one anyway. We've been using it as a towel at the farm this past fortnight so it's got no drying power left. It's only good for covering these egg sandwiches now.' I don't think she quite got my point.

I wondered if Jesus had had the same trouble. 'Are you sure it's all right to wrap the bread in that shawl, Mrs Cohen?' 'Oh yes, Lord, don't you worry. My daughter doesn't need it as a sling now you healed those weeping ulcers in her arm.'

Rather than staying at home and dreading what lay ahead of me, I decided to beat whatever was causing my malaise by getting out and getting on with my new job. My first port of call was the Harsleys; not a long way for me to travel since they lived opposite the vicarage drive in a semi-detached council house, redbrick and immaculately kept. The front garden was a gorgeous display of autumn flowers, autumn crocuses, marigolds, Michaelmas daisies, with a line of sunflowers arrayed along the garden wall, bowing their heads above me, almost out of respect, as I walked up the path.

The door was opened by Sam's wife, Doris, a plump bell-shaped woman to whom I had been introduced the night before. She was clearly a lovely soul, but she gabbled her words without pausing for breath, as if she had never come across any form of punctuation whatsoever. Talking to her was a bit like a conversation over the new satellite link with America; there was a few seconds' time lag before you could respond, not because there was a delay in hearing her but because you needed those few seconds to do the punctuating she had singularly failed to do. 'Ee Vicar it's good of you to come and see us on your first day when you must have so much on come in come in do excuse the untidiness.'

Silence; followed by, 'It looks perfectly tidy to me, Mrs Harsley.' My delayed response gave the unfortunate impression that either I was a half-wit or that I tacitly agreed with her own harsh assessment.

Even so, she was unfazed. 'Sam's out in the back garden pulling up a few onions at the moment do you want to come through and have a look it's his pride and joy now he's retired you'll have to excuse him though because he's not in his verger's best.'

Mrs Harsley's way of speaking was growing on me, since my silence was a little less prolonged this time: 'Yes, yes, that would be lovely. I'd thought of growing a few things myself, so maybe he can give me a few tips.' As I duly followed her through the kitchen and out through the back door, I noticed the place was sparklingly clean, complete with a pot sink that was bleached dazzlingly white, hardly the epitome of untidiness. Lack of punctuation aside, she was clearly a woman who had the highest standards.

'Sam Vicar's come to see us I thought I'd show him your vegetable patch before we got settled in the front room I warned him you weren't in your Sunday-best.'

Sam straightened up and grinned broadly, clearly accustomed to Doris-speak since he replied instantly, 'T' Vicar won't mind my working clothes. There won't have been much Sunday-best around for him or anyone in East Hull.'

The back garden was as perfectly arranged as the front, vegetables neatly in rows with leeks standing to attention, thick, black soil which was well raked and hoed with not a weed in sight. I spent some minutes admiring Sam's handiwork, genuinely admiring it rather than feigning praise, since I had tried my hand at vegetable growing in my former garden in town and knew the high price of even modest success.

Besides which, I can't stand those clergy who enthuse about everything, irrespective of whether it has any merit or not. I had come across a Methodist minister like that in Hull, the Reverend Samuel Heap, no doubt a descendent of Uriah. Everything was 'simply wonderful', with the repetitive accolade proclaimed in a whiny voice which made it grate all the more. 'Ooh, what simply wonderful flowers!' vied with, 'Ooh, what simply wonderful tea!' topped off with, 'Ooh, what a simply wonderful meeting!' I often felt like belting him one in the mouth to see whether he would say, 'Ooh, what a simply wonderful punch!' He grated with me because his verbal profligacy devalued the coinage of praise. If it was good I said so, when it was bad I kept silence.

We trooped back into the house, Sam sheepishly placing his muddy boots on the newspaper his wife had laid down by the back door. 'Now don't you be coming into the front room with those filthy clothes on get upstairs and change,' Doris sternly ordered. 'Don't think I'm being hard on him Vicar he keeps a tidy garden I keep a tidy house.' Each to his (and her) domain was obviously the recipe for their successful marriage.

The front room was clearly rarely used. The upholstery was too firm, the carpet pile too deep, the cushions too neat, the curtains too ornamental, the firebrick too soot-free. Nothing in the room signalled the bedded-in feel brought by human possession. I felt both awkward and honoured to be there.

Doris made it clear that further honour was in store. 'I'm so glad you've come today Vicar because I always bake my Christmas cakes early to give them time to season.' Her voice trailed off as she left the room. I could hear her rummaging around in the kitchen and then she was back, bearing a plate on which was an enormous slab of fruitcake and an equally enormous slab of cheese. 'I'd like you to be the first to taste this year's batch.'

I felt humbled that she should accord me such privilege when she hardly knew me. I also felt terrified that, given the precarious state of my stomach, I hardly fancied one bite, let alone the plateful that lay before me. Yet to refuse the obvious honour could only cause the greatest offence.

Doris must have sensed I was hesitating because she immediately piped up, 'Oh Vicar I am negligent you need something to wash it down with and I've got just the thing.' She unlocked the cabinet door, took out a large wine glass and then rummaged in the back of the sideboard. To my horror she brought out a half-full bottle of sherry, the sugar-encrusted top indicating that it had been opened many Christmases ago. Relief flooded through me as it looked as if she wasn't going to be able to get the seized-up top off at all. But my deliverance was short lived. The top gave way with a sharp crack and she proceeded to empty the bottle's contents into my glass. Even a soldered-on cap would have proved no match for Doris' not inconsiderable weight and strength. The sherry didn't so much pour as glug out in treacly globules. Doris placed the glass beside my plate and settled herself down in the chair opposite, a ringside seat for the first tasting of the Christmas cake 1965. Only a miracle could save me now.

It came in the guise of Sam. Still getting changed upstairs, at that very moment he shouted down, 'Have you seen my braces, Doris?'

'Do excuse me Vicar he'd never find the nose on his face without me there to point it out to him.' As she thumped up the stairs I sprang into action. I wrapped both cake and cheese in my handkerchief and stuffed it into my jacket pocket. Next I tipped the sherry into a flower pot sporting a wilting rubber plant, which looked in such a bad way that at least the wretched stuff couldn't harm it further. I held my breath as the viscous liquid nestled on top of the soil, looking as if it would never soak in. But then, as it gradually disappeared, I quickly sat back down and consumed the remaining crumb on the plate, just as Doris returned. 'Well you certainly made short work of that Vicar and the sherry too.' She was praising me rather than criticizing me, 'There's no greater compliment to a woman than a man who makes short work of her cooking.' She positively beamed as she added, 'You'll no doubt be wanting a bit more?'

'No, no, that was more than sufficient. Simply wonderful!' I said, savouring the last (and for me the first) crumb. I resolved to be more tolerant in future of those clergy who enthuse come what may.

Had I refused any cake, I shudder to think what might have happened, because after that day I could do no wrong in the Harsleys' eyes and I grew to reciprocate their admiration. My first impression of Sam as a rather forbidding figure who fiercely guarded 'the Brass' proved false. Beneath the black was a man whose love for his wife, garden and church was deep and uncluttered by other concerns. Like all Yorkshiremen he was blunt, called a spade a spade and expected a great deal from his clergy; but he was none the worse for that.

Doris was a compliment to him in every sense of the word and cherished me like a mother her son. She even boasted to her neighbours about the new vicar's miraculous power over plants, since the rubber plant, until my visit a severe disappointment to its owners, thrived rather gloriously thereafter. Clearly its digestion was stronger than mine.

CHAPTER THREE

The evening after visiting the Harsleys, I strolled into my garden and watched the autumn sun set over the Ings, so marvellously still that it drove me to be still too. Behind me, in the distance, were the Yorkshire Wolds, rounded, protective, yet barely visible in the evening light; ahead of me was an all too visible sea of red. Somehow the scene seemed to beckon me, speaking of both reassurance and challenge. The surrounding hills were my support; the uncharted waters before me were my call.

The whole panorama calmed my anxieties of the last few hours, and I felt overwhelmed by a tremendous sense that it was right to be here. 'It'll be another world after the city, so quiet, so little to do, no hustle, no bustle. You'll fear you'll go mad with the solitariness of it all. But bit by bit you'll begin to cherish the silence and see it as the most precious possession.'

The voice I was hearing replayed in my mind was that of my godfather, Stamford Chestnut, Vicar of a nearby village and Rural Dean of the eight parishes which nestled on Derwent's bank. He had encouraged me to take this job, against my better judgement. His lilting conversation was like a prose poem and almost that alone had moved me to move. If this area could set up such a man, it would do for me. The soothing record continued playing:

'You'll start to value the time you have to focus on people, rather than having to rush from one appointment to the next. You'll drink in the glorious sights of the changing seasons and feel a thirst you never even knew you had, begin to be assuaged. Moving from town to country will be like deeply grieving as the sun sets, only to have your breath taken away by a star-spangled heaven, still more wonderful.'

My reflections were disturbed by Mrs Weighton bustling up the drive in a state of obvious distress. 'Oh Vicar, I was only taking them a magazine; I didn't mean to upset her so.' However calming I might have found gazing at the sunset, I decided that this was definitely not the time to invite Mrs Weighton to dissolve her troubles by sharing the experience with me. Instead I took her inside and led her to my study. I cleared half unpacked boxes of books from a couple of easy chairs, sat her down and let her tell me all.

In my job I have to make snap decisions about people. Very quickly I came to the conclusion that Mrs Weighton might have been careless about tea-towels but was careful over everything else. Careful not in the miserly sense of the word, not grudging or over-cautious, but in the generous sense of the word, literally full of care for those around her, attentive to their slightest need. It was that very sensitivity which had caused her to be so troubled today.

'It's that time of the month again, Vicar,' she soberly informed me. My fears that this was a preface to a tale of gynaecological woe proved unfounded as she explained that she was the parish magazine lady, delivering to all and sundry at the beginning of the month. 'I love the job, Vicar,' she explained. 'I don't just stuff the magazine through the letter box. I usually pop in and have a good gossip and catch up with all the news. It gets me out o' t' farm and proves a real tonic. There's always something new. Today I stood for half an hour with Hannah Everingham, just watching a pair of new born calves. Ee, the sheer wonder of it!'

She gabbled on, distracted from the concern that had driven her to visit me. 'And let me tell you, I don't need even a crumb o' supper when I get back home, what with sampling a cream cake here, a bread bun there. Today, for instance, when we'd finished admiring t' calves, Bill Everingham had insisted, "You just sit your-self down, Iv-y, and have a slice of pork pie!"' She was a dab hand at doing an impersonation of my ponderous churchwarden. 'I daren't tell him, Vicar, I'd already had six cups of tea and four pieces of cake even before I'd crossed their threshold.'

Her cheerful visits must have been a sharp contrast to the dingy magazine she delivered, a totally uninspiring production, to say the least. The Deanery magazine pooled the news from eight surrounding parishes, so that the reader was treated to eight vicar's letters (all of which began 'My dear people, Harvest/Christmas/Lent/Inanity is upon us once again...'), eight flower rotas, eight gripping jumble sale reports, eight warnings of necessary financial stringency from eight grumpy church treasurers... I guess most people consigned this condensed misery to the bin, but willingly paid their subscription just for the fun of seeing Mrs Weighton at 'that time of the month'.

However, her final visit today had been the very opposite of fun. 'Oh, Vicar, I was so looking forward to visiting Kirkwith Manor. The new squire had moved in just the day before you, and I wanted to be among the first to welcome him to the Withs. Doris Harsley's cousin is Tom Huggate, of Huggate, Huggate and Warter, the estate agents in Pocklington. He'd handled the sale of the Manor, and told Doris that the new squire is a professor, or something intellectual, at that University in York, which has just opened.'

She hardly paused for a breath, her dialect a hybrid of broad Yorkshire and the sort of voice most people reserve in these parts for talking to t' parson. She raced on. 'We've never had a professor living in t' village before. I was wanting to check Doris' story out and see what sort of family he had. The last squire's wife was a cut above all us lot, choosy to a tee about her clothes and hardly said a word when I visited each month, except "Thank you" in a haughty, put-you-down sort of manner.'

Clearly first sighting of the new squire, and more importantly, what the new squire's lady was wearing, would have given Mrs Weighton's news reports added stature as she carried them to the rest of the village. But, as her story reached its climax, the angst returned to her voice: 'I walked up the drive, rehearsing what I was going to say should t' new squire open t' door. I tugged at the bell pull, but there was no sign of life. I thought they were all out, and was just about to turn around when the door opened a crack and a little girl peeped out. She was no more than five years of age, and said not a word, staring ahead, vacantly. I could sense there was something wrong, Vicar.

'I was ever so gentle with her,' Mrs Weighton assured me. '"Oh, hello dear," I said, "Is your mummy in, please?" She, she, just burst, burst into tears, sobbing loudly.' Mrs Weighton paused a moment, to check her own emotion.

I made sympathetic noises. 'Don't worry, Mrs Weighton, it must have been a terrible shock. Just take your time, take your time.'

Eventually she regained her composure and explained, 'Those sobs fair wracked me, Vicar. I'm used to children, and I've heard my own children cry often enough. When our Jack broke his arm, you could hear his howls at other side of t' Derwent. But this little lass's cryin' was in a different league entirely. She wasn't so much crying with her eyes as with her whole body.'

'I'm sure you'd be able to comfort her,' I said, rather ineptly.

'No I couldn't. Almost as soon as she started sobbing, she turned and ran into the house, leaving the front door open behind her. I called out several times, but to no avail. I couldn't coax her to return and there didn't seem to be anyone else around. I didn't think it right to intrude any further when something was clearly amiss, so I left the magazine on the hall table and beat a retreat, coming straight to see you. Oh, the poor little soul. What on earth do you think could be wrong with her?'

'I don't know, Mrs Weighton, I just don't know.' I scratched my head, genuinely puzzled. 'It could be anything. But obviously something's amiss. I'll go over to the Manor straight away and check things out. And for goodness sake, don't be so harsh on yourself. You just happened upon…' I shrugged my shoulders as I searched for the words, '…well, whatever it is, it wasn't caused by you. In fact, I think it's rather wonderful, the way you keep in touch with everyone.'

She visibly cheered up at this, and regaled me with more tales of enormous teas and intimacies shared. She went away much more settled, 'Ee, Vicar, it's been good to talk. I feel a lot better about it all now. Poor little mite, poor little mite,' she intoned, shaking her head as she departed.

With the light fading rapidly, I wanted to be off straight away, so was frustrated by having to spend a quarter of an hour rummaging in the garage, extracting my bicycle from behind the newly bought lawnmower and sundry garden tools which the removal men had so helpfully propped against it. After what seemed an age, I was able to set off on my urgent errand.

Following Mrs Weighton's instructions, I pedalled to the very edge of the village, only to be confronted by a ford in full flood. 'So that's why Mrs Weighton had those strange wellingtons on!' I realized. I had presumed that knee-length boots were the latest trend in rural fashion and hadn't twigged they had a strictly functional purpose. Mrs Weighton had warned me that the way 'might be a bit damp', but in her anxiety hadn't elaborated what was an understatement indeed when set against the torrent which raged before me.

After pausing for a moment or two, I decided my only course of action was to pedal down the hill as fast as I could and try to splash through. Pleasingly the strategy worked first time, with my wheels slicing through the flood and setting up waves to the right and to the left of me. Less pleasingly the swell of water surged back, drenching my socks, shoes and trouser legs from the knee downwards. 'Squelch, squelch, squelch,' spluttered my bicycle, as I laboured up the other side of the hill onto dry land. In the state I was in, it didn't remain dry for very long, as I propped the bike against a convenient hedge and then poured the muddy water out of each shoe in turn, wringing out my sodden socks and trousers as best I could.

Archbishop Magee once had had a waiter spill soup down his neck at a banquet. 'Is there a layman present who would kindly express my feelings?!' he had blurted out, in admirably measured fury. As I treated the gathering gloom to a colourful selection of language, I certainly didn't need the services of a layman for a bout of surrogate cursing; indeed, he might have picked up a word or two...

'First right, after t' dip in t' road,' Mrs Weighton had directed. Certainly it had been more of a dip than I had expected. Feeling pretty sorry for myself, and annoyed at yet a further delay, I turned up a muddy, wending track which I hoped would lead to the Manor. The track was a long one, flanked on either side by tall rhododendron bushes, which clearly would make a glorious sight in the spring. But on a dark autumn's evening, they made my path seem darker still, a black tunnel through which I seemed to be making no progress whatsoever as I pedalled and squelched, pedalled and squelched.

The cycle lamp, powered by a dynamo which, like me, was barely functioning after its dousing, gave off a faint yellow light, which was all but useless. Worse than useless, in fact, since the strange shadows it cast onto the rhododendron branches repeatedly startled me. No less than half a dozen times I swerved to avoid imaginary fiends lurking in the thicket, twice landing in a mercifully dry ditch and three times getting embroiled in the very hedge I was trying so desperately to avoid. By the final time I swerved, I was descending a slight slope, so had picked up a fair bit of speed. The result was that I weaved from one side of the path to the other, bouncing off a bank here, scraping a branch there, bruising a shin here, grazing an elbow there. I careered around a bend, feeling like the most battered contestant on the Cresta Run, only to have to brake sharply as Kirkwith Manor loomed suddenly ahead.

Silhouetted against the night sky, the place was imposing: the tall chimney stacks were by themselves as high as any normal house; the Elizabethan gable-ends rose impressively like ziggurats in exile from their Mesopotamian origins; the portico and slender windows were of such proportions that a giant could have walked through them without bowing his head. I certainly did not feel like a giant. With footwear and trousers still drenched, and severely dishevelled after repeated encounters with an amazing variety of local flora (samples of which still attached themselves to my person), I felt very small indeed and totally unworthy of this place. When I remembered the distressing events that had prompted my call, I felt doubly apprehensive.

As I rang the bell pull, another sentence from the irascible Archdeacon's *Good Practice for the Pastoral Parson* sprang to mind: 'The priest must always be a professional, must always dress in such a way as to command respect, must always prepare carefully through prayer and study for even the most routine of visits.' A tramp would have looked better dressed than I did, and my 'careful preparation' had consisted of cursing continually for the last half hour. I was only grateful the Archdeacon wasn't there to see this living antithesis of his sage advice.

Fortunately the Squire wasn't the least cowed by my woefully unprofessional appearance. 'Oh, you must be the Vicar. I'm George Broadhurst,' he blurted out, as he answered the door.

'And I'm David Wilbourne. Like you, I've just moved in,' I responded, as I shook him by the hand. For the second time that evening, I found myself rapidly having to weigh someone up. True to Ivy Weighton's suspicions, George Broadhurst had a definitely professorial appearance: loose fitting, corduroy trousers, a tweed jacket which was well-worn if not shabby, half-moon spectacles, perched low down on his nose, with tremendously bushy eyebrows offsetting wispy hair, receding and ruffled. All this was completed by a pipe which, I came to realize as the evening wore on, he hardly ever smoked. Instead he patiently filled it, lit it, emptied it, and then painstakingly gouged it out with his penknife before restarting the whole time-consuming cycle once more.

From the start, he presented rather abstractly, as if the main line of his thought was elsewhere. For instance, he seemed utterly oblivious to my untidy state, almost as if he expected clergy to turn up on his doorstep at the dead of night, looking as if they were in the middle of an SAS assault course. When I inadvertently but inevitably left a muddy trail on the pristine wooden floor in the hallway, he waved aside my apologies, with the sort of air that almost exuded gratitude for my seasoning his oak with ditchwater.

He showed me into a vast room. 'I'm planning to use this as my study, when the local carpenter gets round to finishing the shelves,' he explained, a wry grin breaking through his distant manner. Clearly he was employing the same man who had yet to 'get round' to rehanging the doors in my draughty vicarage.

The piles of books, far higher and more numerous than mine, offered me a chance to really engage him in conversation. 'I see you're a Classicist,' I exclaimed, rather stating the obvious. 'What's your particular area of research?' I had yet to meet an academic who didn't come to life when elaborating his own subject.

Until now. 'Oh, the textual criticism of Greek tragedy,' he replied rather dismissively. And that was that. No further explanation. No inquiry as to whether I was interested in the Classics. No attempt to prolong the conversation. Almost as if he had expended his energy welcoming me and showing me in, and now had nothing more to say. From his appearance I would have expected a more bubbly figure. But even the twinkle in his eyes, which was certainly there at the start, had switched itself off by the time we sat down.

My eyes desperately darted around the room for another topic of conversation. The heap of children's clothes and odd toy scattered here and there prompted my next comment, 'I see you have children.' Not the most profound of remarks, admittedly. I realized I was getting into the habit of stating the obvious, but the silence and the atmosphere were getting to me, and I was desperate to say something, however inept. It sounded even more inept when I had to repeat it due to George Broadhurst's total lack of response: 'I see you have children.'

'Yes,' he replied. He resumed trying to light his pipe and would have left it there, had I not prompted him further.

'How many? How old are they?' I persisted.

He frowned as he returned from his musings to focus on my question, biting on the stem of his pipe, which remained resolutely unlit. Eventually he spoke: 'There's, erm, Emma. She's the oldest – 12 last June. Then the next is Peter; he's eight, er, nearly nine. Sally, yes, yes, she was five last March.' His speech was very halting and vague, and since he continued to bite on his pipe, was delivered through clenched teeth. After telling me about Sally, he lapsed into silence once again and seemed as far away as ever.

I decided to take the bull by the horns. 'It must have been Sally who Mrs Weighton came across,' I said. 'She's the lady who delivered the parish magazine earlier today.' My own speech began to lose momentum as I homed in on the incident that had brought me here. 'She, er, she seemed to think Sally was, erm, quite upset about something.'

George Broadhurst gave a sudden start, and then stared at me for what seemed an age. 'Yes, yes, I was out walking the dogs at the time, but she was still a wee bit distraught when I came back. I think the woman must have startled her. She's been particularly sensitive of late, what with the move and er, what with the move and er, er, everything.' His lips twitched and he gave a nervous smile, more as if to reassure himself than me. Then silence and the pipe reigned once again. Curtains had

33

yet to be draped over the long Georgian windows which ran from ceiling to floor; the dark glass radiated a definite chill, which eloquently matched the atmosphere between us.

'Where do the children go to school?' I asked, trying to draw out more information.

He frowned yet again with the mental effort as I rather tediously forced him to return to the present. He was getting haughtier by the minute. 'Oh, Emma goes to York College for Girls. I drive her in each morning before I go to my office at the university. I haven't had the time to fix Peter and Sally up yet, but, erm, there's a local school at Eastwith, so I believe.'

At that moment, the aforementioned Sally stumbled into the room. Barefooted, rubbing the sleep from her eyes, wearing a night-dress too thin for this cold, damp, autumn weather, she presented a somewhat neglected figure. 'Daddy,' she drawled, 'Simon's been crying for ages. Can you see to him? He woke me up and I just can't get back to sleep.' She yawned loudly as she snuggled up to her father.

George Broadhurst suddenly sparked back into life. Picking Sally up effortlessly in his arms, the twinkle returned to his eyes and he turned to address me. This time it was me who was frowning as I tried to puzzle out who or what precisely Simon was.

'Ah yes, I didn't mention Simon, did I,' exclaimed George Broadhurst, reading my mind. 'He's the youngest, just four months old. Do excuse me, Vicar, I'd better go up and change him or feed him or whatever. I'm afraid my wife's, my wife's...' His voice trailed off. Sally began to cry.

I realized that the Squire was seizing on this opportunity to dismiss me and put an end to an extremely awkward evening. In fact, despite cradling a crying child in his arms, his manner became quite cheery: 'So good of you to call, Vicar, and it's been wonderful to have a little chat. Do please call again when you're passing. By then we should have got things more ship-shape.' And with that I was ushered out.

Determined to have no further altercation with the under-growth, I pushed rather than rode my cycle back up the path. It had been, to say the least, a perplexing evening. A hale and hearty welcome equalled by a hale and hearty farewell, but with hardly anything in between. George Broadhurst's distant man-ner and the incident between Mrs Weighton and Sally certainly suggested that something distinctly odd was going on. I was frustrated that I hadn't even been able to scratch the surface, let alone be any help to the situation. As I wheeled my cycle back to the road, I felt utterly useless. And my depression deepened as I realized that I had still got that wretched ford to cross.

I leant my cycle against the hedge once again, and was just taking off my shoes and socks, which by this time had all but dried, when a Land-Rover drove up and caught me in its head-lights. I must have presented a comical sight. A door opened and a familiar voice called out, 'Well, Vic-ar, it's a fun-ny time o' night to be go-in' for a paddle!'

I smiled a sheepish smile at Bill Everingham. 'I've just been to the Manor. I got drenched on the way, so I was just taking eva-sive action to make sure I didn't get drenched on the way back.'

'Well, you've no need to go thro' t' ford a-gain. Just chuck your bike in-to back o' t' wag-on and hop in. I'll drive you 'ome in a jif-fy.'

Though my churchwarden was somewhat oversized for the role, he definitely qualified as an angel par excellence that night. His Land-Rover effortlessly crossed the ford, and I was back home in no time, bidding him a cheerful good-night.

'Yes, sleep well, Vic-ar,' was his parting shot. 'Oh, by the way, I'm glad I came a-cross you. My Han-nah said to invite you for a bit o' tea to-mor-row aft-er-noon, if you've got noth-ing else on.'

I gladly accepted his invitation and wished him good-night for the second time. I let myself in and immediately ran a hot relaxing bath, before snuggling down for a well-deserved rest. Unfortunately my sleep was troubled by dreams in which I was sinking in a deep mire, watched by a piercingly silent George Broadhurst, a screaming Sally and a Mrs Weighton chanting a litany of 'Oh the poor little mite, the poor little mite...'

'You'll never guess what he did, first thing this morning, Vicar.' I had taken up Bill Everingham's invitation and was sitting in Hannah's cosy kitchen, warmed by a magnificent Yorkshire range. The place pulsated with activity. The delicious smell of baking wafted from one of the range's lead-black ovens, leaving the taste of fresh eggs at the back of your throat as you savoured the odour: just breathing in was a meal in itself. A clothes horse was propped up in front of the fire, white shirts galore steaming as they dried. Had I not encountered Bill and his girth before, I could have mistaken them for small tents. An old sheepdog lay by the fire, pensioned off from duties around the farm, but determinedly gnawing a bone to show some solidarity with the room's busy ethos. A kettle sang frantically on the grate, a good omen that tea was on its way.

Not that I needed a reminder, since Hannah Everingham rushed to and fro between the kitchen and the larder with a procession of goodies: ham sandwiches, pork pies, sausage rolls, half a Wensleydale cheese, a massive loaf, a pat of butter fresh from the churn, a sponge cake, a fruit cake, a curd tart, an apple pie, a large jug of fresh cream, all to be consumed by just the three of us. When Bill had invited me for 'a bit o' tea', I never guessed he had this sumptuous feast in mind. 'Bill needs a biting-on when he's working out in t' fields,' she had explained when I raised a quizzical eyebrow after she returned heavily laden from the pantry for the seventh time. Some biting-on.

As she prepared the meal she chatted on cheerily, with Bill chipping in the odd (inevitably monosyllabic) word now and again as he sat squeezed into an oak armchair by an already crowded fireplace. He looked the very epitome of contentment as he warmed himself, his already rosy face made even more ruddy by the flames. He didn't even seem to be disturbed when

36

his wife threatened to reveal his early morning ritual: 'Shall I tell t' new vicar what you did first thing today?'

'Ay, you tell him, Han, it's one for t' book that is,' Bill calmly responded.

'Well,' Hannah explained, 'Yesterday Bill and t' seven farm hands…' Here she broke off giggling. 'Sounds like Snow White and t' seven dwarfs,' she quipped.

'Ay, we don't look like 'em, though. Get on wi' tale, lass!'

Hannah laughed as she continued, 'Anyway, t' boss 'ere and his men had been busy spreading lime on the fields. Do you know what that is?'

'I always thought it was some sort of exotic fruit juice,' I confessed.

'Not around 'ere it isn't,' Hannah explained. 'It's like a chalky dust, which has proved a time-honoured tonic for reviving t' earth when it's been tired by t' year's harvest. You scatter it over t' ground and it instantly bleaches the dark brown soil and makes it brilliant white. Him and men worked hard yesterday and by time t' sun set all his fields were covered. He went out wit' t' lads to buy them a well-deserved drink, found someone a' paddling on his way back…' At this point Bill winked conspiratorially at me. '…and once he'd sorted him out came home and went straight upstairs. By God, he slept the sound sleep of the labourer whose work is done.

'He was up, as usual, just before sunrise, wiping his bleary eyes as he drew back the bedroom curtains. With a look o' total surprise he wheeled round and addressed me while I was still in bed, "Ee, Han, there's been such a heav-y frost; I've nev-er known it come so ear-ly in t' year!" '

Even though I guess they had already shared the story many times that day, Bill good-naturedly roared with laughter when Hannah reached the punchline. Tears ran down his cheeks as he re-ran the tale, 'Can you cred-it it, mist-ak-ing lime for frost, the very lime I'd put down my-self not a day be-fore? You could un-der-stand it if it were some-one else's fi-elds, some-one else's lime. Ee, I'm a right scatt-er-brain, of that there's no doubt.'

Forgetful maybe; genial undoubtedly. I could only admire the golden qualities so obvious in this simple man. He'd come to my rescue on my first day here, when I was sunk. He'd come to my rescue last night, at the very moment when I needed a boost. He was a big man in many ways, yet humble enough to laugh at himself. All this was topped by an ability to relish family, farm, faith and food, single-mindedly celebrating them rather than souring them by wanting more. He struck me instantly as a treasure beyond price.

My simply being at home with them in their kitchen, relaxing and talking about a hundred and one different things, seemed to mean a great deal to them, almost a hallowing of what they held most dear. I can't say it took much effort on my part, since I enjoyed the visit tremendously, not least the tea, which was typically Yorkshire in its generosity.

However, there had been visits by the vicar in Hannah's childhood, when her father had owned the farm, which had been more formal. She vividly remembered the Rev'd Thomas Eddison, Vicar of Kirkwith immediately before the First World War, deigning to call on his parishioners. 'He had to come in by t' front door.' The disdainful emphasis Hannah put on the word 'he' betrayed what she thought of him. 'Because he thought it beneath him, he deliberately avoided t' working kitchen and stackyard, through which I noticed you approached t' house.' I was both flattered and relieved that the emphasis she put on the word 'you' was adulatory.

'Ee, I was fascinated by his white gloves, t' way they stayed on throughout t' time he was with us, even when he was drinking tea and eating cake. I'd never seen a man with gloves like that before. They wouldn't have stayed clean for five minutes on t' farm.'

'Ev-en if you'd put t' lime on 'em,' quipped Bill.

'And the conversation, Vicar, so awkward, so much silence. Kitchen was always full o' gabbling 'til he came along, then everybody got tongue-tied. My mother would start on one subject and then taper off. There'd be a long pause before she flitted on to another topic, only to taper off again. In the face of his…' I noticed that emphasis again, '…disapproval, my dad hardly said a word. In the end, frustration must have got to him, though, because he rose from his chair and blurted out, "You'll have to excuse me, Mr Eddison, but I've got to shift that pile of manure into t' wagon before t' day's out." And with that he was off.

'The startled Mr Eddison remonstrated with my mother, "Really, I would have thought you'd have encouraged him to be more cultivated than to say *manure*."

'His disapproving sneer as he said that word raised mother's hackles, and she replied with some spirit. "Mr Eddison," she fair hissed out t' syllables of his name, "if you knew how long it has taken me to get him to say manure instead of something far worse, you wouldn't complain so!" Where people have come from, not where they are, is the measure by which they deserve to be judged. That's what my mother always said, Vicar, and I've always believed it o' folk too.'

Hannah's sheer good sense and shrewdness made me feel at ease with her, and more than that, she seemed someone I could take into my confidence. I was still deeply worried about my abortive visit to the Manor the previous night. Somehow I sensed she could help. 'No doubt Bill told you it was me he saved from a drenching by the ford last night,' was my opening gambit.

'Ay, he did 'appen to mention it,' Hannah responded, with a broad grin.

'Well, the reason why I was up that way was that I'd gone on an urgent visit to the Manor. Mrs Weighton had called in earlier in the day and had been worried that one of the children was inconsolably distraught. I set off straight away to see if I could help, but I'm afraid I got nowhere.'

The description of my journey set the tears rolling down Bill's cheeks again. 'Ee, Vic-ar, you nev-er tried to get through t' ford in full flood on a cy–cle? It's a won–der you lived to tell the tale!'

Hannah was more concerned than amused. 'But in the end, you managed to get there. What do you mean you got nowhere?'

'I just couldn't get George Broadhurst, the new squire, to open up. Try as I might, and I did try, I couldn't draw him into any sort of conversation. I mentioned Mrs Weighton and the little girl crying, but even then, he had very little to say. Then the baby started crying, he had to see to her, so that was the end of my visit.'

'What about his wife?' Hannah asked, with a worried look across her brow.

'She wasn't around. It was all very strange.'

'And what did you say his name was? Broadbent? Broad-head?' Hannah asked.

'No, Broadhurst, George Broadhurst. He's a professor at York University.'

Hannah Everingham's eyes immediately brightened. 'I'm sure there was an item in the Pocklington Post about someone with that name who was connected with the University. It might be a bit back, though. I always keep the back copies for a month or two, so give me a few minutes to see if I come across it.'

With that she scuttled off. 'She'll have t' Post for last year or two, more like, know–ing her. She's a real hoar–der is my Han–nah. Pap–ers, birth–day cards, Christ–mas cards, news–pap–ers, they'll all be there, stacked up in t' old ward–robe in our bed–room.'

Bill was clearly a man who knew his wife well, for after a few moments she was back with the look of success in her eye. With pride she handed me a copy of the Pocklington Post, dat–ed 7 June 1965, which included a profile of George Broadhurst, headlined 'Professor for our Times'. 'I knew I'd read about him somewhere, Vicar. But bells are still ringing in the back of my mind. There's, there's something else I've seen. You read that for now while I go and have another rummage.'

The article was well-written, although I was surprised to read that the reporter was particularly impressed by George's approachability and conversational ease. It gave a brief sketch of his career, most notably the background to his recent appointment as Professor of Ancient History. He had been brought over from Saint Andrews University in 1962 to help set up the fledgling Classics Department at York. He had injected such energy and enthusiasm into this task, that his promotion to Professor was inevitable. The profile made much of his humanity, humour and humility, to such an extent that I wondered if it was featuring a different George Broadhurst from the distant and aloof figure I had encountered last night.

The feature had a strong personal slant, and made much of George's charming wife, Jennifer, 'expecting their fourth child any day now'. It emphasized how much they were looking forward to moving into Kirkwith, intrigued by its moment of destiny in 1536, with uprisings against Henry VIII and brother betraying brother. It ended with Jennifer Broadhurst's comment, 'Kirkwith is a peaceful place, having had four centuries' recuperation after its brief entry onto history's stage. We hope our new home there will be an oasis of calm in an increasingly busy world.' She sounded an intelligent woman. What a pity she hadn't been around to smooth and spark things last night.

Just as I was handing the newspaper to Bill, Hannah returned. 'I'm sorry, Vicar, I just can't lay my hands on it. I'm almost certain there's something else, though. I'll have a good search over t' weekend, and when I find it, I'll bring it round.'

'It says 'ere he's an ex-pert in t' text-u-al crit-ic-ism o' Greek trag-ed-y. What on earth's that?' Bill blurted out, as he read the article I had just finished.

'Oh, it's the study of how they copied, by hand, ancient Greek plays, and how the errors they made altered the text,' I explained.

'Well, fan-cy that,' said Bill, nodding his head, 'Fan-cy find-ing e-nough to stud-y in that.' Clearly how academics managed to fill their time was beyond him.

'Tragedy, tragedy,' murmured Hannah, cutting across our conversation, in a world of her own. Her look had turned dark.

'Yes, Greek tragedy, a play which catches sharply the joys and sorrows of life,' I emphasized.

Hannah was oblivious to my comment, obviously on a different tack altogether. 'Oh no, oh no, I hope it's not that, I hope it's not that,' she almost wailed as she rushed out of the room. George and I stared at each other speechless, typical men at a loss for words in the face of a woman's distress. Within a minute she was back. 'Oh Vicar, I'm so sorry,' she said, as she handed me another paper.

This time the headline was 'Fatal tragedy on Hull Road blackspot'. I read, 'A woman was killed last Tuesday when her car was in collision with a lorry on the notorious double bend at Kexby. The woman was later named as Jennifer Broadhurst, wife of George Broadhurst, recently appointed Professor of Ancient History at York. Mrs Broadhurst's new-born son, who was in a carry cot in the back of the car, miraculously escaped without any injury.' The paper was dated 7 August 1965.

Once again I passed the paper on to Bill, who read the report with a look of utter sorrow. We sat in silence as the full horror of the situation dawned. A month before they were to move to the home of their dreams, a month before his first crucial term as professor was due to begin, George Broadhurst was cruelly thrust into grief, at the same time, having to comfort, as best as he could, four children suddenly and savagely bereaved of their mother. The most momentous Greek tragedy had leapt the centuries and been enacted before his sorrowing eyes. Mrs Weighton's litany, 'The poor little mite, oh the poor little mite,' kept ringing in my ears.

I only stayed a little longer at the Everinghams'. Having borrowed a pair of high galoshes from Bill, I braced myself for a second visit to Kirkwith Manor.

42

It was still light when I tugged at the bell-pull. Once again the door was answered by George Broadhurst, who greeted me like a long lost friend, 'Oh, I'm so glad you've come back. You must have wondered what on earth was wrong with me last night. I'm so sorry, I felt so tired, so down. Poor Sally had had such a dreadful day. Do come in and let me tell you about it.'

As we settled into the study once again, I explained how I had come across the report of his wife's death. He seemed relieved I knew. 'I just didn't have it in me to tell it all all over again last night. I'm not sure I could have managed it today either. I'm glad you know. So glad.'

I could understand how he would shy away from having to go over each detail again with a stranger, revisiting all the pain, opening all the wounds which were still fresh, still to heal. But now he knew I knew, he was able to be himself and pour his heart out. All the reporter had said about his humanity, humility and even humour was proved a hundredfold, as I quietly listened, taking it and him all in.

He told me about Emma. 'I do so admire her, David. Two months ago she was still a girl, full of fun, making many occupations, as children do. Then, overnight, her mother's death cast her into adulthood, and she's taken it all on the chin. I'm amazed at her sheer good common sense and ability. She's looked after baby Simon and virtually run the home and organized the move to boot. All on top of her school work. She's kept us all going.'

'For how long?' I thought to myself. Emma deserved to be a little girl and deserved to have the space to grieve. 'What about Peter and Sally?' I asked.

'They're lost,' George readily admitted, 'Totally lost. They've lost their mum, they've lost their home. They spend their waking hours dazed and bewildered, bursting into tears frequently and unexpectedly, crying themselves to sleep at night, sobbing even in their dreams. I, I…' George hesitated. 'More often than not I just don't seem to be able to reach them.'

A silence ensued. Not the awkward silence of the night before, but a silence of deep understanding and empathy, a silence in which mere words were singularly inappropriate. 'And you – what about you?' I gently asked.

He wept. Uncontrollably and utterly, his whole body shaken by the sobbing. I let him cry. 'I'm sorry, I'm so sorry,' he apologized, 'I just don't know how I can go on. So many things to do. So many things we'd worked and hoped for come to fruition. Yet she's not here to enjoy them, to help me enjoy them, to help me cope with them. It's so, so...' He paused for a moment as he searched for the right word. 'It's so intolerable.' He was clearly a skilled wordsmith. The whole of his sorry state was eloquently summed up in that one word, with the added pathos which his pronouncing it gave it.

I suppose we didn't spend much more time speaking than we'd done on the previous night. And yet there was the world of difference in terms of communication. I left after an hour or so, feeling I knew the man, his family and situation. And that the knowledge, however searingly sad it was, was an important start on the slow road to recovery.

CHAPTER FOUR

Yet another restless night, this time caused not so much by what had happened the day before, but rather in anticipation of the day ahead. It was to be my first Sunday as Vicar, so crucially important to be at my best. I celebrated the early Communion at Kirkwith, standing by the altar, the knight and his lady in brass before me, feeling drained before I had even started.

As I repeated the familiar words that Jesus had said as he celebrated a final, fatal meal with his friends, 'Take, eat, this is my body...' several pictures flashed through my mind. Jesus' mud-splattered and blood-splattered body, arched and aching on the cross, juxtaposed with Jennifer Broadhurst's body, mangled in the wreckage of her car. In my imagination, I could hear baby Simon shrieking for a mother who seconds before had been only inches away from him and now was no more. I could see George, white as a sheet, stammering out to his children that their mummy was dead, holding them tightly as incredulity gave way to weeping. I could see him again, on his own now, as I saw him last night, crying.

'What on earth do you want to be a priest for? The Christian faith is so irrelevant to today's world.' A voice from my past, a friend from my days at the bank, incredulous about my plans to be ordained. Yet as I homed in on the greatest tragedy in the history of the world and let it inform the tragedy I had just encountered, I felt there was nowhere in the whole of creation I would rather be.

The question of relevance popped up again at a later service. Ideally a vicar's first Sunday in a parish should be a time for him to set out his stall, to outline his vision for the years ahead, to enthuse those who don't normally come to church, but have simply turned out to see whether the new vicar is any better than the last one. Despite all these laudable ambitions, I found my hands considerably tied. For Church law required me to read to the congregation the Thirty Nine Articles of Religion, which contained such gripping lines as 'General Councils may not be gathered together without the commandment and will of Princes, and even then they may err, and sometimes have erred, even in things pertaining unto God...'

Two elderly spinsters, sitting in the back pew, misheard my original announcement. 'We thought you said you were going to read us the Thirty Nine Steps,' they twittered, as I bade them farewell after the service. No doubt they had been considerably disappointed that there had been no dashing heroes, nor equally dashing heroines, nor handcuffs, nor inhospitable moor. Instead they, and the rest of the congregation, had been faced with 17 pages of tightly typed Elizabethan English from the back of the Prayer Book. These set out, exhaustingly, the doctrines of a fledgling Church of England whose insecurity was all too obvious after she had finally broken with Rome in the sixteenth century.

Whilst such issues no doubt excited Christopher, son of Robert and his ilk, the following centuries had considerably diluted their glamour. By the time I got to the third Article, most of the congregation, having been well trained by the Bishop of Pocklington, were asleep with their eyes open. One exception was Sam Harsley who became more and more agitated the more Articles I read. Clearly his Sunday dinner was at stake yet again. True to form, Bill Everingham fell soundly and obviously asleep before Article Seventeen, immune by now even to the severest of nudges from his wife. What an impact I was making.

The subject of relevance loomed again when my tea that Sunday was interrupted by a loud rap on the back door. There on the step stood a well-dressed man, although the clothes, right down to the trouser turn-ups, had that distinctly old-fashioned feel. The yellowed, weather-beaten face was deeply lined and gave away the fact that he was a gypsy. He stood erect, with the mark of authority about him; I braced myself for the usual appeal for money or food. 'Can you spare sixpence for a cup o' tea, your Reverence?' Given the stream of tradesmen's vans which had splashed a path to my door, food I had in plenty. As for cash, I was probably more stretched than the man standing before me.

But the appeal, when it came, was totally different from what I had imagined. 'We'd like you to christen our babies, sir,' he quietly asked, the note of authority still there in the gentleness. For the first time I looked over his shoulder and saw gathered at the gate a crowd of about 40 gypsies. I detected, even at that distance, that there was an air of hesitancy in their stance. They were supporting their clan leader from afar, no doubt imploring me to say yes. Yet, used to a rejection which was often harsh and brutal, they were all too ready to be rejected yet again.

Had I refused them, I could hardly have remained a Christian, let alone a priest. I gladly directed them to the church, gathered my robes and a jug of water and took a short cut through the back field. Most of the water sloshed out of the jug as I rushed to get there ahead of them. However, my concern about how to have a baptism without the one crucial ingredient paled into insignificance as I gaped agog at the scene which greeted me.

Shiny black horses, ribs all too visible, were slowly heaving caravans along the muddy track; tied to nearly every vehicle by a piece of old rope was a dog, as lean and starved looking as the horses. The caravans, horseshoe-shaped and painted in gaudy colours, rolled from side to side, their gypsy drivers stoically trying to control the horses and avoid slithering into the treacherously deep ditch by the track's side. Children were having the time of their lives, leaping on and off the caravans, daring each other to dart underneath them, avoiding, by a whisker, being crushed by the massive iron-rimmed wheels, then gleefully sliding into the ditch, soaking themselves and each other with the murky black water, oblivious to its filth.

Incredibly all the caravans survived the perilous journey and bunched together in a semi-circle by the graveyard wall, beneath which were the Ings, made red once again by the setting sun. A group largely spurned by society overlooking a red sea: now where I had come across that picture before?

I opened the church and let them in, lit the candles and was about to sneak out again to draw some water from the Ings in my little jug, which was by now almost empty. But at the church door was a collection of larger jugs, presumably used by that invincible body of women, the Flower Ladies. Today I risked their wrath by setting their equipment to a different use. Calling all the children to me, who by this time had scattered to the four corners of the church, I gave each of them a jug and asked them to go out, fetch water from the Ings and fill to the brim the spacious font, which only a few days before had proved so elusive. The job took a lot of supervising, with as much water on the floor and the children as ended up in the font, but I felt involving them was worth it.

I robed in the vestry and as I came out the scene hit me, rows and rows of gypsy faces, well worn, their yellow exaggerated by the candlelight. It was not the only scene which remained with me from that day. I expected the service to be a rowdy and disorganized affair, not least because of the liveliness of the children as they approached the church; in fact there was a reverent hush throughout. I was struck by the way they said the Lord's Prayer, with one voice which avoided the usual mindless chant, 'Our Father, 'chart in heaven…' Instead each and every word was given an intonation as if it had been carefully weighed up over a long period and was meant from the heart.

48

Most of all, I remember the babies, swaddled in yards and yards of yellow cloth, wrapped tightly in little parcels, their tiny faces peeping out at me, eyes bright, full of life. I took my time and baptized each and every one, nine in all. The christening over, I gave the leader and his tribe a tour of the church, using the stained-glass windows as visual aids to remind them of the Christian story.

Some windows lent themselves better to this laudable aim than others. I was not particularly helped by a late Victorian affair which highly romanticized the Last Supper. Seven of the disciples, inappropriately dressed with the splendour of Eastern kings rather than Palestinian peasants, gazed vacantly into space, obviously bored out of their tiny minds. Three, with arms outstretched, looked like priests, celebrating an anachronistic communion. Jesus and the beloved disciple by his side looked as if they were locked in an arm-wrestling competition. The table, which should have groaned under the weight of the Passover feast, was all but bare save for an empty cup and scattered here and there a few pots, which bore more than a passing resemblance to ash trays. Undoubtedly the holiest and most thoughtful of the bunch was Judas, who had a wish-I-was-somewhere -else look in his eyes which I could only sympathize with, but which hardly aided my commentary.

At the east end of the church we stood in silence before a window which needed no explanation. It depicted a baby, wrapped in yards and yards of swaddling cloth, tiny face peeping out, cradled in his mother's arms. In the gathering dusk that mother's face looked as yellow and weather-beaten as those who gazed on. The gypsy leader and I looked at each other, our eyes filling with tears. 'We believe in Him, sir, we believe in Him,' the gypsy quietly affirmed. He didn't have to tell me. I already knew. Ever since then I've reckoned that God had a soft spot for gypsies. Probably because he was born as one.

Stumbling across God does make one feel that one's job has a certain relevance, something that bolstered my confidence for the task that lay ahead of me first thing on Monday morning. For I always reckon that the nearest thing to experiencing one's own death is to be a clergyman taking a school assembly. For four years I had served my probation, dying weekly in East Hull, standing on the stage of the barn-like hall at the local secondary modern, trying desperately to enthuse a thousand distinctly unenthusiastic teenagers who were seated in rows before me. The walk from the door at the back with every eye boring into you seemed like a march to the scaffold. Even though the discipline was strict and the place was silent, those looks voiced the sniggers, the contempt, the anti-clericalism which was bred from generation to generation. No other job under the sun could be opposed with such vitriol as when the invective, 'Yah, Vicar!' was spat out, every consonant having a guttural harshness.

I sensed from my visits to the school that teachers weren't that popular either. At one assembly I talked about hands giving away what sort of person you were, aiming ultimately to get the children to contemplate what God's hands were like. But in the long run up to that conclusion I talked about other hands: miners' hands ingrained with coal dust; mechanics' hands covered with oil; fishermen's hands cracked by the cold; gardeners' hands with soil under the fingernails; mothers' hands as soft as your face, provided you believed the adverts on ITV. I put a final question: 'And what sort of hands do you think teachers have?' An easy one, I thought. They'd all know the answer was chalky, with a blackboard in every classroom.

A boy in the third form timidly raised his hand, 'Please sir, cruel hands.' He lingered over the word 'cruel' with an inflexion which captured both the misery that had been inflicted upon him and the utter hatred he felt for the teaching profession.

'Cruel! Cruel? We are most certainly not cruel,' the headmaster had exploded, interrupting my talk. The sheer force of his denial could only corroborate the boy's complaint.

That the headmaster had said anything at all surprised me, since he usually suffered from a nervousness in front of his charges which did little to calm me: 'G-g-g-g-good morning, school. This morning once ag-g-g-gain we have the Rev'd Wilbourne to speak to us.' And with that, I was on, standing out at the front, my dog collar advertising that I was the most obvious of idiots, with no one to bail me out. Save God…

I drew considerable solace that someone had fared even worse than me. An aged deaconess had seen fit to stand in front of the school and pull a banana out of her handbag, holding it up in front of her. 'Now you all see this banana I'm holding erect before you. I want you to call it names, I want you to insult it with whatever words spring to mind.'

Apparently there was a stunned silence as both teachers and children were struck dumb with incredulity. 'Come along, don't be shy,' she continued. 'You must know one or two rude words.'

With that, all hell had broken loose, catcalls from the older boys opening the door for gales of verbal abuse, the teachers trying to restrain them, the deaconess trying to encourage them: 'What was that I heard? Fog? Fig? Beggar? Burger? Oh dearie me, I must be getting out of touch in my old age. I didn't know such words could be used as insults.'

Haunted by these East Hull nightmares, I set out to cycle the three miles to Eastwith School for my first visit. I gently pedalled along the winding country lanes, hardly meeting another vehicle; in Hull I would have been battling with traffic, spluttering as I breathed in diesel fumes. Quite a lot of the fields had been treated with lime (I smiled as I recalled Bill Evering-ham's heavy frost) which was caught by the breeze and blew across the hedges and ditches, dusting them down like a sprin-kling of icing sugar. Wood alternated with field, with leaves of various hues of autumn gold highlighted by the early morning sunshine. Hardly surprising that the ride soothed my dread of yet another assembly.

I rode into Eastwith, greeted by its redbrick houses, hud-dled together in places, scattered in others. At the heart of the village, several unconcerned farmyards spilled their earth, hay and even the odd hen onto the main street, as if the road belonged to the farm and the farm belonged to the road, the two inseparable. Set into a stackyard wall was a post box with the initials VR embossed on it, oblivious to successive reigns. Clearly time moved slowly in these parts.

I found the school down Ings Lane. The geese calling from the nearby river competed with the excited shrieks of the children as they ran amok in the tiny playground, squeezing every ounce of enjoyment out of the minutes that remained before the school bell summoned them to order. Geoff Goodmanham, the head teacher, met me at the door. Not much older than me, his hair was tousled with wisps pointing in every compass direction, his Harris tweed jacket well worn (sported, as I was to find out as time went on, whatever the temperature). All this advertised him as a man after my own heart, someone who got on with the job rather than over-worrying about their appearance. I warmed to him immediately.

He greeted me enthusiastically, 'David, how kind of you to make time for us when you must have one hundred and one other things on in your first week. It's really good to see you. Come and meet my colleague, Miss South.' He introduced me to Miss South, the other teacher in this two-teacher school, who looked after the tinies.

Geoff was a personable chap; when I rang him to book today's visit he'd insisted that I use his first name from the outset. I could only match his friendliness and insist he call me David. So the formal way in which he addressed Miss South struck me as significant: she clearly belonged to the generation of schoolteachers who never flaunted their Christian name, if they ever had one at all. In my mind's eye I imagined her as a baby, being baptized. 'Name this child,' the vicar would have barked.

'Miss South,' her cowering mother would have replied.

'Miss South, I baptize you in the name of the Father...'

My mind snapped back to the present as the infant made the quantum leap to middle age and addressed me. 'Good morning, Mr Wilbourne,' she said, in very proper tones as she very formally shook my hand.

'Good morning, Miss South,' I replied, in equally proper tones. 'And how long have you been teaching here?'

'Thirty-seven years,' she replied, in a matter of fact way, her steel-blue eyes retaining their firm gaze, as if the figure were neither something to be proud or ashamed of. 'I was only thinking the other day, Mr Goodmanham, that I've taught a parent or grandparent of every single child in this school, save the two townies who joined us last year.' The way she said 'townies' hinted at her loathing for these invaders whose ancestry she didn't have a personal hold on.

'You'll have seen a few educational fashions come and go in thirty-seven years,' I commented.

'Indeed,' she said firmly. For a moment I thought she was going to leave it there, but she went on, 'I've never been one for fashion, educational or otherwise, Mr Wilbourne. You can observe that from my clothes.' Those eyes suddenly flashed a twinkle of humour. 'I teach children the basics, year in year out, no frills. Experts come along and tell me I'm wrong, that I ought to try this method or that method. Other experts come along and wax lyrical about what I'm doing, as if they've never encountered it before. I take notice of neither and just get on with it. I was taught to teach by Mr Burgess, headmaster here during the Great War. What was good enough for him is good enough for me.' With that firm statement of intent, which brooked no discussion, she departed to ring the bell for the start of morning school.

'She reminds me of my infant teacher from twenty-odd years back, firm but fair,' I remarked to Geoff, when she was well out of earshot.

'Oh, she's pure gold,' Geoff confirmed. 'Nearly everybody in these parts sees her as a third parent and often with more sense than their first two put together. You'd be surprised how many seek her out for guidance, long after their schooldays, with posers such as "Should I get married?" or "Should I apply for this job?" or "Should I sell mum's house?" She's certainly been invaluable to me in my first two years here, not least in her avoidance of fashion.' I was pleased to see from his broad grin that here was someone who shared my sense of humour.

Geoff proudly showed me round his school, a typical late Victorian building endowed by the local philanthropist. The limits of the philanthropist's generosity were now beginning to show: eighty years of winds whipping up off the Ings had begun to make the cheap red bricks flake. Geoff picked up one of the flakes as he showed me round the outbuildings. 'You'd be surprised how much trouble these wretched things cause. The children have great fun with them skimming them across the river and throwing them at each other. Not so much fun for me though, when I have to cart some wounded child off to hospital. Nor for the managers when they are faced with the bill for new brickwork, month by month.'

'We have the same trouble with many of our churches,' I quipped, 'except that most of my crowd don't throw debris at each other, or at least not very often.'

We wandered inside the compact, if moulting, building. There were two classrooms with high ceilings and high draughty windows, a small kitchen which doubled as a staff room and a hall which served both as a canteen and gym. It was in that hall that we gathered today, a fire blazing in the hearth, twenty-seven children sitting before me cross-legged, Miss South at the piano, Geoff with me at the front, beaming with pride over his charges.

Geoff duly introduced me. 'Now then, boys and girls, we're very fortunate to have our new vicar, Mr Wilbourne, with us today. Can we give him our usual welcome?' I knew my name took some getting used to, so I wasn't surprised to hear at least twenty different variants: 'Good morning, Mr Welborn,' vied alongside 'Good morning, Mr Wilburn,' alongside 'Good morning, Mr Wilbraham,' even alongside 'Good morning, Mr Wilberforce.' I simply smiled indulgently; they'd get it right in the end. At least they hadn't addressed me as Reverend Wilbourne, as if I were a preacherman who'd escaped from a Wild West set.

Developing the subject of getting to know one another's names, I focused on the cruelty of name-calling. I had decided to try and redeem the fateful assembly that had gone so devastatingly wrong for the deaconess in East Hull. Like her, I held up a banana, but suggested the children insult it by calling out the names I had written out on card beforehand. They very obediently chanted, 'You're yellow!' 'You're spotty!' 'You're crooked!' with not an obscenity to be heard.

Giving the banana careful scrutiny, I commented, 'Well, calling it all those names doesn't seem to have affected it in the least, does it? But let's just check it's OK on the inside.'

I handed the banana to Geoff, my unwitting stooge. As he peeled it, the banana fell apart in neat slices in his hands. I quickly drew my conclusion whilst the children were still agog at this obvious piece of magic: 'Yes, calling it names didn't affect its outside, but inside it was all cut up. Just like people are all cut up on the inside when you make fun of them.'

As the children were returning to their classrooms, and Geoff was trying to wipe his sticky hands on his tweed jacket, he whispered to me, 'How on earth did you pull that trick off?'

'I'm no magician, Geoff,' I reluctantly admitted. 'I spent last night carefully piercing the skin of the banana with a needle. I then wriggled it around inside, to slice through the soft interior, whilst leaving the exterior intact.' Though I didn't realize it, I'd stumbled across keyhole surgery 20 years before its time.

I spent the rest of the day simply enjoying that little school, sitting in on the lessons, talking to the children as they worked, helping put out the chairs and tables in the hall to prepare for dinner, eating a delicious meal which had been prepared by Mrs Ludlow, the school cook. The braised steak was served with creamy mashed potatoes, lump-free, a unique achievement in my long and usually bitter experience of school dinners. There was the inevitable cabbage, but it had been lightly cooked, unlike the anaemic, over-boiled variety I usually encountered, with both goodness as well as colour steamed out of it. It was followed by a generous portion of treacle sponge and custard. Throughout the dinner, Mrs Ludlow hobbled in and out, gently encouraging the little ones with 'Come on, love, have another forkful,' offering a plentiful supply of seconds to the larger ones, who needed no encouragement whatsoever.

Following lunch, Geoff took his mug of tea outside to supervise the children's play and make sure flakes of Victorian Red weren't used as weapons. I stayed in the kitchen-cum-staff room and, whilst Mrs Ludlow bustled around us clearing up, I stood with Miss South by the window. We both watched Geoff in the playground as the children vied for his attention. He had a friendly and natural manner which indicated a genuine interest in those around him. Even when a fragment of brick glanced off his shoulder, he kept his cool, having a quiet but effective word with the red-faced and remorse-filled culprit.

Miss South spoke in hushed tones. 'Vicar, we have never had one like him in all my years here. There's not one ounce of guile in him. He simply lives for these children.' Given her rather stiff and formal manner, this praise for Geoff seemed high indeed. She continued in a similar vein, 'Do you know, since he took over as Head, he's worked wonders, breathing life into the place, encouraging the potential and skills of each individual child. Before him we hardly ever had a child go on to grammar school. But last year three out of the six leavers passed their Eleven Plus – they would never have done it without him.'

Miss South broke off as we watched Geoff soothe the sobs of a little girl who had scuffed her knee. 'Just look how he cares for them, Vicar. He wants them to pass, but they're not just examination fodder in his eyes. He values each and every one of them. He doesn't half bolster their confidence, accepting them so totally and unconditionally. I, I...'

Again Miss South broke off. But this time there was no accident in the playground; her moistening eyes indicated that it was something within her rather than outside which had made her pause. Eventually she continued, although haltingly: 'I, I, only wish that he and June could, could have one of their own.'

At that moment Geoff burst in, carrying the little girl with the bleeding knee. 'Mrs Ludlow, do me a favour and just pop a bit of Savlon and a plaster on Mandy's leg. You'll be as right as rain then, flower,' he reassured the child as he set her down on a chair. 'You might as well ring the bell, Miss South, and I'll get them in from the yard.' Miss South rushed off to begin afternoon school, leaving me intrigued.

I spent the rest of the afternoon hearing individual children read. Just before home-time they returned the compliment and demanded that I read them a story. They chose a highly imaginative account of David and Goliath, which they clearly relished. It was a touch too gory for my liking, however, complete as it was with pictures of giants with severed heads and shepherd boys smugly holding aloft swords dripping with blood. The scene might have turned my stomach, but it had no adverse effect whatsoever on them as they pored over the picture's contents, 'Hold the book up again for us, please sir! Just look at that giant's head rolling around in the mud. Is that a puddle, or a pool of blood?'

Never mind my gentle assembly about cutting people up on the inside. Their clear preference was for cutting people up on the outside, and as much of it as possible. I could only hope that like the God of the Bible, they would mellow with age.

Having endured a day of my company, I would have thought Geoff would have been glad to see the back of me. But not a bit of it. 'You'll be having a bit of tea with us before you go?' Seemingly unwearied by a full day's teaching, he eagerly led me to his home which adjoined the school. As I walked with Geoff up their front path, I noticed that the buildings matched in every way, right down to the flaking brickwork.

His wife June came out of the kitchen to greet us, a shade diffident, but also perky, attractive, and as smart as her husband was unkempt. Her slightly rounding figure and rosy complexion suggested that she was in the early stages of pregnancy. I didn't say anything, though, since before now I had been caught out in this area. An innocent question such as, 'When's the baby due, then?' would be met by a black look, with my being firmly told that the baby arrived six months ago, or that no baby was expected at all.

As we chatted over yet another Yorkshire tea of sandwiches and cakes galore, I only hoped that my cycling back home would burn off some of the pounds undoubtedly gained by being so well fed. 'Have another salmon sandwich, David,' Geoff pressed me.

I resisted his generosity. 'Oh no, I've had more than enough already.'

'Oh go on, just another one. Someone's got to keep June company. You're eating for two, aren't you darling?' Geoff looked fondly across at his wife, who blushed a deep shade of beetroot. So my hunch had been right, she was expecting. Yet why had Miss South been so tearful? And why did June have an air of anxiety about her? Things didn't entirely square.

'And, and, when's the b-b-baby due?' I stuttered. The standard comment, though sounding terribly daring on my bachelor lips.

'Towards the end of February, if all goes to plan this time.' As June uttered the last two ominous words, her eyes filled with tears.

'This time?' I gently prompted. I sounded calm, but inwardly I was panicking. Pregnancy, childbirth, 'women's troubles' were a closed book to me, situations for which my training hadn't prepared me in the least. Ask me about the Virgin Birth, and I could reel off theory after theory. But a real woman with real problems...

June took a deep breath and visibly steeled herself to reply. Yet when she did speak, there was a certain strength amidst the sadness, as she told me her story in a matter-of-fact way: 'I've been pregnant three times before. The first was a still-birth, there was absolutely nothing that could be done. The cord had just wrapped around his neck, and that was that. "It's extremely unlikely it'll happen again," the doctor reassured us, "Better luck next time!" As if we were having a flutter on the horses. The next time I went and miscarried. Geoff and I wondered whether continuing to teach whilst I was pregnant was too stressful, so when he got this job and we moved here, I gave up teaching and concentrated on home-making. Then eighteen months ago, I had another miscarriage. Now I'm expecting again, but...'

Her lip began to quiver. I was impressed that she had held out for so long. '...but we're not building up our hopes too early. They've been dashed too many times before.' With that June rushed out of the room, followed closely by Geoff. I wanted to follow too, but I realized they needed the space to comfort each other without my intrusion. I remained, alone, feeling awful, cursing myself for putting my foot in it, forcing her to revisit all that grief.

It was some time before Geoff returned. 'She's put the kettle on for a fresh cup of tea. She's...'

'I'm sorry, Geoff,' I interrupted. 'I'm sorry I pushed her.'

'Good heavens, no, don't apologize. I was going to say, she's better than she's been for a long time. Being at home makes her introspective, makes her dwell on it all. She was bottling it all up, refusing to talk about the miscarriages, the still-birth, even to me. For some reason she opened up to you. True, she's been weeping, but I don't think weeping's ever hurt anyone. But what's more, she's my June again. For months I've felt only part of her was with me.'

At that moment, June came in with a pot of newly made tea. Geoff was right, she did look different. She was more relaxed, less up-tight, the anxious air had evaporated. 'I'm sorry about all that, Vicar. Pregnant women go a bit odd from time to time. You'll find out soon enough when you have a wife of your own.' This time it was me who blushed a deep shade of beetroot.

'It's funny, you know, but it's the kindness that gets to me,' she confided. 'It's quite a strain, everyone you meet asking, "How are you?" That tilt of the head, that concerned inflexion in their voice really drives me nuts. The concern is genuine enough, but it's too much to bear. It's bad enough living with my sorrow if I lose this baby, without having to carry the disappointment of those around me.'

I listened attentively, but tried my best not to look 'concerned'. My neck ached with keeping my head vertical. My concentration drifted as I thought how privileged I was. I had been in so many situations like this, with people casually sharing their innermost secrets only moments after our being introduced for the first time. I didn't fool myself that it was because of any quality I had. Far from it, I was pastorally inept, socially gauche. It was something to do with the role, as if it shouted out, 'Trust me, I'm a priest!' And they did. The particular face might keep changing as vicars came and went, yet in their eyes the character remained the same. I often felt a bit of a Dr Who figure, that somehow, someone else had played this part before and paved the way.

'...the Broadhursts?' I came to, realizing that Geoff was putting the question to me.

'Sorry, I was lost in my thoughts, what were you saying about the Broadhursts?' I confessed.

'I was just wondering if you've come across them,' Geoff explained. 'I think they moved into Kirkwith about the same time as you. Mr Broadhurst is coming to see me tomorrow about two of his children starting here. It's funny, because in these parts it's usually left to the mother to make those arrangements.'

Geoff only had the barest details, so I was able to fill him in with the whole sorry story, explaining why the two children's start of term had been so delayed. Both Geoff and June listened attentively throughout; at several points in the conversation, June was in tears, her heart wrung out for the pity of it. She would make a superb mother.

By the time I left Eastwith it was dark. The moon was full and guided by its light and a rather dim front light powered by dynamo, I cautiously made my way home. From time to time I caught the dim shadow of a creature running across my path, a harvest mouse, a shrew, a weasel with its long thin body which made it look like a shrew stretched out. In the half-light I couldn't really be certain what the tiny creatures were. I could make the front light brighter by pedalling faster, but that was hardly a wise course of action when an unidentified obstacle lay ahead. Larger creatures were more easily recognizable. I saw a hare, only a little more startled than I was, which spurted across the road from the fields, ears and body longer than a rabbit's, legs more muscular. Overhead flew a barn owl, ghostly white in the moonlight, on the hunt for the tiny mammals that my bicycle was good enough to flush out from the undergrowth. A real frost now competed with the lime from the fields, making the road twinkle like a thousand diamonds and me freeze.

Before going home I called at the Manor to see George Broadhurst and tip him off about my conversation with Geoff. It was a delicate matter, since I didn't for the moment want to give the impression that I had been gossiping about his business. But he wasn't in the least offended, but quite the opposite, seemed relieved that I had told part of his story. Once again, I found myself admiring his generous spirit. 'Actually, I'm very grateful to you, David. You just can't imagine how very difficult it is to tell the whole story from scratch, time and time again. I was so glad that when you came the other night, you knew already. I'm glad the school knows now. It'll make tomorrow so much easier. But, er… do you mind if I make a confession?' George looked very serious indeed.

'Er, no,' I said, warily. Whilst people baring their soul was an undoubted privilege, once was probably enough for one day.

'The thing is, I'm dying for a drink. I'm afraid I'm a Guinness addict. I've got a few bottles in the fridge. Would you like to join me?'

Relief made me laugh out loud. Not only because I was spared another heart-to-heart, but also because Guinness was my favourite tipple too. An hour or so later I wobbled home on my bicycle, a warm feeling of well-being undiminished by the dim headlight and still moderately raging ford. Stout was undoubtedly good stuff.

CHAPTER FIVE

'I'm the Archbishop of Canterbury, you know.' The old chap looked at me with a fixed stare and immediately stuffed the Communion card I had given him down his trousers. Whilst the action seemed a curious qualification for a post I knew to be already filled by someone with even whiter hair than the man before me, I felt it wiser not to agitate him.

The morning wasn't going well. An emaciated old lady wandered around the room staring out with vacant eyes chanting, 'Wha, wha, wha!' non-stop. As those who live in a cathedral close soon become oblivious to the cathedral's clock chimes, fortunately I soon grew accustomed to the noise of this resident Red Indian and was able to carry on regardless. What gave me a headache were the protests and outrage of the other old people in the room, who loudly and repeatedly tried to shut her up. Anything I said was punctuated by, 'Be quiet, the vicar's here; can't you show some respect?'

I was trying to celebrate communion in the pensioners' home at Eastwith. I had called in at the place the day before, during afternoon play-time at the school, and had had a chat with Matron, a heavily made up woman with bleached hair who smoked throughout my visit. The arrangement was that I would come back the next day, giving Matron and the staff ample time to identify those who wished to receive the sacrament and gather them together in a suitable room.

That at least was the theory. In practice when I arrived I found that no preparations had been made whatsoever. Matron and the staff rushed around shouting, 'Do you want to take Communion?' at each resident, shaking them awake if they were asleep, firing the same question at them regardless of how disorientated they might be as they came to.

'Do you want to take Communion?'

'Yer what?' one old man replied.

'I said "Do you want to take Communion?" ' Matron raised her voice by several decibels.

'I'd rather have a pee.'

'Yes, but when you've been, do you want to take Communion?'

'Oh, go on then,' the man replied, rather as if he was acquiescing to a second Rich Tea biscuit.

All the communicants were dragooned in this way and eventually herded together in the TV room, hardly the most numinous of places. One old lady definitely decided she wanted to have nothing to do with this religious nonsense, so wheeled her chair at great speed to the double doors, unfortunately getting jammed in the exit with a jaundiced old man who was wheeling himself in. They shouted obscenities at each other, each turning the wheels of their chair with such determination that they became locked together all the more. The only thing Matron could do was to drag them both off in this very antithesis of a love-seat and let them battle it out in another room.

Although broadcasting began much later in the day, the set was on with about half a dozen residents avidly watching the test card and listening to the accompanying music. I tried to turn the thing off, but was shouted down by the telly-addicts. I did however manage to reduce the volume, but even so, Communion was accompanied by background music. 'Tea for Two' vied with the Collect for Purity, Eartha Kitt trilled 'I'm just an old fashioned girl' along with the Confession, and Jesus' words over the bread and wine were accompanied by Cliff Richard singing 'Bachelor Boy'. All this was accompanied by the Red

Indian and her critics, so that the service proved a cacophony of
several voices:

'Almighty God, unto whom all hearts be open,'

'*Tea for two, cha, cha, cha, cha, cha, cha...*'

'All desires known,'

'*Wha, wha, wha, wha, wha, wha, wha...*'

'And from whom no secrets are hid,'

'*Shut up, show the Vicar some respect!*'

'Cleanse the thoughts of our hearts,'

'*Cha, cha cha.*'

'We acknowledge and bewail our manifold sins and
wickedness...'

'*...and an old fashioned millionaire!*'

'Likewise after supper he took the Cup, and when he had
given thanks he gave it to them, saying...'

'*...I'll be a bachelor boy, until my dying day.*'

It was almost like all the machinations of one's brain being
played out loud with no editing whatsoever, the subconscious
aired, random thoughts broadcast, wild ideas swirling around
without suppression: a nightmare indeed.

But that was nothing compared to the point where the
inmates received the bread and wine. One old dear, after I had
put the consecrated bread in her hands, tried to stash it away in
her handbag. Whilst I had written off to experience the loss of
the Communion card lodged down the Archbishop of Canterbury's trousers, I took a dimmer view of this offence, so had to
resort to struggling with her to try and get the bread back
again. 'Gerorff! Help, he's pinching me stuff!' she shrieked in
complaint. Fortunately no one came to her assistance, so we
avoided a major brawl. Even so, a priest fighting with just one
communicant seemed a travesty. Jesus' Last Supper with his disciples was a fraught occasion to say the least, with dark betrayal,
torture and death lurking in the wings. If they managed to
avoid fisticuffs there, then the precedent ought really to be honoured on subsequent occasions.

Another old man chewed the consecrated bread for a few seconds before he came to a halt and assumed a thoughtful look, quite a rarity in that place. Then he took the masticated bread out of his mouth and handed it back to me, with saliva dripping off it, with the comment, 'No thank you, sir, I'd rather not if you don't mind.' No amount of cajoling from me would get him to eat it, so I put the bread back on the paten and smuggled it home with me; I would decide what to do with it later.

As if that wasn't enough, another old lady's hands shook so much as she received communion that the bread slipped off them and disappeared down her ample cleavage. Rescuing the body of Christ from handbags was one thing; risking accusations of sexual assault was another. I opted to have a quiet word with Matron after the service, suggesting she retrieve the bread when the old lady undressed and encourage her to eat it.

I came away from that place feeling spiritually shell-shocked. I cycled home in a daze, oblivious to the marvellous countryside which only the day before so enthused me. I dug a little hole in my garden, buried the chewed-up remains I had smuggled out of the home, and then went inside and lay on my bed, thoroughly exhausted.

I grieved for a service which had had such a glorious potential, but had proved a travesty. I grieved for the sheer misery of all those old people. In the days before Alzheimer's and dementia were in common vocabulary, it was simply assumed that most people became like that, that nothing could be done for them. Such places only compounded the disorientation. Separated from their home with all the memories it contained, separated from their roots, brainwashed by a television blasting out at all hours, little wonder their personality fragmented.

Even talking to old people in such places was fraught with pitfalls. You didn't want to draw attention to what they were missing, so several topics of conversation were taboo subjects. You could hardly enthuse about your bracing walk in the Dales when they were stuck in a wheelchair, imprisoned in a hot

66

house, day in day out. What the weather was doing outside those four walls was, quite frankly, irrelevant to them, since their environs were the same stifling temperature, winter in, summer out. Pain was something which loomed, the pain of separation, the physical pains of old age, but pain called for silent sympathy and could hardly be a talking point.

They could talk about their memories, if they had a memory, or their family, but even here you had to exercise some care. In East Hull my fellow curate and I used to visit a very gracious old lady who had been in a home for many years, and although she was a lovely soul she had effectively lost contact with the outside world. We used to talk about what was going on in her former church, the characters she had known, and then we moved on to her family. She had a favourite son who was quite poorly with cancer, and the inevitable question we put, week in, week out, scratching around for something to say, was, 'And how's your son?' which would set the woman off on a long description of his ailments.

In the course of time, the son died and I took the funeral, with his mother sitting at the front hunched up in her wheelchair, the most heart-rending of sights, a parent who had survived her child. My colleague was away on holiday, but I briefed him on the sad developments as soon as he returned. Unfortunately, on his next visit to the old people's home, during a long silence, he reverted to the time-honoured formula, 'And how's your son?'

'Oh, he's not too bad,' the old lady replied, clearly also conducting the conversation on automatic pilot. Then her senses returned and she chirped, 'He's dead!' as if death was just another ailment that her son was suffering from. The tragedy was that even before he died, in one sense her son was already dead to her, as was virtually everything else outside the four walls of the home which was not her home.

Dwelling, as I did that evening, on the loneliness of old age inevitably led me to focus on my own loneliness. It was a wonderful job, sharing people's joys and sorrows, laughter and tears, welcome at any meal table or family hearth. But at the end of the day, it was a terrible shock to have to leave all that and return to an empty, cold house. Sometimes the silence was refreshing, a retreat from all the clamour. But more often than not, it mocked me, 'Everyone else you encounter has someone, but you have no one!'

'You want to get a dog, Vicar, living in that rambling house all on your own. It'll do you good to have a bit of company.' Sam Harsley had accosted me as I cycled back from Eastwith; we had talked about this and that, nothing in particular, until entirely out of the blue, he had spouted forth his unsolicited advice. Primed as I was by my experience at the old people's home, I had taken it to heart. So much to heart, that I found myself scanning the 'Pets for Sale' column in the York Evening Press. I didn't particularly fancy the corgis, alsatians and poodles, who saturated the column; but one entry caught my eye:

For Sale. Welsh Collie pup. Myrtle blue. Mum quite enough to cope with, so we have to bid the son a reluctant farewell. £3. 10s. to a loving home.

I'd owned a sheepdog as a boy and had fond memories of a devoted yet independent pet. The offer seemed just the ticket, so I rang the owner in York and agreed to fetch the pup the next day. It would do me good to have a break after such a busy week.

Even then, standing around on the pavement at 7.25 on a foggy morning, stamping my feet to keep them warm, was a funny way to begin my day off. Yet I had no alternative but to get up early and catch the one and only bus to York. I could hear the slow steady chug of the bus engine, an eerie sound which grew neither louder nor softer as time seemed suspended. But then suddenly its headlights pierced the fog and it drew up, its interior lights compounding the rather ghostly sensation in the gloom. Since Kirkwith is a dead-end village in every sense of the term, the bus had to execute a tricky turn in my drive, narrowly missing backing into a ditch, before it eventually pulled up alongside me and I hauled myself aboard.

The bus wended its way through most of the Vale of York, covering some 18 miles and taking over an hour to reach the city walls. At this time of the year it also took you from the dark of night through dawn to the light of day, although the thick yellow fog muffled the effect on this particular morning. An already slow service was made even slower by being so user-friendly, stopping at the end of virtually every garden path, with the driver getting out to help the infirm up the steps, and waiting, with horn tooting, for regular passengers who came hurrying along, toast and marmalade in hand, finishing off their breakfast as they ran.

The trip was conducted in silence, most of the passengers still emerging from sleep and therefore resistant either to making conversation or responding to it. This served to make the journey drag all the more, so that it seemed an age before the bulbous bus squeezed through the Barbican, the arched east gateway through York's ancient city wall. It disgorged its cargo outside the market (already in full swing at this early hour), with Ron the driver cheerily bidding farewell to each passenger. He was clearly a very trusting man, since a significant number of those alighting from the coach promised, 'I'll pay you tonight, Ron.' Presumably they would have the funds to pay the 3s 4d return fare when a visit to the bank had made them more solvent. Unfortunately such visits to the bank didn't make some of them more honest. Sam Harsley, in waxing lyrical about 'our local bus service', had mentioned one or two deceitful characters. 'Ee, Vicar, they're real scamps. They promise to pay Ron on t' return journey, but then go and hitch a lift back in a friend's car or a farm lorry, so Ron never gets his money. Ron's as forgetful as he is trusting, so he can't remember who's paid and who hasn't. They ought to keep a list, but Ron ain't one for administration either.'

Sam's description of the whole enterprise had been both fascinating and amusing. 'T' company started in 1862 with a coach and 'orses. Comin' o' automobile might have changed t' world, but it didn't alter their timetable by a minute. In fact, they say that galloping horse could beat stuttering engine and get to York in just under an hour. Though I think that's probably a bit o' folk-lore that's stretched the truth a bit,' Sam commented, with a twinkle in his eye. 'The buses they have are a bit cronky, though.'

'What's the company called?' I had asked.

'It's known locally as Ron Ran Run, because Ron has always ran the daily bus run to York,' Sam very helpfully explained. 'Ron Ran Run, bit of a tongue twister in't it?' he chuckled. 'Then there's Ron's elder brother, Sid. He keeps to t' local school run because of his poor eyesight. You must have seen him, chuggin' around Kirkwith, Beckwith and t' other hamlets at t' speed of a tractor, harvesting Eastwith's school's scattered pupils.' Sam had paused to savour his agricultural allusion.

'But isn't it terribly dangerous?' I had asked.

'Nah,' Sam had replied. 'Providin' parked cars don't surprise him, he does fine. All t' locals know it's wiser to move their vehicles off t' road at going-to-school and coming-home time,' he had reassured me, mistaking the cause of my anxiety. Clearly they were only worried about their cars, not the kids; no one seemed to have any concern about children in transit in those days.

'Now the third brother is Harry,' Sam's lecture had continued, as he proved a fount of information. 'He runs the local garage and he's a dab hand at t' mechanicals. Without him, no one could coax those two elderly buses into giving service. T' school bus was bought in 1935; second hand, I think it was. T' York bus is a flashier model, bought new in 1947 and so barely run in.' Again Sam had had that twinkle in his eye which considerably lightened his otherwise quite formal delivery.

'Do you know, in both buses th' windows are wedged tightly shut. Folk say that's 'cause heaters have packed up long ago, so they try to keep t' summer's heat in to warm 'em through t' winter. Doesn't work though. After bein' in Ron's bus your feet are like blocks of ice from about now until April.' I resolved to put on two pairs of socks whenever I travelled with Ron Ran Run.

'Have you ever been to t' Blackpool illuminations, Vicar?' Sam's little lecture had taken a surprising turn.

'No, that pleasure in life still awaits me,' I admitted.

'Well, you don't need go as far as Blackpool. You just go to Wilberfoss on a dark night when Ron's turning off t' busy Hull road. Ron does as Harry tells him an' idles t' engine just above tickover, to preserve it. He never goes more than 30 mph, if that. When he turns off t' main road, the string of car lights following stretches for miles. A fair few kids who live near the junction turn out just to see the sight. It's a real treat, believe me.'

I mused on Sam's words as the bus chugged away. My day out in York was to be a long one, since the bus didn't set off back until 5.30pm. That left quite a lot of time to kill, since I wasn't picking the puppy up until four. I lingered in the market for a while, intrigued by all the activity, serenaded by the calls of the stallholders; that they were completely incomprehensible to anybody but themselves deterring neither their frequency nor their volume.

After drinking my fill of the scene, I walked back to the Barbican, climbing up the steps onto the wall. On the wall's top, the wide walkway enabled me to do a clockwise circumnavigation of York, with my circuit of the city only broken by the Rivers Ouse and Foss. Last night's TV news had featured the opening of the Post Office Tower, complete with rotating restaurant treating its customers to a spin around London. In a similar vein, I decided to have a spin around York. I was grateful though, prone as I am to motion sickness, that it was my feet which did the moving whilst the walls remained mercifully static.

Even though the early morning mist still clung to the medieval houses and shops, it had lifted enough for the towers of the Minster to be clearly visible, like a ship with three solid stone masts looming out of a sea of fog. Soon that fog was gone altogether, as the sun broke through and presented me with a breathtaking panorama.

The Minster was never out of my sight, its disproportion to the rest of the buildings in the town really quite startling, as if the standard measures had somehow been recast when it was built, with what was normally an inch measured as a yard. I actually found this disparity quite unnerving, recalling my childhood worry when a newly presented toy car jarred with the scale of my other toys. Somehow its proportions threatened my neat, ordered world, and I felt disturbed. It was that same disquiet now as I gazed on the Minster. Whatever your religious state or lack of it, its presence made a bold statement about the infinite in the midst of the finite.

Having said the Minster was never out of my sight, in a strange way I felt I was never out of its sight as I walked around the walls. It appeared rather shy, watching me from a distance, disclosing parts of itself, a rose window here, a chapter house there, only when it felt it could trust me or that I could take what it had to reveal. Towards the end of my walk, as the walls penetrated the Cathedral precincts, the Minster seemed too near, almost as if I had violated its space, that there needed to be a distance between the two of us, that I was unworthy of this privilege of being so close. By the time I came down from the walls I had stopped thinking of the Minster in terms of it and more in terms of thou, not a you, but a thou of deep respect.

I saw other things beside the Minster during my two hour amble, and yet its presence throughout filtered how I saw those other things, heightening the value of them. The Wolds to the east, the Dales to the west, the Moors to the north, with Kilburn's White Horse beaming in the sun's rays, presented a frame to the canvas that drew me to wonder. The normally disparate parts of the canvas itself seemed to have a unity to them: Terry's chocolate factory belching out sweet smoke; the curving railway station with trains big and small coming and going; Archbishop Holgate's Grammar School, my old school, nestling in the shadow of the Minster; the modern tenements with rooms at the walls' level, whose inhabitants looked out at people looking in; the spires and towers of numerous churches, of much smaller scale than the Minster, but whose unmistakable family likeness made it obvious that she had spawned them up and down the city: all these things somehow belonged together with the Minster as their focus.

The only thing that jarred the harmony of this scene was the River Ouse, which cut through the city like a sharp knife. Never really able to overcome its genesis in the rugged terrain of several of the Yorkshire Dales and angry at its confused parentage, as it surged through York it always seemed to blow a fierce wind which chilled your very soul. Even the Vikings, who had the audacity to sail up the Ouse to pillage York, could never really match its ire. As I shivered that morning by its bank, I longed to return to the Derwent, a river more at ease with itself, its assurance reflecting its origins in the rich, grassy moors above Scarborough, its youth spent wending its way through the rounded wooded Wolds, before reaching its adulthood in York's gentle Vale.

The rest of my day was spent on more mundane activity, browsing in bookshops, lunch in Terry's, the chocolate factory's shop window in the centre of York which also boasted a restaurant serving wholesome meals at reasonable prices. Whilst sitting eating my meal by an upstairs window I looked out at Betty's Cafe across the road, in 1965 very much Terry's inferior, but thirty years later one of the most prestigious string of restaurants in the North.

Bill and Hannah Everingham had told me how they had stopped off at Betty's for afternoon tea, and Bill, his appetite being what it was, had ordered a cream cake between the two of them. After a fairly long wait a surly waitress brought a tray, poured out the tea and put the cake, whose diameter was no more than five inches, in the middle of the table. Bill's face had taken on a dark, troubled look. 'Ex-cuse me Miss, I think you've got t' ord-er wrong. I ord-ered a cream cake; all you've brought me is a flipping big bun.' Bill ended up buying two flipping big buns to sate his appetite, and having washed it down with a thimbleful of tea, vowed he would drive home for his afternoon refreshment in the future.

After lunch, having found a pet shop, I bought the few requisites needed by a budding dog owner. Armed with a basket and a carrier bag of dog food, I nudged my way through the crowded streets, and eventually, with arms aching, found the terraced house where I was to pick up the puppy. As soon as I rang the bell, there was an intense barking from the other side of the door, a deep, resonant woof accompanied by a yelp, taking alternating turns. Eventually the door opened and the dogs' owner briskly introduced herself. 'You'll be Mr Wilbourne. I'm Mrs Sawyer. We talked on the phone. This is Susie, my lively collie dog and this is her pup – call him what you will. The way he chews the furniture, we call him any swear word that comes to mind more often than not.' She suddenly noticed my dog collar. 'Oh, I'm terribly sorry, I didn't realize you were a man of the cloth.'

'Don't worry,' I reassured her. 'Even the most perfect pet can try the patience of a saint.'

'Ay, well this one ain't perfect and I'm certainly no saint,' she quipped. 'But though a bit boisterous, he's a loyal, comical little dog. He takes after his mum. I've got my hands full with her, so I couldn't be doing with two of them. How are you going to get him home?'

'I've come from Kirkwith on the bus,' I answered. 'I thought I'd sit him in the basket on my knee.'

'Kirkwith, Kirkwith, Oh yes, I know where you mean. He'll last the journey. He's just about house-trained. It won't take much more than 30 minutes will it?'

'Actually it takes an hour,' I informed her.

'Good heavens, but it's no distance. What on earth are you travelling in? A hearse?' Again she blushed as she realized her tongue had run away with her. 'Oh, I'm sorry. I didn't realize what I was saying. I suppose you have a lot to do with hearses in your line of work.'

'Just a little,' I said, smiling in amusement.

'Have you got time to come in and have a cup of tea before your bus goes? It'll give you a chance to get to know the little fella.'

I accepted her invitation and was ushered into a spacious lounge. I noticed the carpet, threadbare in places, the cotton chair covers, torn to tatters at their base, the chair and table legs, scratched and worn. This shabbiness jarred with Mrs Sawyer's appearance, which was smart in the extreme.

Over a cup of tea I made friends with both dogs; they seemed delightful creatures and made a big fuss of me. But as I got up to go, and Mrs Sawyer handed me the puppy on its lead, Susie's good nature turned to ire as she snarled and snapped. Mrs Sawyer grabbed her collar in the nick of time, otherwise I am certain she would have savaged me for stealing her off-spring. I bade Mrs Sawyer a hasty farewell before taking to my heels, dragging the whining puppy along behind me. As I hurried through York's famous snickleways, Susie's fierce barks rang in my ears, a more than eloquent requiem for her lost pup.

The bus journey back was as noisy as this morning's had been quiet. Exhausted by his trek across York, the little pup slept all the way, nestling in the basket on my knee. Because I was new and largely unrecognized, with my scarf covering my dog collar to keep out the evening chill, I was able to enjoy snippets of news whose bearers were uninhibited by the presence of a clergyman.

A voice from behind me wafted by. 'It must be his. T' child looks just like him with that blond hair and blue eyes. She and her husband are as dark as the ace of spades.'

'Ee, I'm not so sure,' came her neighbour's response. 'She's stuck up and as cold as cold can be, that one. I can't imagine her own husband getting near her, let alone anyone else's…'

I decided to turn a deaf ear to further revelations, but was thwarted by a penetrating voice. ' "Don't you think you can get me out o' 'ouse as easy as that, you lazy swine," my Joe said to him. "If you think I'm moving, wit' missus expecting, when I've worked me fingers to t' bone for you these past dozen years, you'd better think agin." He truckles to no man, my Joe, not even t' boss. "Don't think you can move your son and his fancy piece into me 'ome and do me out of a job. That lad wouldn't last a day on t' farm without me to guide him." He told him straight, just like that. He sorted him out good and proper. We've had no trouble since.' I made a mental note to handle very carefully any forthcoming baptisms where the father was called Joe.

'I doubt if she's cleaned it this side o' Christmas. The grease in that cooker must have been an inch thick. Shelves and table were covered wi' dust. It's a little wonder those kids are always having t' trots. They blame t' sickness on somethin' in t' water; too much muck in t' kitchen more like.' I made another mental note not to eat anything when visiting dodgy looking homes.

I tried to concentrate on choosing a name for my new dog, but a conversation with a churchy theme enticed me to eavesdrop once again. 'The cheek of it. He's only been vicar of Fangton five minutes, and then he flatly refuses to christen our Sophie's baby, when she's lived there all her life. Just 'cause she doesn't go to church. She's got better things to do with her time than spend hours chantin' psalms and looking as miserable as sin. Little wonder nobody goes with a po-faced vicar and congregation like what we've got.' I silently thanked God that I was vicar of the Withs and not Fangton.

The passengers also displayed an impressive wider horizon. 'What on earth did the Queen think she was doing giving an MBE to those good-for-nothing Beatles when a good haircut was all they deserved? If she'd given me one I'd send it back in disgust.'

'But what would she ever give you one for, Mabel? You have to have done something big for the country to get one of those.'

'Oh do you? And what have the Beatles ever done for our country other than run it down?'

Someone else chipped into this conversation, 'What does MBE stand for, anyway?'

Silence reigned for a few moments as the bus to a man and woman racked their brains. 'Mentioned By Elizabeth' seemed the most popular suggestion with 'May Boost England' a close second. Their ingenuity amazed me.

A snap opinion poll amongst the bus passengers revealed that most were totally mystified as to why Harold Wilson should oppose Ian Smith's wanting to govern Rhodesia. Comments like, 'It's our land anyway,' alternated with 'Just look at the mess they made after they let them have the Belgian Congo back.'

Shrewd political commentators blamed it all on the government: 'That Labour lot are soft in t' head. They should never have been voted in after t' war. T' country's gone to dogs. We 'ad an Empire on which the sun never set, then those fools gave it away for nowt.' Needless to say, the Withs were a solid Tory stronghold.

Further entertainment was provided by the bus's foreign correspondent, who explained about a recently found map which conclusively proved that the Vikings had discovered America, apparently called Vinland in 'them days'. This sparked off a great deal of speculative follow-up. For instance, it did much to explain the prodigious sexual appetite of 'them Yanks' stationed at a nearby camp during the war: 'It must have been all that hot Viking blood soaring through their veins.' Although at least one lady still had her doubts: 'That Arnie, who got our Carol into trouble, looked more like an Eyetie than a Viking, with his swarthy looks and smooth tongue and his "Warnt anee silk stockings, maarm?" '

Our Carol's getting into trouble prompted another conversation, which was conducted in hushed tones. 'She's on it, you know, our Samantha's on it.'

'On what?' whispered another voice.

'On it, you know, on-the-Pill.' The last three words were breathed out in staccato fashion.

'But she's only 21. I didn't even know she was courting.'

'Ay, she is sure enough. She's going around with someone called Eddie who works at the aerodrome. He's got his own flat there, which is part of the trouble. She's terribly keen on him. And he's terribly keen-on-it.' Again the hushed staccato tones.

'But what does your Jim think of it all?' The whole bus waited with bated breath for the answer.

'Think, think? He'd have his belt off to her if he even got a whiff of what was going on. She's still a little girl in his eyes. The apple of his eye in fact.'

'Well, I'm afraid his apple's got a worm in it.' The whole bus guffawed at this double entendre.

Throughout all this banter, I maintained a dignified silence. The implicit and not so implicit racism I didn't intend to let pass by, but by the time I had a counter-speech ready, the rest of the passengers had moved on to a wildly different topic. It was a veritable firework display of a conversation and the hour sped by. I felt my education, and store of bad language, had been broadened considerably.

I opened up the house and settled the puppy into its basket in the kitchen. Not only had I spent the return journey eavesdropping, I had also decided on a name for him – Dewi, David in Welsh. It seemed apt to name a Welsh collie after the saintly bishop who had roamed the Welsh hillsides shepherding his human flocks.

I cooked a tea of yet more lamb chops from Mr Hinchcliffe, butcher of distinction, with Dewi bounding around my feet.

I then relaxed and watched 'The Saint' on television. It was the usual plot: scene set in Act I; all but crucified in Act II; resurrected in Act III, with a halo over his head heralding the end. I had that funny feeling I had come across that theme somewhere before. I switched over to the BBC for Michael Aspel reading the news before I took Dewi out for a stroll and settled him down for the night. I put a hot water bottle in his basket and set a ticking alarm clock near him, as a comforting sound. Soon after I retired to bed, happily exhausted by my day.

I recalled how my first boss had been a stickler for working every hour that God sent, driving himself and his assistants terribly hard, allowing them little if any time off. Asking my colleague to do an 'urgent' visit on his appointed day off for the third week in succession, he was surprised by his splenetic reply: 'Fine, no problem. But while we're about it, are there any other of the Ten Commandments which you would like me to break?' Keeping a Sabbath rest does us all good.

I awoke the next morning to find Dewi had chewed the hot water bottle to bits, dousing the kitchen floor with its contents, or at least what I hoped were its contents. The alarm clock was in a bad way too, since the puppy had clearly spent most of the night trying to crunch it like a bone. I was grateful the clock was still intact, with none of its parts missing. To cap it all, Dewi had had a bout of diarrhoea, no doubt brought on by his being separated from his mother combined with an indigestible diet of rubber. As I cleared the mess up, I was followed around by him, wagging his tail, looking very pleased with himself indeed. 'It is not good for man to be alone,' God proclaims in the Book of Genesis. If he had to mop up a fetid kitchen, I guess he'd think again.

CHAPTER SIX

The whole kitchen was thick with the smell of cooking, a stew steaming on the hearth, Grandma stirring it, a handsome candle and holder in her hand so that she could see what she was doing. I guess she actually couldn't see that well. Every few seconds tallow from the hot and thick candle dripped into the stew, no doubt making it exceedingly nutritious.

It was Saturday night and I was visiting the Weightons' farm. It was over a week now since Mrs Weighton had tipped me off that something was amiss at the Manor. Though I had had a brief word with her after church on Sunday, I thought, at the very least, she deserved to have fuller details about the Broadhursts' situation. It had been a busy week, and I felt bad that I had postponed my call until now, but Mrs Weighton wasn't offended in the slightest. Rather she was immensely grateful that I should bother to tell her anything at all, a response which I found very humbling.

'Now sit yourself down, Vicar. How very kind of you to call,' she had said, as I stumbled through the back door which led straight into the ramshackle farmhouse's dark kitchen. Doris Harsley had told me how the Weightons had 'escaped being electrified'. At the time she was treating me to a survey of homes in the parish, whose condition and cleanliness abysmally failed to reach her high standards. This included nearly all of them as far as I could gather. Doris' statement considerably puzzled me until I worked out that it was all to do with electricity being brought to the village way back in 1947. Whether the Weightons had failed to pay the connection fee, or were too far from the main road, or had simply been forgotten was a matter for much local conjecture. But whatever, the outcome was that their farm had no electricity, with coal and wood fires, a Yorkshire range, oil lamps and candles serving them very well indeed, as they had done their ancestors for centuries.

Despite Mrs Weighton's kind invitation, sitting myself down in her kitchen was easier said than done. The supply of seats was plentiful; that was not the problem. For there in abundance were wooden chairs, comfy chairs, stools, even a sofa with the stuffing spilling out (I learned later that their pet rat had escaped one day and used the sofa as a nest, undetected for weeks). But none of them was free.

Two large sheepdogs, muddy from working in the sodden fields, were asleep on the sofa, growling and snarling in their dreams so fiercely that I felt they were best left undisturbed. Mrs Weighton's husband together with two burly sons and a farm hand occupied the four chairs around the table, eagerly awaiting the meal that Grandma was so expertly cooking by the fire. Copies of the Farmers Gazette, which must have run right back to the turn of the century, were stacked up precariously on three of the stools, with two kittens sleeping peacefully on the fourth. On one of the comfy chairs there was a pile of clothes awaiting ironing, on the other a screwed up tea-towel. I was almost certain that it was the very same tea-towel which had been used to cover Mrs Weighton's contribution to the bunfight following my service of welcome. Perhaps they only had the one. At the end of the day I opted for the arm of the sofa, sitting down upon it gingerly so as to avoid having a bite-on part in the sleeping dogs' dreams.

Having declined to take tea with them, I relaxed as best as I could on my perch and enjoyed the banter around me. The day had been spent clearing and dredging ditches and there was much talk of 't' digger playin' up' and 'so and so's septic tank o'erflowing into t' fields'. The latter subject, which included

81

careful description of the contents of the said tank, seemed a topic of conversation hardly compatible with a mealtime. Although, thinking further about the meal's preparation, maybe it wasn't so incompatible after all.

Notwithstanding their tempting cuisine, the Weightons clearly were kindly folk who welcomed every waif and stray. 'Do you know Vicar they make a space at their table for every passing tramp,' Doris Harsley had breathlessly informed me. 'Any dog, cat or even vermin which turns up on t' farm is treated as a family pet.' That their hospitality extended to rodents earned the Weightons five stars in Doris Harsley's *The Withs' Guide to decrepit dwellings* (a document circulated by oral transmission), which I guess made a lot of people wary of visiting the run-down farm.

Which was a pity, because many people whose homes were rodent-free and far better turned out than the Weightons lacked their *joie de vivre*, and it would have done them good to have encountered it. Their attention to the outcast and those on the edge of society was impressively Christlike and put my prejudices and sheer snobbishness to shame. I also guess that when Jesus supped with sinners, prostitutes and tax gatherers, he wasn't unduly fussy about what he ate; having encountered the heartiness of the Weightons' table, I began to wonder precisely where my own faddishness about food got me.

The Weightons' sheer generosity of spirit meant that they encountered people whom others, who meted out their hospitality, missed. As the menfolk put their feet up after the meal, I got chatting to Mrs Weighton while she cleared up in the kitchen. Since the place looked more of a mess at the end of her ministrations than it did before she started, I guess 'clearing up' was a misnomer. 'How many people work on the farm?' I asked, to cover up an awkward pause in the conversation. I had been struck dumb with horror as I watched her washing up in a bowl which looked as if it contained soup rather than clean water.

'Oh, just my Fred and the two lads and Hans. And me, when I've got a minute. I usually end up feeding t' calves, whilst they do the heavier work,' she replied, scrubbing at a particularly persistent gravy stain with the all-purpose tea-towel.

'Is Hans a relative, then?' I put the question, because in my limited experience not many farmers would entertain their farm-hands at their table unless they were related. Certainly not Joe's boss of the Ron Ran Run bus fame.

'Oh no,' Mrs Weighton replied, with a sweet smile. 'Although I suppose he's like a brother to us. It's a long story, Vicar. You'd better settle yourself down on that stool over there while I tell you it all.' I removed the bag of sugar and two bags of flour and dusted the seat down. Mrs Weighton watched, amused. 'Are you sitting comfortably now? Then I'll begin,' she quipped.

She fondly rattled on about him for the next ten minutes. He was simply known as Hans. His real Christian name was unpronounceable by Yorkshire folk suspicious of foreign names at the best of times, and so he was greeted as Hans, answered to Hans, even signed his Christmas cards as Hans.

His origin was shrouded in some mystery, not because he wasn't forthcoming about his past, but because you couldn't always keep up with his broken English. 'It doesn't seem very courteous, always asking him to repeat himself,' Mrs Weighton had explained. 'But as far as we can make out, he was born in the German-speaking part of Romania, "Transylvania, vere the vampires come vrom!" ' There was a glint in Mrs Weighton's eye. I recalled her impersonation of Bill Everingham, a week or so before. She was clearly a versatile mimic, which made listening to her telling Hans' story a great pleasure.

Before the last war the Nazis had conscripted him into the German army, but when Rommel's force in Egypt had been routed, Hans was captured and shipped to Britain. Since he had no sympathy at all for the Nazis who had uprooted him, he was categorized as a low risk prisoner of war, billeted in a camp near Kirkwith and allowed to work on the land as a farm labourer.

Initially it had not been an easy time for this apparent German, working alongside Englishmen. Those old enough to have lost family or friends in the Great War and whose grief was still sharp vented their wrath upon this very convenient scapegoat. There were some younger men who were itching for combat but had to stay on the farms because their work was a reserved occupation. This Nazi suddenly being delivered into their midst seemed an answer to their militaristic prayers.

'Ee, he had a hard time to begin with, Vicar,' Mrs Weighton explained. 'We took to him right from the start. He was a friendly, simple soul, and proved a hard worker. His attempts to get his tongue round our language made us laugh, which was a real tonic, because there wasn't much fun around here during wartime.'

All the bullying Hans had survived, mainly because of the kindness of the Weightons, who treated him as a friend rather than a foe and shamed the rest of the Withs. It was a testimony both to their kindness and to the even harsher conditions he must have endured in Transylvania that following the war he elected to stay on in England. The ever kind-hearted Weightons permanently employed this hard worker, housing him in a tied cottage, which to Hans was like a palace, often entertaining him at their table.

He was a man who enjoyed simple pleasures, strolling the winding mile to Beckwith of an evening, invariably ending up in the Stack, the parish's one and only pub. Over a pint or three he regaled the locals with his tales of Transylvania, 'Vere the vampires come vrom!' Since most of the locals had never ventured further than York, his stories widened their horizons considerably and he proved a much sought after drinking companion. The mile back to Kirkwith proved far more winding on his return, although like all good Transylvanians, Hans could hold his drink as well as any Yorkshireman.

The bullying he had endured during the war had subsided and been replaced by immense popularity, with Hans being adored by young and old alike. 'He's a cheery sort, but it's not just that,' Mrs Weighton had confided, looking thoughtful. 'He's got some fascinating yarns which keep folk spellbound, without a doubt. But I think the real reason why he's so liked now is that he's adopted here as his home. He's given the place a vote of confidence, and they love him all the more for it.' I was aware that this had only happened because the Weightons had first extended their vote of confidence to him, an enemy in their midst whom they had the nerve to welcome.

As Hans had got to grips with English, he'd also picked up some funny phrases along the way, whose nuance he'd obviously misunderstood. For instance, as Mrs Weighton came to the end of her tale, Hans popped his head around the door, before he took his leave for his nightly expedition to the Stack. His final and startling words to me were, 'Well, bugger off then!' This valediction he clearly took to be the Yorkshire equivalent of *auf Wiedersehen*. Hans' angelic smile, entirely devoid of malice, drained the phrase of any evil intent. Even so, it was a novel dismissal.

With Hans gone, I was able to chat to Mrs Weighton about George Broadhurst and his four children. Tears ran down her face as she heard the grim details. And then all of a sudden she brightened as an idea came to her. 'The last thing that man wants to be doing of an evening is to come home to a cold house and have to cook tea for all those children. Grandma can look after things here while I pop over t' Manor, light all t' fires and get a wholesome meal on the go.' Her suggestion was impulsive and characteristically generous. I promised to have a word with George as soon as possible and broach things with him. She had come to Hans' rescue; maybe she could do a similar job in this case. I would have to alert him, though, that because the Manor was 'electrified', candle-tallow stew would sadly be off the menu. I felt certain he would be able to live with his disappointment.

Just before I left the farm the otherwise taciturn Mr Weighton spoke up: 'You haven't seen our pride and joy, have you, Vicar?' For a brief moment I feared I was going to be introduced to a further Weighton delicacy, a pear and paraffin pie, or something of that ilk. Or perhaps there was a third sheepdog, even more ferocious than his two brothers still sleeping and snarling on the sofa.

Mrs Weighton put paid to my speculation. 'Ay, she's singing with t' school choir this afternoon, but she should be home any minute. You'd like our Rebecca, she's an intellectual like you.' I wasn't quite sure what qualified me to be an intellectual in the Weightons' eyes, but I soon found out. 'I couldn't help noticing all those books stacked up in your study. You know, when I came to see you about t' little girl at the Manor. Our Rebecca's a bookworm too. She hardly ever had her head out of a book when she was a child, then all that studying at university, and even now, she's always reading. "Keeping up with her subject," she calls it. "You'd have thought you'd know it all by this time," I said to her, only last week, when she was still reading after midnight. "Oh no, Mum," she replied. "You can only be a good teacher if you're learning yourself." '

'What does she teach?' I asked, trying to feign just a casual interest.

'German, at the Mount School in York,' Mr Weighton dourly informed me.

'Ay, she learned the language from an early age, with Hans being around,' his wife explained further. 'Apparently, she's even got a Transylvanian lilt to her pronunciation; a very rare quality.' Mrs Weighton had that gleam in her eye again.

'She's a funny lass, mind you,' she added, to temper the praise. 'Very particular, always tidyin' her room; it's the teacher in her I suppose. But she often has a go at me, in her gentle way of course, about whether this is OK to eat, whether that is OK to eat. I dropped a roast potato on t' floor t' other day and she wouldn't have it after that. "Now then, Rebecca," I said. "A bit o' dirt isn't goin' to kill anyone." But she still didn't have it. A bit like you and that tea-towel, if you know what I mean.'

I blushed as I realized that my reservations about Mrs Weighton's hygiene hadn't gone as unnoticed as I'd thought. I blushed further as Rebecca walked in at that very moment, for she was ruddy, of beautiful countenance and goodly to look at. I knew just how the prophet Samuel must have felt, when David, his future king, was brought in from the fields.

PART TWO

++++++++++++++

CHAPTER SEVEN

Our mistake was to cast Paul Broadley as a shepherd. Though one of the youngest boys at Eastwith School, he was by far the naughtiest. It had to be said he looked very much the part, decked out in his father's dressing gown, with a Marks and Spencer's tea-towel wrapped tightly round his head. The dressing gown cord was a little long, however, which meant that he repeatedly tripped over the thing as he stumbled to his place, looking like a very drunken shepherd indeed. Once he was seated on the ground (to coin a phrase), safely out of the range of the restraining arm of Miss South, Paul whiled away his time by trying to lasso the brass eagle on the lectern.

My first months at the Withs had flown by, almost as if I had gone to sleep in October and had woken up to find it was Christmas. Indeed I had to pinch myself to check I wasn't dreaming as I sat in Kirkwith Church on Christmas Eve. Eastwith School was staging its final production of a Nativity play which had successfully toured Eastwith and Beckwith churches on the previous two nights. Well accustomed to the plot, my wandering mind raced over all that had happened to me in the last three months.

Undoubtedly, one of those things that had happened to me was Dewi. He was growing into a lively dog who chewed and chased everything that could be chewed and chased. The stream of tradesmen's vans now had a sheepdog escort as they drove up and down the drive, a sleek animal who was far fleeter than the speed their stuttering engines could deliver. Those, like the postman and paperman, who came by bicycle, found their heels snapped at as they furiously pedalled. 'What untidy postmen you have in these parts,' my parents had observed, when they came to stay with me. 'The bottom of that man's trouser legs are in tatters.' I didn't have the heart to tell them it was Dewi who had done the damage. I tried to restrain him, I tried to keep him in whenever I was expecting a visitor, but to no avail. Fortunately both chewed-up men were very understanding. 'Now don't you worry, Vicar,' Charlie the postman reassured me. 'I've got a collie just like that at home. There's only three rules with sheepdogs: they'll roam, they'll nip and they'll worry, and there's nowt you can do about it. So don't keep apologizing for him. T' missus can stitch up me trousers. There's not much for her to do at home now that t' children have left.'

He was right about the worrying. Dewi focused all of his flocking instincts on me and whittled when I was not around. In the North, whittling means to fret as well as to erode, and in that respect it was a word which summed Dewi up to a tee. Having gnawed at most of the furniture in the kitchen, one evening when I was out he decided to set about my study. Though thwarted by the sturdy metal filing cabinets and desk, the desk-top contents he found far more exciting. He savaged a Prayer Book, consuming whole portions of the Burial Service, before assuaging his thirst by lapping up the contents of a bottle of ink, which he had cunningly tipped over. He was then sick over my newly fitted carpet, which hitherto had been a delicate shade of beige. Despite my scrubbing at the thing intensively on my return, beige islands in a sour sea of blue were henceforth the order of the day.

Though Dewi gave the vicarage a lived-in feel (and smell), my loneliness was still acute. I had confided my concern to Stamford Chestnut, who had encouraged me to come to this forlorn spot to start with. Instead of sympathizing, he had given me a stiff lecture. 'Now don't go feeling sorry for yourself. It's all very selfish, this wanting company, this wanting someone to talk to, this wanting someone to encourage you. What about what the other person wants? And you can't hurry love. You just have to wait.' It was only when I had heard the Supremes trilling those last two lines on the radio that I realized where he had drawn his homely philosophy from.

Whilst not hurrying love, I did try to engineer another meeting with Rebecca Weighton, but without much success. She attended church regularly, listened to my sermons raptly, and shook hands at the door enthusiastically, eyes sparkling. Frustratingly, though, the church door, with its staccato exchanges, was not the ideal place to proposition her. 'Good morning, Bill, and thank you for reading the lesson so mean-ing-ful-ly... Good morning, Doris, you played that last hymn with great spirit... Good morning, Sam. Yes, the brass has brought in a tidy sum this last week... Good morning, Mrs Weighton. Good morning Rebecca. By the way, are you doing anything next Tuesday night?' Even in my imagination, let alone in reality, such a turn in the conversation didn't seem on. I found myself visiting the Weightons' farm quite frequently, on some errand or other, but each time Rebecca I did not see. However, like God, I had great hopes for Christmas Day. I had accepted Mrs Weighton's invitation to dinner, laying aside any concern about culinary hygiene.

So, unwittingly, had George Broadhurst. He had eagerly tak-en up Ivy Weighton's offer of help, which meant that he and the children came home to a warm house and meal each evening. 'I've written to the Water Board about the quality of their sup-ply,' George confided in me about a month after Mrs Weighton started 'doing' for them. 'We seem to be having a lot of tummy upsets, and I think I've narrowed down the culprit.' I kept my own counsel, only hoping that in time the family would become immune to all the strains the infamous tea-towel carried.

June Goodmanham too had come to the Broadhursts' rescue. Whilst George was teaching at the university, she minded baby

Simon, looking after Sally and Peter as well, between the end of school and their father picking them up. She was proving an immensely able surrogate mother, her confidence surprising her and growing day by day. Predictably, she had been a marvellous presence backstage before each performance of the Nativity play, calming Geoff's very understandable panic as he tried to assuage the stage fright of his charges. Once Geoff had accepted June's sensible advice and had taken off his heavy Harris tweed jacket (which I understand was a very rare event indeed), he regained his cool. And he needed it.

As on the two previous nights, on Christmas Eve the children performed to a packed house, with proud parents squeezed a dozen to a pew. Older brothers and sisters stood at the back, also proud in their way, but prone to giggle when 'their Karen' appeared with fluffed-up wings or 'their Tim' walked on, face blackened with boot polish. Sam Harsley had dutifully got up before six that morning to stoke the boiler, so the place was piping hot even before the cast and audience started to assemble. With us all inside the atmosphere was as stifling as a greenhouse on the hottest August day, in sharp contrast to the severe frost outside. By the end of the evening the holly, which was rather gorgeously entwined around the dog-tooth chancel arch, began to wilt and look in a very poor way indeed, its red berries popping in the heat.

Not surprisingly all the congregation had a ruddy glow to their faces, but none were more rosy than June Goodmanham, on the verge of her eighth month of pregnancy. By no means gross, she nevertheless had that lovely rounded look to her which exuded maternity. I had asked her to read one of the Lessons, the one from Luke where the angel Gabriel surprises Mary with the news she is to give birth to God's Messiah. She had read it beautifully in a measured way without over-dramatizing, simply bestowing on the reading the poignancy of her pregnancy:

'Hail, thou that art highly favoured, the Lord is with thee: blessed art thou among women.'

Paul Broadley's success at the seventh attempt to lasso the eagle brought my wandering mind back to focus on the play. His success was rewarded with a ripple of amused applause from a congregation who should have known better than to encourage him. The cord, now running from shepherd to lectern, effectively roped off a major part of the stage area, with the result that the angels had to be diverted. The latest publication by leading biblical scholars which poured scorn on angels' very existence, Geoff and I had ignored, and instead plumped for blonde-haired little girls dressed in white sheets with cotton wool wings. Five-year-old Sally Broadhurst was one of their number but was confused by the re-routing and accidentally brushed her wing against a candle and became a very fiery angel indeed. Bill Everingham, for once not slumbering in his churchwarden's seat at the front, suddenly found himself with a walk-on, or rather rush-on part, bravely beating out the flames with his gloved hands. His quick thinking prevented a comic scene from turning into a tragic one. Even though it was difficult to look pale in this sweltering temperature, George Broadhurst turned ashen as the spectre of death returned to haunt them in the midst of this jolly Christmas interlude.

As well as Bill Everingham, the other saviour was Doris Harsley, who was playing the harmonium for us that night. She had had the recent good fortune to watch the film *A Night to Remember* when the Mothers' Union had had its pre-Christmas trip to the Mecca Cinema in York. Amongst other things, she had been much impressed by the Titanic's orchestra playing to the very last to instil as much calm as possible as the ship slithered down to its icy grave. Taking her cue from them, whilst our own high drama was going on she treated the congregation to twelve verses of 'Away in a manger' when the norm is usually no more than three. Undoubtedly this steadied the congregation whilst calm and order was restored and the play resumed.

The only casualty caused by her quick thinking was her husband Sam. Already sweltering in his black and heavy verger's gown, beneath which was his equally black and heavy woollen suit, he looked ready to burst after he had pumped sufficient air into the organ to blast out a dozen verses of the carol. He had no need of Brylcreem for the rest of that evening; his sweat alone was more than sufficient to plaster his hair down.

There was one further hitch as Jesus' interrupted nativity resumed. The moment of any birth, let alone that of the son of God, is always a delicate event to stage for family entertainment. June had carefully instructed the Virgin Mary (played by Sharon Dubbins, aged ten and a half) to pick up discreetly the baby doll from the cot by her side at the appropriate moment.

Unfortunately the appropriate moment came and went and no child appeared: the cot was small, the doll was large and was clearly wedged tight. Despite the muscular frame which had meant that generations of Dubbins had been champions of the bale-throwing competition at the Howden Show, no amount of heaving by the good Sharon would release the thing. Joseph (played by Lee Moss, aged eleven and a quarter, and known to be slightly keen on Sharon) was quick to assist, putting his knee on the cot and pulling with all his might. A final massive tug did the trick, although Jesus' sudden birth sent Lee toppling over and falling into the huge Christmas tree behind him. For several tantalizing seconds the tree rocked, together with the bin in which it was anchored, threatening to crash down on the cosy nativity scene. Some wag at the back shouted 'Timber!' but mercifully the tree stayed itself and for the second time on that holy night disaster was averted.

There were some moments of high drama as well as farce. A hush happened to fall on the church as the time drew near for the Wise Men's visit, which gave the loud rap on the west door an even more dramatic effect than was intended. In fact many were so startled that they literally jumped in their pews, their nerves already frayed by candles torching angels and by Lee's brief but productive foray into obstetric practice.

It was me who opened the door, introducing an icy but welcome blast into our overheated building, with the snow, which had just begun to fall, billowing in. There shivering on the church step were three exotic travellers. Their robes, which bore more than a passing resemblance to the magenta velvet curtains from Eastwith School, were profusely decorated with largish pieces of silver paper. I guess these were unwittingly provided by the sages' mothers, who would find their stock of aluminium foil depleted when they came to prepare their turkey for the oven on Christmas morn.

As the three kings rustled into church three treble voices, crystal clear, pierced the hush as they sang 'We three kings of Orient are'. Each king sang his solo perfectly, processing down the aisle as he did so, and knelt with great reverence before the muscular virgin (miraculously recovered from her protracted and complicated delivery), presenting their gifts of gold, frank-incense and myrrh.

The gold was a gold-plated Victorian chalice from Eastwith Church. The incense burned in a thurible and wafted upwards in great clouds of smoke as the king swung it. The myrrh was a phial of precious scent, formerly owned by Jennifer Broadhurst, George's late wife; the king who carried it was Peter, their son.

Myrrh was a precious ointment used in Palestine to anoint dead bodies in preparation for burial, so traditionally the gift was seen to foreshadow Jesus' suffering and death. I had talked to George at length about the symbolism of that particular gift on that particular night: that the Christ child, whose birth we celebrated, was no stranger to pain and agony but embraced it all and somehow, in the heart of all the undeniable sorrow, conferred on it a God-given dignity. Peter performed his part impeccably, unstopping the phial and letting the drops of his mother's precious scent fall on the baby Jesus. Of course, it was only a worthless doll which had almost ruined the show, surely a travesty to see immensity there. Yet two thousand years before it was in a worthless stable and in a worthless manger that history itself had hinged. I caught George Broadhurst's eye. The significance, though shared very privately between the two of us, was vast. Never had the lines of the carol more meaning than they had that night:

> Trace we the babe, who hath retrieved our loss,
> From his poor manger to his bitter cross;
> Then may we hope, angelic hosts among,
> To sing, redeemed, a glad triumphal song.

The play came to its end; the actors and actresses went to sit with their mums and dads; there had been laughter, as there should be at Christmas; the cast had performed their part sometimes clumsily, sometimes movingly, the supreme point made well at the last. A silence, a holy silence, fell on the crowd for the last time as they bowed their heads for the blessing:

'May the blessing of God Almighty … be upon you, and those you love, this Christmastide and for evermore.'

At least those were the conventional words. But as I said them, the words of our oft-sung carol, 'Away in a manger', kept ringing in my mind, especially 'Bless all the dear children in thy tender care'. Inevitably I thought of the Broadhurst children. But I also thought of all the dear adults: George Broadhurst in his loss, sharpened at this time of rejoicing; June Goodmanham in her hope, yet a hope which had been cruelly dashed so many times until now; Jennifer Broadhurst, in a heaven where she basked in God's love, but bereft of her husband and children. As I thought particularly of them, I also focused on the congregation before me. 'God bless us all, God bless us every one.' Tiny Tim's words from *A Christmas Carol* rather than a Christmas carol always moved me to tears, coming as they do from one so frail, so vulnerable, yet with massive generosity of spirit. Tears were in my eyes now for the joys and sorrows that lay ahead for them all.

I stood at the door and wished two hundred people 'Happy Christmas' as they tramped out into the thin covering of snow.

Children eager to get home and hang up their stockings and pillow-slips and chase an elusive sleep; mothers with sprouts to peel and stuffing to mix for tomorrow's feast; fathers joking about how early they would be woken up the next day; old people who would happily take on ten times the hassle if they only could return to Christmases past. One of the last out was Hans, who shook me warmly by the hand, looked me in the eye and said, 'Well, bugger off then!' Behind him was Rebecca Weighton, the amusement in her eyes reflecting in mine.

The billowing snow proved just a sprinkling, which was just as well because later that night I had to cycle to Eastwith to celebrate Midnight Mass, my robes in a rucksack on my back. The covering of snow on the roads was unblemished by other tyre marks, although the dim light of my cycle lamp picked up a variety of animal and bird tracks. I pulled up to investigate where two sets of tracks merged in a bloody flurry on the verge, one obviously that of a rabbit, the more powerful hind legs leaving a firmer print than the forelegs, the other that of a fox who had clearly caught his quarry by the roadside and had his Christmas dinner early.

I parked my bicycle by the church door and walked in a little bow-legged after a three mile ride on a chilly night. My hands were numb with cold, but I wouldn't have missed such a magical journey for the world. Ron, of the Ron Ran Run bus service was churchwarden at Eastwith and was there to greet me. 'Vicar, why on earth did you cycle on such a cold night? If only you'd given us a ring, we could have sent Sid out to fetch you. He's at a bit of a loss during the holidays with no school run to do.'

Remembering what Sam Harsley had had to say about Sid's eyesight in the daytime, I shuddered to think what sort of journey I would have had with him driving by night. 'That's kind, Ron, but I love cycling, whatever the weather. Besides, the exercise keeps my weight down, what with all these Yorkshire teas that people are always plying me with.' The longer I was a vicar, the more diplomatic I was becoming.

The church was a sweet little Georgian redbrick building, basically a high-ceilinged assembly hall with an altar tacked onto the end. Although it was 'electrified', tonight it was lit entirely by candles, and the effect was simply lovely. Shadows flickered as I prepared the altar, with magnified images of hands and chalice projected onto a nearby wall. As we began the service, people clustered around the pockets of light to follow the words of the opening carol, singing with great gusto, 'And in thy dark streets shineth, the everlasting light'. In that dark church it was their faces that shone, yellow, in the candlelight. My mind flashed back to my first Sunday and the gypsies with their 'We believe in Him, sir, we believe in Him.'

As midnight approached I was acutely aware of the great privilege of simply being here with these people as we marked the birth which had made the world of difference to us all. I stood at the door at the end of the service, as cheery as the rest, exchanging the compliments of the season with all and sundry.

As I made my chilly way home through a fresh covering of fallen snow, I recalled one detail of the service at which I could now safely laugh aloud. That in itself must have made a funny sight, a rucksacked vicar weaving along the road on a snowy Christmas night, giggling uncontrollably. In the gloom of the church I had badly over-estimated the number who would like to take communion and so had consecrated far too much wine. According to strict Church law all that wine had to be consumed on the premises. I became increasingly concerned as I got to the end of the rail and came to Ron, my last communicant, with over half a chalice of wine still remaining, I knew that I couldn't possibly drink it all and be sufficiently clear-headed for all that lay ahead of me the next day, and so I added some words to the set text:

'Drink this in remembrance that Christ's Blood was shed for thee, and be thankful.' My bold voice was followed by a *sotto voce* from the heart:

'Ron, could you help me out please and drink it all?'

The congregation couldn't fail to have heard Ron's good-natured but loud response, 'Of course I can, Vicar. Very generous of you. Cheers!' Even though I squirmed at the time, why shouldn't we say 'cheers' to the Lord on his birthday?

It was well after 1am when I reached home. I gave Dewi a large mutton bone for his Christmas present, his tail beating a veritable tattoo on the kitchen floor in thanksgiving. Deciding I ought to acclimatize myself for what lay ahead, I treated myself to one of the mince pies Mrs Weighton had given me. Having washed it down with a scalding hot cup of tea, I retired to bed to snatch a few hours' sleep before dawn brought another run of services.

Christmas morning had a magical feel, a quiet holiness, with each gathering less busy than the previous night, but none the worse for that. It seemed no time at all before it was noon, and I was shaking hands at the church door for the last time. 'Look at the gold watch that he gave me I've always wanted one,' proclaimed Doris Harsley, as breathless as ever.

'Ay, let's hope she gets my dinner on time in future,' Sam quipped, following close behind. 'She's got no excuse now.'

'Happy Christmas, Paul,' I said to the unwitting star of last night's play. 'What a lovely teddy bear; who gave it to you?'

'Her,' Paul growled, nodding towards his mother. He obviously wasn't best pleased. When you're trying to project an image as a young tough, it doesn't help to have parents thrust cuddly toys upon you.

Hannah Everingham rushed past as we were talking. 'Lee, Lee,' she called, 'You've left this behind.' She was waving a blue balaclava, complete with a bobble. 'Who made this for you, then?'

'Me auntie,' Lee Moss replied, looking even surlier than Paul Broadley. I guess he was intent on losing this distinctly untrendy present at the first opportunity.

'Now you put it on; it'll keep your ears nice and warm,' his mother fussed. Lee gave her a look that could kill. 'Now don't you dare look at me like that. Just 'cause it's Christmas doesn't mean you can't be smacked.'

As I strolled back into church, those episodes swirled around in my mind. Doris' gift, much longed-for, but which would actually call her to account. Paul's gift, which he probably secretly liked, but publicly was embarrassed by. And finally, Lee's gift, which would soon be forgotten, at least if he had anything to do with it. I found myself staring at a poster stuck on the church wall, drawn by a Sunday school child, depicting the Nativity scene. It bore the caption, 'Jesus, God's gift to the world'. I felt someone was trying to tell me something.

Having changed out of my clerical gear, I set out for dinner at the Weightons' farm, with perhaps more eagerness than was usual for one of their invited guests who knew what to expect. 'Well done, Vicar, you've managed your first Christmas,' Mrs Weighton, complete with almost clean pinny, fussed over me. 'Ee, you must be feeling so tired. Just you sit down and relax, and let us do all the work.' As on my first ever visit, despite the generosity of her greeting there was actually nowhere to sit. Once again the two sheepdogs slept the sleep of the just on the sofa, their snarls and growls dissuading me from even thinking of disturbing them. The stools were still the repository for the Farmers Gazette, the tottering towers ten copies higher since my first encounter. Underwear of various dimensions still awaited its ironing on one easy chair, whilst on the other the tea-towel was enthroned. As before, Mr Weighton, the two Weighton boys and Hans all sat around the table in exactly the same places, permanent fixtures. Grandma was stirring the gravy, boiling in a pot over the fire; mercifully the daylight that particular Christmas day was broad, so she didn't need a candle to see by. Once again I perched cautiously on the sofa arm, until extra chairs were brought in from the bedroom so that we could all have a place around the table.

I had only accepted their kind invitation on condition that I provide the wine. I had calculated that four large bottles of sweet white would be enough to neutralize even the most determined germ. However, the way Hans knocked back the drink made me wonder whether any of the rest of us would ever reach the qualifying level for bacteria destruction. This concern notwithstanding, I was resolute to suspend, for today at least, any worries about food hygiene and set out to enjoy the meal from the very outset.

And a very fine meal it was. The tenderest roast goose, with all the trimmings, was served with sprouts, carrots, cauliflower, roast potatoes, mashed potatoes, all grown on the farm and absolutely delicious. This was duly followed by a magnificent plum pudding over which Mr Weighton poured a generous supply of brandy, so generous that the ensuing flames roared towards the ceiling before subsiding as suddenly as they had begun.

My qualms about the standards of catering briefly returned when I bit on something large and hard as I was chewing my first mouthful of Christmas pudding. As surreptitiously as possible I managed to get the offending morsel back on my spoon only to discover it was a threepenny bit wrapped in tissue paper. 'Vicar!' Mrs Weighton shrieked. 'You've found the threepence. That means that good luck will be yours for the entire of 1966.' Everybody heartily congratulated me as I sat there feeling rather bewildered by it all. Having initially thought that the coin had been accidentally dropped into the mixture by short-sighted Grandma, it required a giant leap of reason to grasp that the threepence's inclusion was intentional and that my finding it was the very best omen possible.

After lunch I made as if to help with the washing up. 'Men don't wash up 'ere, lad, that's mother's work,' Mr Weighton sternly lectured me. His wife joined in the conspiracy against herself.

'Ay, Vicar, we'll have none of that. Now you leave clearing t' table to me and simply sit and relax in a more comfortable chair,' she cooed. Yet again, she seemed oblivious to the fact that all the chairs were already taken in one way or another, so I found myself perching on the arm of the sofa once more. Rebecca sat on the other arm and gave me an amused, understanding look. She leant across the still sleeping collies and whispered, rather awkward in her boldness, 'I was thinking, even if baby Jesus himself visited us, there would be no room for him to sit down.'

Hans had brought his guitar with him and, after much encouragement from the rest of the family, eventually strummed 'Silent Night', singing the words in his lilting Transylvanian German, '*Stille Nacht, heilige Nacht.*' Rebecca softly accompanied him, singing in harmony. I'm sure our Lord himself would have been happy to stand or even perch for such a performance. As she sang, my heart pounded, providing a percussion which I was sure must have been audible to the rest of the household. If it was, then they were courteous enough to pretend not to notice. The only hostile sign was from one of the sheepdogs, who awoke from his slumbers and fixed a beady eye on me, his message unmistakable: 'You make one move, pal, and I'll savage you.' It was bad enough overcoming my shyness, without having a hostile guard-dog to boot. I decided to await another day. Yet again.

I returned home to find my sheepdog had not only demolished his mutton bone but had also savaged the Christmas tree. Dewi proudly bore in his mouth the fruit of his labours, a branch which was far too big for him, barring his entry into any other room since it kept on jamming across the doorway. He wrestled with determination, emitting a continual low growl which kept on changing pitch, like one of Ron's buses, labouring up a hill. His performance made me laugh: the best Christmas gift of all.

The next days flew by: lots of sleep; relatives visiting; long walks with Dewi in a landscape which shimmered with low December sunshine; thank yous said and delivered to almost every With resident who had played some part or other in the keeping of Christmas; a hangover of Christmas services marking a disparate group of saints, including Stephen, the first to die for the crime of being a Christian, John, who wrote it all down, and the Holy Innocents, babes born in the wrong place at the wrong time, who got in the way of the paranoid Herod, out to do to death the son of God before he even began.

Late on Holy Innocents' Day, I was woken just before midnight by the phone ringing. The voice at the other end was shaky, full of emotion, 'David, it's Geoff here, Geoff Goodmanham. I'm at the Maternity Hospital in Howden.' He began to sob. 'June's given birth, prematurely, to a little girl.' More sobs. 'They've told us she won't survive the night; will you come and christen her?'

I tried to sound calm, fighting the tears myself. 'Of course, I'll come, Geoff. I'll be with you within the hour.'

I quickly dressed, packed my robes in my rucksack once again, and set out to cycle the eight miles to Howden. A gentle breeze from the north sped me on my way, the night mercifully clear, crisp, trees silhouetted against a starlit sky, a glorious backdrop for my distinctly inglorious errand. I drank from my surroundings in all their fullness to strengthen me for what lay ahead.

The tower of Howden Minster couldn't loom quickly enough, and yet in a paradoxical way it loomed too quickly. Emotions were warring within me. Half of me wanted to be with them so very much. The other half wanted to stave off confronting the trauma, the soul-crushing grief. It dawned on me why Jesus delayed going to Bethany when Lazarus, his dear friend, was dying.

Leaving my bicycle near the main door of the cottage hospital, I went straight to Matron's office. As she led me to their room, there were few words between us, not even 'Have you had a pleasant Christmas?', nor 'It's a clear night'. No trivia at such an immense time.

There lying on the bed was June, looking exhausted. She cradled her tiny, premature baby in her arms. Beside the bed was Geoff, hair as ruffled as ever, Harris tweed jacket as crumpled as ever. His eyes were red with crying. He fixed me with a bewildered, pleading look. 'David, she's only two pounds; she's not got a hope. The doctor has told us she won't survive the night.'

What could I say? The little girl was nearly two months before her time. Thirty years later she might have stood a chance, but in 1965 premature care was still at a very primitive stage. I had never come across one so small and so early surviving. The doctor may have been blunt, but he was right.

My mind flashed back to the Nativity play, just four days before but seeming an age away. Then the couple had been so vibrant, had held the show together, June the epitome of expectant motherhood. Now they were a sorry sight indeed, June clutching her dying child, Geoff looking helplessly on. Racked with deep grief for them, I was immensely grateful for the words my office gave me, because those very words carried me; without them I would have broken down and wept. I spoke softly, 'June, Geoff, let's christen her.'

Matron was in attendance, and Sister fetched a kidney dish brimful with water whilst I put on my cassock and white stole. I took the frail little bundle from June, far too small for the white shawl which was wrapped round and round her, and held her in one hand. I said the words I had said so many times before, yet they seemed so heavy, so very heavy. 'Name this child.'

'Elizabeth,' June said, and then broke off weeping.

'Elizabeth Mary,' Geoff's gentle voice supplied the full name.

'Elizabeth Mary, I baptize you in the name of the Father, and of the Son and of the Holy Ghost. Amen.' I continued to hold the child in my palm and gazed at her. Tiny eyes, tiny ears, tiny fingers, tiny feet, all so wonderfully made; perfection seemingly for nothing.

Then a movement caught my attention. As the water trickled down her face to her lips, a little tongue came out of a little mouth and licked the drops.

The movement caught Matron's attention too, and she didn't just gaze on. 'This one's a survivor, she's not going to die,' she barked in crisp tones. 'Get Mr Stokes here,' she ordered Sister.

'But he'll be in bed by now. And Dr Harris said there was not the slightest hope, anyway,' the Sister stammered.

She was right to be nervous, for Matron brooked no discussion when she had made up her mind. 'Get him here now!' Each word came out like a gale. Faced by her in full flight, even God would have complied.

Events moved fast and furiously, and the rest of that night and the days beyond have a dream-like quality. Mr Stokes, fresh from his bed and bleary-eyed, carefully examined the child and agreed with Matron. Then came the mercy dash by ambulance to St James' Hospital, Leeds, where the baby was put into intensive care. I went along in Geoff's car following the ambulance and spent the long night with the couple, returning home the next day when it was clear that Elizabeth's life no longer hung in the balance. Even then, anxious days followed: breathing difficulties; feeding problems; severe jaundice.

Then, as 1965 gave way to 1966, the baby began to rally; she came out of the incubator and by mid-January came home. Needless to say, the whole village rejoiced. On returning to Eastwith, the first thing June did was to bring the child into school. Twenty-nine children gazed on admiringly. Even Paul Broadley stopped being naughty for a moment and stood silently before the tiny child. 'Look, Miss South, she's got mini-fingernails!' But Miss South could not look at that moment; she had caught something in her eye which was making it water. The red bricks themselves seemed to cheer, weeping flakes of joy. But none cheered as much as Geoff and June.

Eighteen years later, on 28 December 1983, I was a guest at Elizabeth Mary's coming of age. Because she had been such an obvious choice to be Elizabeth's godmother after the crucial role she had played in her birth, a much diminished Matron was there too. By now she was a retired old lady who walked only with the help of a stick. It was difficult to imagine that she had done a job which was now carried out by five hospital administrators with a fifth of her clout. Certainly none of them could have got Mr Stokes out of his bed on a wintry night.

After her shaky start, Elizabeth had grown up to be a healthy lass, beautiful, bright, now about to go up to Cambridge with a scholarship. She was the only child of her parents. June had had two further miscarriages and then called it a day.

Some while after that party, I sat in on a Church of England General Synod debate at York University on the baptism of infants. There were many powerful speeches informing us that it was silly to baptize babies, since a very necessary part of baptism was the response of faith by those to be baptized in promising that they would follow Christ and turn away from evil. A baby shouldn't be baptized because it obviously couldn't promise anything.

One speaker lectured us that too many people pandered to the foolish superstition that baptizing babies had some magical effect, as in 'Our Tracy hasn't half come on since she was christened...' I recalled that magic night in 1965 when I baptized the dying Elizabeth, two pounds in weight and two months too early. I must confess, I felt a considerable sympathy for those too many people and their superstition. Seeing a christening bring a child to life is prone to make you biased.

CHAPTER EIGHT

The deep tenor bell of Big Ben rang twelve times, the pensive pause before each chime driving you to reflect on the lost opportunities, the things left undone, the hurts unhealed, the resolution to do better next time around. I was at the Manor seeing in the New Year with George Broadhurst in a drawing room which was considerably warmer than when I had first encountered it three months before. A fire blazed in the hearth, heavy velvet curtains hung over the floor-to-ceiling windows, banishing the chill. George's generous portion of whisky was no longer an essential anti-freeze, but was none the less welcome. Hard though he had worked to get it in order, the room lacked a certain something when compared with other homes and other rooms I visited. A woman's touch, I suppose, so lacking in my home too. As we tuned in to the Home Service to herald 1966, one woman's absence hung heavily in the air.

One change that the new year would bring was certain. With the arrival of baby Elizabeth, Geoff and June would have their hands more than full, keen though they were to continue their kindness to the three younger Broadhurst children. George had always known that the arrangements with June would be temporary, although Elizabeth's premature arrival had made them a little more temporary than he anticipated.

I tried to lighten our intense and sombre reflection by telling George the story of Mr Soames, who had been vicar of the same tiny parish on the Yorkshire Wolds for 42 years. In his eighty-sixth year, he received a letter from the Archbishop of York, making a tentative suggestion in the gentlest of ways:

My dear Soames,

From time to time I go through the clergy files at Bishopthorpe and as I perused your file I noticed that you had recently celebrated your eighty-fifth birthday. I write to offer you my belated good wishes on reaching this most venerable age.

I was wondering whether, after such a long and immensely valued ministry in your parish, the time perhaps has now come for you to retire. Please don't feel I am exerting pressure on you in any way whatsoever, but I firmly believe that all of us, in the twilight of our years, deserve lighter responsibilities and a little rest.

Your sincere friend and Archbishop,
Cyril Ebor.

Mr Soames' reply had been terse:

Dear Archbishop,

I have no intention of retiring. When Archbishop Maclagan, the Archbishop before the Archbishop before your predecessor, instituted me into this living in 1907, he never mentioned in any way whatsoever that this was to be a temporary appointment.

Yours sincerely,
Charles Soames.

I was pleased that George laughed for the first time that night. The pressure was on, however, to find an alternative now that his own temporary appointment had come to its end. And workable though it had been, I had increasingly noticed that as autumn turned into winter, George had looked more and more drained. Dealing with massive personal grief, absorbing the grief of others, running a new university department as well as a new home undoubtedly presented a major challenge. I sensed that rather than being the sort of energizing challenge one could rise to, it was a debilitating challenge which was grinding George down.

As we quietly talked in the minutes after midnight, George rather shyly shared with me something that had happened over the Christmas season. 'I'd taken the children out for the day, looking up our old friends in York. I thought it would do us all good. It gave Ivy Weighton a break from cooking for us too.'

'It would give the children's tummies a chance to recover as well,' I silently thought to myself.

'Our last port of call was Pam,' George went on. 'The children love her, because not only was she Jennifer's closest friend, but also she was the infant teacher at the school Peter and Sally used to go to. Since Jennifer died she's been so good, keeping in regular contact, offering the children a soft shoulder to cry on.' George was telling all this in a matter of fact way, but then he paused for a moment to gather himself as his own grief caught up with him. I think it dawned on us both that he needed a shoulder to cry on too.

He eventually resumed. 'They love Pam's golden retriever almost as much as they love her. So they were delighted when she suggested they take her out for a good long walk. Pam and I stayed behind to look after Simon, who was asleep in his carry cot. I quickly realized that she had engineered our being alone, because almost as soon as the children had got out of the door, she got down to some serious talking.' As he ponderously said the last two words, George raised his eyebrows, like a naughty schoolboy who had been caught in the act.

'She was pretty blunt, stressing that things couldn't go on as they were. She as good as told me that I would be no good to the children whatsoever unless I took steps now to avoid the breakdown of health I was apparently hurtling towards.' George had half a grin, half a grimace. Clearly he was amused by Pam's forthrightness, yet at the same time her words had gone home.

'She was absolutely right, of course,' he admitted. 'I'd known deep down for a good few weeks that I couldn't carry on at this pace. But I kept on putting off doing anything about it, primarily because I hadn't the first clue what could be done. Pam put it all into focus for me, almost as if she was sorting out a disorganized child. "Now look here, George," she insisted. "What you need is someone permanently at home to give the children regular, sustained care. This headteacher's wife who minds them, this woman who comes in to do your tea, it's all right as far as it goes, but it's too piecemeal. Emma needs the space to be a teenager and not have to be a mother before her time. Simon needs someone to cherish him. You've got more than enough on your plate at the university. You need a home to recharge you, not deplete your energies." '

'Phew, what a woman!' I exclaimed. The fact that George had remembered her speech almost verbatim was evidence both of her forthrightness and how she had hit the nail on the head.

'That's only the tip of the iceberg, because she didn't stop there,' George explained. 'She not only eloquently diagnosed the problem, she also proposed a cure.'

'Really?' It was my turn to raise my eyebrows now. I would have defied the archangel Gabriel to have come up with a solution to all George's problems.

'To put it simply, the cure was herself. She offered to resign her post as an infant teacher. Though she dearly loves her job, she has the humility to realize she's not indispensable, that there are hundreds of others who could do the work as well as her. She did feel, however, that she was uniquely qualified for another post – my housekeeper!' George paused as he dropped this bombshell.

'What do you feel she'd bring?' I gently asked.

'Oh, lots of things. She's got the children's confidence for a start, having nursed two of them through starting school, feeling homesick and missing mum. And she can certainly run a home, combining work with looking after her mum and dad, until they died two years ago. I suppose coping with their death has primed her for dealing with the grief of others. She's certainly a good listener, when she isn't telling me my fortune! Her faith is very deep, David. I think that's motivating her. Although she wouldn't for a moment use such flowery language, I sense she sees her offer of help in terms of Christian service, a costly and sacrificial one.' George's cool, analytical mind had obviously been sifting all this for days.

'Have you got any reservations?' I asked, my eyes getting heavy. We were now well into the first hour of 1966, and I was aware I'd got an early service the next morning.

'Oh plenty!' George said, candidly. 'She's a strong personality; will she bully me? She likes the children well enough, but how will she cope with us 24 hours a day, day in, day out? How will she get on with me? After all, professors are funny old chaps. And will having an attractive young woman under my roof lead to gossip?' George's wildly shocked intonation on the last word made me laugh out loud. He laughed too.

'I don't know, George,' I commented, adopting a serious tone. 'In one way it seems heaven-sent. But I can see it's a big step for you. Let me have a think about it when my brain isn't fuddled by sleep and your malt. I'm more than happy to act as an honest broker between the two of you, if you think it's worth a go.'

'That's not a bad idea at all,' he responded enthusiastically. 'You could both come over for supper fairly soon and we could thrash it all out.'

Having agreed with him on the night after next, if Pam was free, I wished George yet again the happy new year he deserved and cycled home. I found Dewi still happily gnawing his

Christmas tree and got to bed as quickly as possible, aware that only five hours later I would be on the go again.

When I got up the next morning, the night had seemed so short that I had to pinch myself to make sure I wasn't still dreaming. Certainly I felt as if I was in a nightmare. There they were, Doris Harsley, Hannah Everingham, Ivy Weighton and her daughter Rebecca, faithfully gathered in Kirkwith's cold church for a Communion on the first day of the new year. There I was, standing before them, blushing and stuttering, cursing the fact that the Book of Common Prayer marked this day by keeping the feast of Christ's Circumcision.

In 1966 circumcision was not a word which easily slipped off the tongue, especially if you were a twenty-seven-year-old and very shy bachelor who had attended a single-sex school, studied physics at a single-sex Cambridge college and trained for ordination at a single-sex theological seminary. Thirty years later, in an age so liberated that the word condom can be freely aired at an Archbishop's tea party, such reticence may seem remarkable. But in 1966 I died each time I had to say the wretched word. In the course of that service I had to say it not once (which would have been bad enough), not twice, but no less than 15 times.

Each time I saw the word coming up, I steeled myself, convincing myself that I was not going to stutter, that I was going to carry it through nonchalantly without a flicker of embarrassment. And each time I failed and like an idiot kept stuttering the first syllable, 'Cir, cir, cir, cir,' finally almost sneezing it out, 'Cir, cir, cir, cir, shircumshishum.' My female congregation kept their heads resolutely buried in their prayer books, although I noticed Rebecca's shoulders were shaking uncontrollably. By the fifteenth circumcision I was feeling distinctly faint, and carried off the rest of the service in a state of suspended animation, the whole church bathed in a strange bright light on that dull January day. I thanked God that I only had to go through this charade one day a year, and that he had called me to be a priest and not a rabbi.

Circumcision had proved a problem since my first day as a priest. My boss had sent me to visit the children's ward in the local hospital where we were chaplains. I had bounded in, and began talking heartily to one mother sitting by the bed of her son, who had a sort of tent arranged over his lower half. 'And what's this little chap in for?' I had asked, tilting my head to the degree prescribed by our pastoral tutor at college to indicate my utmost concern.

The mother blushed, looked away from me and addressed the bleak hospital wall: 'He's been circumcised.'

I blushed too, muttering something like, 'Hope he's soon better,' before beating a retreat to the next bed. Unfortunately I hadn't learnt my lesson. There too was a young boy, tent over his lower half, his mother sitting by his bedside. 'And what's he in for?' I said, my heartiness reduced but not extinguished; yet.

The same blush, the same looking away, the same 'He's been circumcised.'

Three circumcisions and four operations to-lower-an-undescended-testicle later, I vowed two things. The first was that I would never, even in moments when I was at my most frustrated with parish life, yearn to be a hospital chaplain. The second was that I would never, ever again, in all my ministry, ask a patient what they were in hospital for.

As I stood at the church door, eyes downcast, shaking hands with my departing and thoroughly female congregation, I made a third vow. Either to support Prayer Book reform, or to be off sick on future New Year's Days.

I returned home and slept off my embarrassment. I pottered about for the remainder of the day, with Geoff Goodmanham driving me over to Leeds the next day to see his bright yellow baby in an incubator, whose every movement was watched over by a tired but obviously happy June. In fact, all three of us stood staring at the little mite who'd caused us so much trouble just four nights before. Few words were said. Our homage was silent; of the deepest sort.

That night I set out for supper at the Manor with my mind made up. I felt that George had crossed a major bridge, albeit prompted by Pam, in admitting that there were substantial issues that had to be faced to ensure his family's survival. Given that massive outside help was absolutely essential, Pam's was the best offer around. The fact that she was a skilled carer and teacher, who knew the children well, put her head and shoulders above any other candidate. Not that there were any other candidates.

I was glad that I had come to such a conclusion in theory, because from the very first moment George introduced me to Pam, I realized that any chance of objective assessment went out of the window. She had a vitality about her which exuded warmth. Her slight physique was more than compensated for by a bubbliness which made her character immense. She made you feel that she was interested in you, her steel-blue eyes gazing attentively as you spoke. Emma stayed up while we had pre-supper drinks; the two clearly got on like a house on fire.

Once Emma had gone to bed, our conversation took a serious turn. 'What do you think of my proposal, David?' Pam asked, putting it as directly as that.

I felt I could be direct in return. 'I think you are offering to respond to a major need in a major way. In all my future ministry, I guess I will seldom, if ever, come across anyone else who will be prepared to respond as you have. But it's for you and George to decide whether it's on or not.'

'I'd be very grateful if we could make a go of it,' George quietly but firmly said. Obviously he had made his mind up too.

'Well, that's great,' I replied. 'In that case, I think you've got to agree some proper terms, like setting Pam's quarters, salary and days off, for instance. I also think, for both your sakes, you ought to agree to a probationary period, say six months, after which either of you can honourably withdraw.'

'Oh, I think that's absolutely right,' Pam interrupted. 'Although, since one of my reasons for coming is to give the children some security, we'd better keep the probation side to ourselves, rather than make them feel we are all somehow under test conditions.'

'Yes, I agree with you there, Pam,' George added. 'David, we thought about setting a *terminus ad quem*, as well, when Simon reaches school age. By then, we'll all be five years older, and Pam's major work here will have been accomplished. I think it only right and fair for her to think about resuming her teaching career at that stage.'

My presence actually felt superfluous, since they seemed to have it all sorted out. But it was a good evening, with good company, heightened by the promise that the Broadhursts' fortunes were on the upturn. The meal, a goose casserole prepared by Ivy Weighton at the farm, was good too, at least until I gulped down what I suspected was a large piece of candle fat. Following the meal, I gratefully accepted George's offer of a large whisky in the hope that the alcohol would sozzle any germs.

Any expectation that my role that night was as the adviser, George and Pam the advised, was quashed over coffee. 'But what about you, David?' Pam asked, as directly as ever. 'George pointed out your vicarage when we went for a stroll this afternoon. Those eaves! You don't live in that rambling house all on your own, do you?'

'Oh no, I've got a dog!' I described a few of Dewi's exploits, at which they both roared with laughter.

But Pam would not be fobbed off. 'But who've you got to talk to? You must feel so drained when you've visited all these people and absorbed all their problems. I know what I feel like when I return to an empty house at the end of the day, and I've got colleagues to talk to and don't carry the burden of priesthood. Who ministers to the minister at the end of the day?'

'There's always God, I suppose. He's quite understanding most of the time.' She was touching a nerve, and I was guarding myself by being flippant.

'Well, he's not bad, I suppose,' Pam acknowledged. 'But, David,' she continued, a twinkle in those blue eyes, 'I think a warm-hearted chap like you also deserves someone a little more local.'

I blushed and she blushed and we left it there. I came away from the Manor feeling that it was not only George and the children who would never be the same once Pam moved in.

Pam's words were still ringing in my ears as I trudged to Kirkwith Church the next Saturday, with marriage on my mind. Sam Harsley had told me how, in the fiercest heatwave, he always kept his cream in Kirkwith church to stop it going sour; surrounded by trees, set by the river, the building had the permanent chill that ideally suited it for the role of improvised larder. The present cold snap had turned the larder into a deep freeze, with Sam reluctant to stoke up the boiler as generously as he had done on Christmas Eve. 'We don't get enough folks to warrant it being warm,' was his excuse. Which struck me as a curious sort of logic, and not an attitude which was likely to encourage more people to come. Folk would think twice about turning out to hear even the Pope if he was preaching in a fridge.

Given the low temperature in church, it was definitely not the time of year to get married. I felt for the bride and bridesmaids in their frail finery, doomed to shiver through the entire service. The bride-to-be was the distinctly unvirginal Mabel Dubbins, sister of the infamous Sharon of the Nativity play fame. Despite her muscular frame, her rounding belly was evident to all and sundry at last week's wedding rehearsal. Whether it be sunshine or snow, of necessity the marriage would clearly have to be soon.

At least the snow had stopped. Dawn had been heralded by angry-looking clouds which billowed and then dropped their load over the four inches of snow which had already settled overnight. But by noon the sun had broken through and the church looked like a picture from a Christmas card, decked in white, surrounded by frozen ings which stretched as far as the eye could see, Kirkwith's own Arctic wastes. Ducks, geese and swans made a funny sight as they slithered and waddled on the ice, crashing down hard as their legs slithered from under them. Mindful of their need for fresh water, Sam had trudged backwards and forwards from his home, transporting bucket loads to fill the trough by the church wall.

The wedding was to be at one o'clock. I arrived an hour early to help Sam set the place up. It was then I noticed the waterfall cascading down the inside wall of the south aisle. Inevitably, since he knew every nook and cranny of the church and virtually every year of its history since the Norman invasion, Sam had come across the problem before. The gutters must have been frozen solid with ice, so that as the sun shone and the snow melted on the roof, it was forced to find a different route to earth, drenching the south aisle in the process.

In an hour's time, the church would be full. Weddings were few and far between, especially at this time of year, and in a little village were missed by no one. I would have to act quickly if I was to avoid turning a wedding into a mass baptism.

What was needed was for someone to climb up to the roof and shovel the snow off. We had a bit of a problem in that Sam was afraid of heights: 'I'll do anything I can for t' church, Vicar, anything. But one thing I can't do is climb a ladder. No more than two rungs up and my head starts swimming and I start sweating like a pig. I've been to t' doctors with it, but there was nothing he could do. It's me impetigo, you see.' I guessed he meant vertigo, otherwise his 'sweating like a pig' could only worsen his skin's condition.

Despite his aversion to climbing ladders, he was quite happy to hold one whilst I climbed up to the roof, armed with a shovel from the boiler house. Fortunately I was kitted out in the right gear, wellingtons and a warm overcoat, so once I had gingerly climbed over the parapet and walked along the gangway, I began my mammoth task. With the urgency of a stoker trying to fire the Flying Scotsman for a record run, I shovelled snow as rapidly as I could, hurling it well clear of the church. To prevent his verger's black turning into a snowman's white, Sam retreated into the church to bail out the flooded aisle as I worked above.

After shovelling for twenty minutes, I noticed a figure in the graveyard, cigarette in the corner of his mouth, mackintosh askew, a camera round his neck. Even back in 1966 weddings were incomplete without the inevitable cameraman. 'Hello,' was my cheery greeting from on high.

'Hello, mate,' he replied. Once he realized he wasn't being addressed by angels, he took on the camaraderie of a fellow workman. 'Have you seen the wretched Vicar? I wanted to take a picture of 'em walking down the aisle, but parsons are touchy about flashin' in the service.' He gave a seedy laugh.

Raising myself to my full height, I directed a shovel-full of snow at him which fell bang on target, extinguishing the cigarette in an instant. 'I'm the wretched Vicar,' was my rejoinder. 'I'll be with you in a minute.' After that he proved the meekest photographer I'd ever encountered.

The congregation arrived in dribs and drabs, unaware how close they had been to having a walk-on part in Noah's flood. Mindful of the Archdeacon's unfortunate experience on my first night, all cars were parked at the Hall, with everyone walking the last half mile on the snow-covered track. Their delicate footwear looked extremely indelicate by the time they had trudged to the church door.

As one couple passed me, I heard the woman giving her husband a stern lecture, 'Now you're not to have a drop at t' do afterwards. T' roads are crawling with t' police armed with that new breastalizer.'

'It's never called a breastalizer,' her husband dared to interject.

'Yes it is,' his wife corrected him. 'It's called a breastalizer 'cause they get you to suck on it and if it turns purple, they'll know you've been drinking. Then bang goes your licence. Who'll drive t' tractor after that, with you off t' road, I ask?'

Fears about drink apart, everything else seemed to be going swimmingly (perhaps an unfortunate adverb under the circumstances). Despite the weather, the bridegroom, the best man, the bridesmaids (Sharon Dubbins among them) and even the blushing bride herself, with father on her arm, all arrived on time. At one o'clock precisely, I was standing in the porch, with the burly bride arm in arm with her burly father, with her equally burly bridesmaids behind her. I was about to nod to Doris Harsley at the harmonium to strike up the Bridal March for us to process in, when a little man with a massive beer belly rushed out of church and tried to squeeze past us. What with his beer belly and the Dubbins ensemble assembled in the porch, it was a fair struggle.

Gasping for breath, he addressed me. 'Bloomin' hell, I've left the missus at home. You'll have to hold on, Vicar. She'll kill us if we start without her.'

It transpired that 'the missus' was the groom's mother, so carelessly left behind by the groom's father in his panic as he ferried everyone else to get to the church on time. Fortunately they only lived at Beckwith, a mile away, but even then, we stood shivering in the porch for 20 minutes whilst Doris treated us to her extensive repertoire on the harmonium. 'The Golden Chord' alternated with '*Ave Maria*'. The tunes were repeated so many times that they became ingrained in my memory; even 24 hours later, I could still hear Doris playing. By the end of the twenty minutes of pumping the organ, Sam had worked up a sweat which his 'impetigo' would have been proud of.

'The missus' duly arrived, followed by a sheepish 'Mr', who had clearly been treated to a piece of her mind which had endured the whole journey and promised to continue well into the service. Her litany, consisting of just one sentence with varying emphasis, droned on and on: 'He left me!' She looked like a pantomime ugly sister who had escaped from a performance of Cinderella. Had I been her husband, I would have opted for being hung for a sheep instead of a lamb, and would never have bothered retrieving her, enjoying the wedding free of her company.

When her litany continued beyond the first hymn and threatened to drown out the magisterial words of the service, I decided that enough was enough and broke off to address her. I spoke softly, so only she could hear: 'Madam, I am really sorry that your husband accidentally left you at home. But these things happen. He realized his mistake and we held up the whole ceremony while he came to collect you. You're here now. If you go on like this, you'll ruin not only your own day, but also probably the most crucial day in the life of your son and daughter-in-law. For their sake, I ask you to calm down.'

My little speech did the trick, although 'the missus' had found a new victim for her wrath, giving her husband and me alternating glares for the rest of the service. Doris was very kind in her comments afterwards. 'Vicar you did absolutely right I felt like giving you a round of applause when you sorted that woman out.'

There was one further hitch. As we were singing the last hymn, just before we retired into the vestry to sign the registers, I noticed the bride had gone deadly pale, and was swaying on her feet. I signalled to her husband to attend to her, but he was oblivious, eyes staring straight ahead in a daze, probably wondering what his mother was going to do to them following the service. It was Sam and I who took hold of the portly girl, shuffling her into the vestry where we sat her down. The time-honoured cure for a faint, head between knees, was not possible due to her substantial girth, but in due course she came round and was able to sign her name not too shakily.

When it was all over, Sam guffawed loudly as he no longer had to restrain his mirth. 'What a wedding! A waterfall down the aisle, t' vicar on roof shovellin' snow, a photographer hit by the biggest snowball I'd ever seen and an abandoned mother-in-law. And if that weren't enough, all topped by a fainting bride. If we hadn't got hold of her, Vicar, I reckon crash which followed would 'ave shaken t' pillars. I was watching an American wedding on t' telly last night, where t' minister drawls at t' end, "You may now kiss the bride!" 'Ad he been 'ere today he would 'ave 'ad to 'ave changed it to "You may now catch the bride!" ' He laughed so much, his face became red and blotchy with the exertion. I feared the day might have brought his vertigo on after all.

CHAPTER NINE

'I want to see life in all its fullness,' the Bishop of Pocklington's letter had emphasized. 'Please, please, don't put on a special show for me. I simply want to see the parish as it is.'

I had decided to take him at his word, so the first port of call for his day's tour was Eastwith's old people's home. I had done the decent thing and tipped off Matron beforehand. However, given the scant preparation she made whenever I visited the place, I felt fairly confident that life in all its fullness was precisely what the Bishop would encounter.

I could not have been more wrong. We were effusively greeted at the door by a much changed Matron. The bleached hair had been replaced by a more natural tint, any make-up was subtle rather than laid on with a trowel, and the cigarette which normally hung out of the corner of her mouth, ash trailing, had been banished entirely. Her normally broad Yorkshire had been traded in for a cut-glass accent which would have done justice to the Queen's Christmas Day broadcast: 'Oh Bishop, how good of you to visit us when you must have so many calls on your time. The residents are so, so delighted. They have been talking of nothing else for the last week. Undoubtedly, it will be the highlight of their year.'

The Bishop beamed; I was sorry to see that flattery and flirtery would obviously get you everywhere. Matron duly introduced him to a cigarette-free staff, who all looked as delighted as she to meet him. We were then led to the lounge, where again a miraculous transformation had taken place. In the centre of the room the usual coffee table littered with half-finished drinks, sweet wrappers, cotton wool balls, and even the odd set of false teeth had disappeared. In its place was an altar, covered in starched white linen with a brass candlestick at each end. The place smelt clean, with a pine aroma. The usual scent of urine and stale tobacco, which I thought had been specially impregnated into the plaster-work when the home had been built, had totally gone. Most miraculous of all the changes was that the television had been turned off. After weeks of its background music serenading me, I had begun to wonder whether they supplied a special custom-built model for old people's homes without an on-off switch. Today my hypothesis was proved wrong. 'What a delightful place,' the Bishop pronounced. 'You must work so hard to give it this special touch.'

'We do our best, my Lord,' Matron oozed. 'We try to make sure this home has the comfort and the cleanliness of our own homes. I tell my staff that nothing less is acceptable.' I was overcome by a choking fit.

Having robed in Matron's office, the Bishop processed back into the lounge to celebrate Communion. Now the veneer would come off and he would see life as it really was. I braced myself. The residents were sitting around as usual, but they were scrubbed clean, perched expectantly on the edge of their seats. Immediately I realized that something was missing. Not only had the television's background noise been routed. The Red Indian's war cry had also been silenced. She sat in the corner, saying not a 'wha', looking highly drugged. They had obviously been funnelling the cough mixture into her since dawn.

But she wasn't the only one who had changed. The Archbishop of Canterbury had decided to abdicate his see for the day, and meekly took his Communion card off me without showing the slightest inclination that he was going to stuff it down his trousers. Everyone there piously joined in with those parts of the service they were supposed to say, and more surprisingly kept quiet for those parts of the service they were not supposed to say. That same sense of piety invaded the way they took their Communion, each one savouring the bread and wine as if they had hungered and thirsted for it for days. No one tried to stash the bread away in their handbag, no one dropped it down their cleavage, no one handed it back bearing imprints of their teeth.

The Bishop was so impressed by their reception of him that he felt moved to preach one of his 'My good people, this...' homilies. Even then, their attention was rapt throughout, apart from the Red Indian, who by this time had fallen into a deep linctus-induced sleep, alternating her snores with the occasional 'wha' as she dreamed of wigwams and plains, with lithe-limbed, war-painted chiefs returning from their raid and choosing her as their squaw. Certainly her dream was far more exciting than the Bishop's little sermon, which after twelve minutes was making even my eyes feel heavy.

Once the Communion was ended, the Bishop spoke to each old person in turn. No obscenities, no confusion, just 'My Lord, how very good to see you,' chanted by each inmate. They intoned the words so perfectly that it was almost as if Matron was before them like a schoolteacher, pointing to each word on a blackboard:

'My – Lord – how – very – good – to – see – you.'

After we had made our farewells and strolled down Ings Lane to the school, the Bishop commented, 'What a supreme joy it must be to minister to such lovely people in the twilight of their lives.' I have to admit that reeling from the home after my weekly visit, 'joy' and 'lovely' were not the first words that sprang to my mind.

The Bishop had visited Eastwith School two years before, just after Geoff Goodmanham had taken over, and had attempted to conduct a question and answer session on a predictably religious theme. The event was a total flop in that the Bishop had persisted in asking questions but the children had persisted in not answering, despite both Geoff and Miss South willing them on. Apparently the scope of the Bishop's inquiries had been rather narrow, and Geoff assured me that he had prepared the children well this time around, should the Bishop repeat the exercise.

Geoff's welcome was effusive, as he swung open the heavy school door with a gusto which sent several slivers of red brick showering down upon us. 'You want to get the Archdeacon to look at the fabric of this building. It's a bad advertisement if our Church schools are falling down,' the Bishop commented. I shivered involuntarily. After the debacle when I had been installed as vicar, I had been trying to put off any further meeting with the Archdeacon for as long as possible.

Geoff had arranged the children in the hall, a blazing fire in the hearth trying to stave off the chill draughts from the ill-fitting windows. Having been introduced to the children, the Bishop embarked on his expected interrogation.

'Now children, I want to ask you a few questions about your faith. Who made the world?'

Twenty-nine hands eagerly shot up. Rather unwisely, the Bishop chose Paul Broadley, whose being miscast as a shepherd had had such a devastating effect on our Nativity play. I held my breath, fearing the worst. I noticed that Geoff was in a bad way too, nervously and frantically pulling at his left ear lobe. Neither of us need have worried.

'God, sir,' Paul replied, with a cherubic smile belying the naughty boy we all dreaded.

'Good. Very good indeed,' said the Bishop. 'Let me try a harder question. Who turned water into wine at a wedding?'

Once again, twenty-nine hands shot up instantly. This time the Bishop picked Peter Broadhurst. Again I feared the worst. Not an easy question for an eight-year-old. Geoff too was clearly apprehensive, anxiously tugging at his right ear lobe this time. But once again our anxiety was misplaced:

'Jesus, sir.' Peter confidently answered, winning a further accolade from the Bishop.

The next question was even tougher, couched in language which few of the children would have encountered before: 'Whose face was transfigured on Mount Tabor, so that it shone more brightly than fuller's bleach?' But again the children were unfazed; twenty-nine hands shot up as before. Unfortunately the Bishop chose the muscular Sharon Dubbins, whose family were renowned for their bale-throwing prowess and pre-marital activities, rather than their mental agility. 'This is where we come unstuck,' I thought. Geoff obviously thought so too, tugging at his right ear lobe yet again. I would have to have a word with him about that; funny I hadn't noticed it before.

'Please sir, Jesus,' Sharon calmly answered. I could have fallen off my chair.

The questions went on and on. Geoff had been right about their narrow scope, since the answer to them all seemed to be either God or Jesus. But what I found astounding was the children's admirable knack of plumping for the right alternative every single time. The Bishop was immensely impressed, and rightly so. I only wished Geoff would relax and stop fidgeting.

Out of fifty questions we only had one wrong answer when the Bishop chose David Harsley, the grandson of verger Sam. David was a sweet little child who waddled around Kirkwith come rain or shine, sporting wellingtons which invariably were on the wrong feet. When I first met the boy at his grandparents' home, his grandma's teasing made him blush: 'Our David doesn't know his right from his left.'

'Who sent a flood to destroy the earth?' the Bishop sternly asked.

'Jesus, sir,' David had replied. Geoff's fiddling with his left ear took on such gargantuan proportions that he looked in danger of pulling the whole thing off.

'No, that's not quite right,' the Bishop gently remonstrated.

'Oh God!'

'Yes, you're absolutely right,' said the Bishop, taking David's expletive as his corrected answer.

The Bishop was wildly enthusiastic about the school's astounding improvement in the sphere of Religious Knowledge. As we walked over to Geoff's home to see June and Elizabeth, home from hospital only the day before, his praise knew no bounds. 'Wonderful, absolutely wonderful. I've never been to a Church school quite like it. Every question right. Such an improvement since last time. You've made a remarkable impact, Mr Goodmanham.'

Whilst the Bishop cooed over the tiny baby, I managed to have a quiet word with Geoff about his ear trouble. I'd noticed that the problem at least had subsided once we had left the school building. For a moment I thought my questioning induced a relapse, since he immediately lifted up his hand towards his face. But with a grin he whispered, 'Left ear for God, right ear for Jesus!' So that's how he'd done it. One is always heartened when a hint of slyness pierces an otherwise guileless exterior.

Since the Bishop was particularly keen to visit a farm, our next port of call was the Weightons. His limousine slithered and squelched up the muddy drive, sinking to its axles in the stackyard. As he stepped out of the car he sank in mud, which totally engulfed his shoes and left a tide mark on his trouser turn-ups, once he had managed to slough most of the stuff on the foot-scraper by the back door. I was impressed that his dignity remained throughout.

He insisted on taking his shoes off before he entered the kitchen, an unnecessary gesture given that there was far more mud on the kitchen floor than there was on his footwear. Mrs Weighton's welcome was as warm as ever, 'Bishop, come in, come in, take a seat and rest your legs. The vicar's been telling me what a long day you've got ahead of you.'

As usual, there was nowhere to sit. The Bishop attempted to shift some of the Farmers Gazettes from one of the stools but only succeeded in starting an avalanche. Although magazines galore cascaded down and gathered in a pile around his feet, the tower on the stool seemed undiminished. Mrs Weighton waved aside the Bishop's profuse apology. 'Don't worry, we'll see to 'em later.' Yet she did nothing to clear him a space. Turning from the stools, the Bishop made as if to move one of the ever-sleeping sheepdogs off the sofa. In a rather comic scene, one of the dogs woke up, leapt off the settee and gave the Bishop's stockinged heel a painful nip before leaping back onto his cushion to resume his slumbers. It was the Bishop's turn to wave aside Mrs Weighton's apologies, giving the impression that being savaged by ill-tempered hounds was part and parcel of everyday episcopal life.

He gave up trying to find somewhere to sit and hobbled over to chat to Grandma, who, as ever, was stirring her stew by the fire. It was when the Bishop leant over the pot to admire its contents that the accident happened with his pectoral cross. Hanging around his neck, it kept to the vertical like a plumbline and dangled, unbeknown to him, in the thick brown gravy. The four men watched from the table, thoroughly engrossed by the spectacle, but as taciturn as ever. Even though I was more articulate, I somehow couldn't find the nerve to tell my Father in God that he was dunking his cross.

It was Mrs Weighton who broke the impasse. 'Ee Bishop, you've got your thingy in the pot.' Not being entirely sure which 'thingy' the good Mrs Weighton was referring to, he shot upright. As he did so the cross lifted itself out of the casserole and swung back against his chest, dribbling a trail of scalding gravy down his purple stock and onto his worsted trousers. For the third time that morning, I admired the Bishop's ability to keep his dignity despite considerable adversity, clearly a qualification for high office.

Mrs Weighton quickly picked up 'the tea-towel' off the comfy chair and proceeded to wipe the Bishop down. Hardly at its cleanest to start with, the cloth just spread the mess, blending the brown in with the purple and black and giving him a camouflaged appearance. He began to look more like an army chaplain on manoeuvres than a bishop. I noticed, though, that as Mrs Weighton wiped the cross clean, it shone like new and looked far brighter than it had done before its unfortunate immersion. However unpalatable Grandma's concoction was, without a doubt, it would take the world by storm if marketed as silver polish.

Before our departure, the Bishop attempted to discuss farming with the four men seated around the table. Any exchange was hampered not only by the men's answers being limited to monosyllables but also by the Bishop's all too evident ignorance of anything to do with agriculture.

At one point, Brian, one of the Weighton boys, nearly fanned the flames of a conversation. As a sideline he ran a nursery in his large greenhouse, which was effectively a lean-to against the long farmhouse wall. There he grew lettuces and tomatoes entirely under glass, making a little money supplying local greengrocers. So enthusiastic was he about this project that he rose from the table (I had begun to think the four men were a permanent kitchen fixture) and offered to show us around. The Bishop was keen to see further life in all its fullness, and once he had prised his muddy shoes back on, took off with Brian for his guided tour. Having listened attentively to Brian's brief but lucid description of his work, he rather unwisely decided to show his grasp of horticultural detail by asking an intelligent question. 'Now tell me,' the Bishop inquired, pointing to row upon row of seedlings arranged on the greenhouse shelves before him, 'do you have to water them at all?'

'Ay,' responded Brian, 'we have to water 'em.' It wasn't so much the way he said it as the pitying look he shared with the rest of us. In the ecclesiastical world the Bishop might have walked as a giant; in Brian's rustic world, the only one that counted for him, he was little less than a midget.

The incident reminded me of a similarly urbane Elizabeth Fry, the nineteenth-century reformer. When she was being shown round a farm, she pointed to a beast in its stall, and quizzed the farm hand who was with her, 'And what precisely is that?'

'Oh, that be an heifer, ma'am,' the farm labourer drawled.

'Yes, yes, yes,' Elizabeth Fry barked impatiently, 'I know that already, my good man. But tell me, is it a male heifer or a female heifer?'

By the time we adjourned for lunch at the vicarage, the Bishop was looking a little worse for wear. With feet of mud, if not of clay, hardly able to bear to put his bitten heel down on the ground, and with Grandma Weighton's potent brew spread around his midriff, he looked a sorry sight indeed. Despite his earlier bad experience with one sheepdog, he made great friends with Dewi, who fussed over him like a mad thing, licking him half to death. A bishop with the pervasive odour of meat about him must have seemed irresistible to the young dog. I had prepared a lamb stew the night before, and while this came to the boil, I got the Bishop to remove his shoes so I could wash the worst of the mud off in my back yard. We were calling at the Harsleys that afternoon. Knowing how acutely house-proud Doris was, I felt the Bishop would not make the best of impressions if mud on the carpet was the only memento he left of his visit. Having delayed Sam's Sunday lunch in the past because of preaching too long, the Bishop already had a considerable handicap to overcome, without making things worse.

With the dinner still bubbling in the oven, I eventually persuaded the Bishop to remove his sock so I could attempt to dress the wound on his foot. 'No, no, it's nothing,' he attempted to reassure me. 'It'll be all right, it's hardly anything more than a scratch.' All men have a reserve about having their ailments treated by others, especially by other men, but the Bishop seemed particularly reluctant. At first I thought it was because he didn't want to appear weak before someone who was junior to him. But then, when he finally took off his sock, I realized it wasn't that at all.

His foot was horribly disfigured, two toes missing, the other toes terribly gnarled. His shyness about letting me see was a combination of shame and modesty: shame about the shocking state of his foot; modesty about how it had got into that state in the first place.

From the gentle way he told his story it was clear that he had shared it with few others. 'As a lad, I was very keen on King and Country, and was a willing volunteer in the Great War,' he explained. 'I soon became disillusioned when we ended up in the Dardanelles campaign, trying to put the Turks to rout at Gallipoli. As casualties increased and the situation became more and more desperate, an already harsh discipline became even harsher, with each rank taking out their frustration on their subordinates. We had a bully of a sergeant who insisted on kit inspection, morning, noon and night. After yet another inspection, my rifle, and that of two of the closest friends I have ever made, were found to be not quite as sparkling clean as that despicable man felt he had a right to expect.' Hitherto, the Bishop had come across as the mildest of men; his venom now was poignant indeed.

'You have to realize,' the Bishop continued, 'we were in an army where defeat was so obviously on the cards, it was a matter of when rather than whether. We had seen our comrades' bodies blown to smithereens in battle. We hadn't slept or fed properly for days. Having a rifle in the pristine state expected on a parade ground seemed quite frankly irrelevant.

'But not to that brutal sergeant who ordered our punishment.' Again, the venom weighed heavily. 'Each dawn, for three successive days, we were tied to a wooden cross, hauled up in full view of the enemy, and left to hang until they cut us down each nightfall. Even if the enemy's snipers missed such very convenient target practice, in the freezing, damp, conditions, exposure lurked in the wings, threatening to do the enemy's deadly job for them.

'By some fluke, I survived. The loss of two toes through frostbite seemed of small consequence compared to the loss of

life suffered by my two dear friends. As I hung there, in excruci-
ating pain, inevitably my thoughts turned to another who hung
on a similar cross, nineteen centuries before. Up until then, I
hadn't had much time for the Christian faith. As I realized, from
my lesser Calvary, just a little of the hurt and rejection that Jesus
went through, faith was born which fired a lifetime.'

The Bishop's testimony would have sounded phony from
any other lips. But because of his searing experience, simply
told, it had the mark of unshakeable conviction and integrity.
'You know, it dawned on me in that sorry place, that Jesus had
gone through all this, not because his rifle was dirty, but to
show he loved us. That Jesus had lived and died so that we
might treat each other with the respect due to a child of God.
That Jesus had said that those who live by the sword will die by
the sword. That even the worst death, a death which I had tast-
ed myself, could not put a stop to Him then and never would.
All these things turned me. What I was died on that cross. I was
cut down a new man.'

It was an intensely moving story, and I hated myself for
mocking this sweet, gentle man with his 'My good people,
this...' and 'My good people, that...' It was little wonder that
following his harsh experience, the answers to all his questions
were Jesus and God; those two, and those two alone had
ensured his survival. As I bathed his deformed foot with a towel,
I felt searingly humbled, as if the roles were miscast. I was simply unworthy to be doing this for him: 'You should be doing
this for me, Lord...'

After that, the rest of the day changed gear. No longer did I
feel I was touring the parish with a rather bumbling fool.
Instead I treated the Bishop as if he had a hidden treasure within him because of what he had suffered all those years before. A
vulnerable holiness had been disclosed to me, which I wanted
to protect rather than laugh at.

All that morning I had been troubled by something that
didn't quite add up. However much a whitewash our visit to the

old people's home had been, one thing that Matron could never have controlled was the response of the old people themselves. On the boundaries of sanity, it was almost as if they had recognized goodness in the Bishop and had come back from the brink, showing what they were capable of becoming. My weekly visit to that home was unadulterated hell; today I had seen a glimpse of heaven.

Perhaps another glimpse of heaven peeped through at the Harsleys'. I knew something was different, but I couldn't quite put my finger on it at first. We were ushered into the pristine front room, complete with flourishing rubber plant, by a Doris who seemed remarkably relaxed. As at the Weightons, the Bishop had offered to remove his shoes, which I hadn't quite restored to their original shine. But Doris would have none of it: 'You keep your shoes on, Bishop. You're visiting a home, not some palace where you have to go round on tip-toe, frightened even to breathe.'

'Good heavens,' I blurted out. Instead of gabbling away without the slightest deference to a comma or a full stop, Doris had started punctuating her speech. It also suddenly dawned on me that not only was Doris speaking like the rest of us, but also her house-proud self had been kicked into touch for the afternoon.

She mistook the reason for my exclamation. 'Yes, you can't fail to notice, can you?' She explained things further to the Bishop who was looking puzzled. 'You see that plant, Bishop? It was ailing until the Vicar called; ever since his visit, it's thrived.' The Bishop was almost successful in feigning amazement; only I detected the curl of his lips which were threatening to break into a smile.

Sam saved the situation by telling us another story on a horticultural theme, about Mr Eddison, the vicar whom Hannah Everingham remembered for being so stand-offish all those years ago. 'Each May, on t' Sunday before Ascension Day, he used to walk round t' fields, blessing t' forthcoming crops. You have to understand,' Sam explained, 'in an age before pesticides and insecticides and soil nutrients, the success of any harvest was a very hit and miss affair, literally in t' hands of God. His blessing therefore was a much sought-after commodity.

'However, in 1912,' Sam went on, as if the year were yesterday, 'Mr Eddison had a nasty bout of 'flu at Rogationtide, with the result that t' crops had to cope without his benediction that year. Do you know, t' harvest was a bumper one, the best ever. T' farmers were already deeply resentful of t' parson for taking his tithe. That resentment paved t' way for another nail in t' Vicar's coffin: it dawned on them that it was precisely the lack of Mr Eddison's blessing that had led to that year's success. They turned a convenient blind eye to t' damp spring and long hot summer and t' fact that harvests had been plentiful outside t' narrow confines of t' Withs.

' "Keep Eddison from blessing t' crops" was their clarion call t' next spring. Poor Mr Eddison must have been bewildered as he wandered round t' fields, as this farmer and that farmer whispered in his ear, "No need to bless anything here, sir. We're letting it lie fallow this year." The only fields the poor man was allowed to bless was the marshy scrubland near the Derwent. The general opinion of t' farming community was that nothing in all creation, not even Mr Eddison's blessing, could make this area worse than it was already.'

It was a story with a depth of pathos, which Sam caught well. 'The real tragedy was that Mr Eddison never cottoned on to why he had been shunned, or even that he had been shunned at all. He still walked around his parish, ready to dispense blessings to all and sundry, not realizing that his parishioners didn't want 'im anymore. He did however manage to corner one old chap, working in his allotment. He couldn't run away as fast as t' others, you see, "I see you and the Lord have laboured together to produce a wonderful crop," Mr Eddison remarked. Being shunned hadn't stopped him being pompous.

'The old man straightened up. "Ay, sir, we have. But you should ha' seen state of this allotment when t' Lord had it all to himself." '

We all chuckled at Sam's story. But the Bishop then added a postscript, 'Mind you, we don't have to look very far in today's world to see the state of the allotment when man has it to himself.' I admired his nerve in being able to move us on from laughter to thoughtfulness. The carnage in central Africa and Vietnam, with its harrowing pictures nightly on our television screens, sprang readily to mind.

That day's visit might have encouraged Doris to punctuate her speech, but there are some things that even a bishop cannot change. 'We've still got some fruitcake left over from Christmas; will you have a piece along with a glass of sherry?' An ominous invitation which drove me to revisit the first time I had come here, a little worse for wear after sampling Mrs Weighton's culinary delights. The Bishop gladly accepted Doris' kind offer, and last autumn's scene was replayed before my eyes: the same disappearing of our hostess into the kitchen; the same massive slabs of cake and cheese brought forth; the same rummaging in the sideboard; the same bottle, with the same viscous liquid glugging out. Being the man he was and I wasn't, the Bishop drained his glass to the dregs, thoughtfully licking his lips afterwards, trying to place the taste.

Strategically I was well positioned next to the rubber plant, so when no one was looking, I tipped the contents of my glass over its roots in a fashion which was rapidly becoming time-honoured. Weeks later I heard from Sam that he and Doris had decided that my legendary way with rubber plants was shared by the Bishop. 'We thought it was funny at the time, the way he kept looking at it, smacking his lips. We think now he must have been blessing it, because since then it's grown half as big again.'

After the Harsleys, we paid a quick call to the Manor. Pam was by now well established. Her school in York had waived

136

her notice because of the exceptional circumstances and she had moved in with the Broadhursts by mid-January, living in her own separate suite in the spacious east wing. Following my advice, she and George had agreed on a six month probationary period, with George generously matching the salary she had been paid as a teacher.

As I knocked on the front door, I could hear the delighted squeals of the children, a sound I had sadly never heard before on my previous visits to the Manor. A harassed but happy looking Pam answered the door. Not cowed by the Bishop's presence, she eagerly invited us in. 'We're just having tea, come on through. You can join us for fish fingers and baked beans if you like.'

'I don't know about you, David, but I feel quite replete,' the Bishop explained to Pam. 'We've just had a large piece of Christmas cake and I think I'd like to savour the sherry wine we were proffered for just a little longer. I haven't come across a bouquet like that for a long time.'

'Nor will ever want to again,' I thought to myself.

We simply watched tea, which proved a command performance. George and Emma had yet to return from York, so Pam was feeding the three younger children, whilst at the same time entertaining them with a Sooty puppet. Sooty got up to some exceptionally naughty antics, including pulling the Bishop's hair and tweaking his nose, with the Bishop heartily entering into the spirit of fun. In between mouthfuls, Simon gurgled with delight, Peter and Sally laughed out loud. Given the state of those children just months before, it was a miraculous transformation, such a naturally happy scene.

We couldn't stay long, but as Pam was showing us out, with squeals of laughter still echoing behind us, the Bishop took her by the hand, exclaiming, 'My dear, it is a wonderful thing you are doing here, simply wonderful. In the name of God, I thank you.' From anyone else it would have sounded so pompous. It seemed so genuine from this man that it moved me to tears.

It moved Pam to tears too, as she responded, 'I'm doing very little, Bishop. I thought of it as my duty; it's turning out to be sheer joy.'

We rounded off our day with a question and answer session at Kirkwith Hall, where the Bishop was the lone batsman and the audience bowled him assorted googlies. The topics were fairly predictable. 'Why do you drive a limousine when Jesus rode around on a donkey?' vied with, 'Why don't you visit the parishes more often?' 'Why can't the Church be firmer on moral issues?' vied with 'Why can't the Church be more with it?' Few of the questioners took much notice of what had been said before, quite oblivious to the fact that their point was often diametrically opposed to the previous one. It was all rather tedious until Hans bowled a mischievous corker:

'Bishop, vot do you vink of the undead?'

At first, because of Hans' peculiar accent, the Bishop misheard the question. Assuming that he had said 'What do you think of undies?' he launched forth to attack pornography and the need for a certain privacy and due decorum. His answer understandably lost Hans entirely, who repeated his original question with some explanatory gloss.

'You misunderstand me, Bishop. I come vrom Transylvania, vere the vampires come vrom. Do you believe in Dracula and the undead?'

The Bishop waited for a moment, unsure whether to take Hans seriously or not. When it came, his reply was ponderous. 'I believe Bram Stoker's novel to be a story and only a story, a mixture of horror and romance. As for the undead, when I served as a soldier in the Great War, I saw a lot of dead bodies, too many, far too many...' The Bishop paused, as his ghosts haunted him, before continuing. His timing placed the audience in the palm of his hand, their silence pregnant. 'Even fifty years later, I seldom sleep without a nightmare disturbing me with scenes from that war. Every night I see the dead horribly maimed, I smell their putrid stench, I hear the cries of those with fearful injuries pleading for their loved ones, begging for death itself to overtake them. I suppose you could call them the undead. If so, I believe in them, because they are real enough to me.'

He paused again, before continuing, 'So real, that novels like *Dracula* dishonour them with their false descriptions. I have no wish to read a fictional travesty when reality, an albeit grim reality, is so near me. All I can do is commend all those, whose death I can never forget, to the infinite mercy of God. If he could raise his Son to glory, when he had been so terribly mutilated on the cross, then he can raise them up too.'

He had moved Hans, a fellow soldier; he had moved us all. Hans' valediction lightened the heaviest of moments. 'Vank you, Bishop, for that. Bugger off, then!' The whole hall, which had seconds before been so near to tears, roared with laughter, a laughter which was fuelled by Hans' bewilderment as to why anyone should find what he had said so funny. It was a fitting end to a day which had been both sweet and sour; life in all its fullness, without a doubt.

I was surprised when my leisurely breakfast the next day was interrupted by Mrs Weighton. Her face was blotchy, her eyes red and swollen. 'What on earth's wrong?' I asked. Selfishly, I was fearful for Rebecca.

'It's Hans, Vicar,' she blurted out, punctuating her speech with tears. 'He's dead.' Of necessity, her sentences were short. 'He's dead, dead,' she repeated, unable to take it in. 'He didn't turn up for work at six o'clock. He's never been late before. Fred went to t' cottage to rouse him and found him on t' kitchen floor. We got Dr Seaton out, but Fred knew there was no chance. He was so cold, so cold. He's been as good as family for so long. I don't know what we'll do without him. I just don't know. It was a heart attack, Dr Seaton thinks.' I let her prattle on, distraught myself that she was distraught.

Grief, as always, had many faces, and I saw them all in the days ahead. The Weightons mourned a man they had stood up for, against the crowd, who had become their faithful friend and worker on the land. Rebecca Weighton mourned a man who had been around the farm since her childhood, who treated her as the daughter he had never had, and whose encouragement set her on her career. The Withs mourned a fascinating character who could swear at a bishop and get away with it.

It was a couple of days later that I learned from a calmer Mrs Weighton that grief would dawn not only in the Withs. 'He often talked to me, Vicar, about the family he had left behind in Transylvania, who hadn't had the 'lucky' break that he had in making it to the West. They moved to improved conditions in East Germany after the war, but once the Iron Curtain was brought down, a further move became impossible, even if they'd wanted it. And from asides Hans made, I guess they were not as keen as he was to leave German things behind. Even then, they had clearly been a close-knit family; Hans missed them as much as he loved us.'

Mrs Weighton was a generous soul, able to think of others even when she herself was immersed in grief. 'I'm going to get in touch with them, Vicar, his family in East Germany. They need to know he's died. And they ought at least to have the chance of coming over to his funeral.'

Rebecca, like her mother, was able to rise above her own grief, and make the necessary calls to East Germany in the days that followed. Her fluency in German meant that she was able to negotiate the labyrinth of government departments so that visas could be issued to Hans' family for them to travel to England for his burial. I signed a document which was sent on to the East German embassy in London assuring them of the compassionate reasons for issuing such a visa. To our immense surprise and to the East German government's credit, a visa was quickly issued. Rebecca suspected that a prime reason why they were so swift and lenient was that they felt Hans' family could be trusted. After all, they had been amongst the few people to emigrate to East Germany, in a decade when most of her citizens had desperately wanted to flee her borders.

All these complex arrangements meant that Hans' funeral was delayed somewhat; it eventually took place a fortnight after his death. A further complication was that 19 of our visiting East Germans spoke no English whatsoever. I strongly felt that I owed it to Hans to give them a word in their own language during the service, so revisited my School Certificate German which had lain dormant these last twelve years. It was rusty, to say the least.

The prayer I chose for translation was a beautiful one I use in season and out of season at funerals, simply because it always seems so apt. Written by Cardinal Newman, it reads:

> O Lord, support us all the day long of this troublous life
> until the shadows lengthen,
> the busy world is hushed,
> the fever of life is over,
> and our work is done.
> Then, Lord, in thy mercy,
> grant us and those we love,
> safe lodging, a holy rest and peace at the last.
> Through Jesus Christ our Lord. Amen.

Having translated it into German, as a double check I decided to translate it back into English, meticulously looking up each word in the German/English section of my dictionary.

I got no further than the first phrase, because to my horror I found that I had cast 'O Lord support us', as 'O God, give us a truss'.

It was at that point that I decided I needed expert counsel. The obvious choice was Rebecca Weighton, although initially I held back from asking her. In part it was not wanting to overload her at a time when, as well as grieving herself, she seemed to be conducting single-handed negotiations with half of Germany.

But there was another reason for my reluctance: I felt shy with her. In a job which exposed me to all manner of life and death, to all sorts and conditions of men and women, where an instant rapport and ease of conversation were essential tools, this awkwardness seemed strange, out of place. Yet I could not deny it.

I was a great addict of Noggin the Nog, a cartoon the BBC showed before the tea-time news about the adventures of a rather disarming Viking king. Last night he had been courting Nuka, daughter of the King of the Midnight Sun, and his words to her father had struck a chord:

'I have come far, through hail and wind, through snowstorm and sea mist, past the black ice on the edge of the world to ask your daughter to marry me. Well, now I'm here, I feel a bit shy. Will you ask her for me?'

As well as the shyness there was a heaviness, an immensity, as if in these comparatively routine points of contact, a future was involved. I had only had the feeling twice before. In my upper teens a telegram had arrived for me on Christmas Eve. I remember carrying it unopened to my parents, acutely aware that in many ways the rest of my life was contained in this rather scrappy brown envelope. I opened it with trembling fingers and read:

JESUS COLLEGE CAMBRIDGE —STOP— AWARDED
ENTRANCE EXHIBITION —STOP— TO READ NATURAL
SCIENCES — STOP—

I think the word 'stop' spoke more profoundly to me than anything else on that telegram, as I paused on the brink.

Two years later another letter elicited similar feelings. With its York postmark I knew instinctively it was from Archbishop Michael Ramsey, and once again I realized that it carried my future. Again I opened the envelope with considerable trepidation and read:

My dear Wilbourne,

Having received a report from the selection conference
you recently attended, I am glad to endorse its recom-
mendation that you proceed with your training for
ordination. I wish you every blessing in the ministry
that lies ahead of you, that all that you think and do and
pray may be to the glory of God.

Yours sincerely,
Michael Ebor.

I felt now the same apprehension I had experienced before
opening those two missives, and I dithered about taking a further step. Rescue came as I remembered Stan and Jean, a young
couple from Hull. I had got to know them well after I baptized
their first child. Like me, they were great fans of fish and chips,
and we often patronized a nearby shop whose fish and chips
were superb. The shop was run by a homely couple in their late
fifties who were suddenly visited by terrible tragedy, in that
their daughter and grandchildren were killed in a car crash. Following the funeral, Jean couldn't bring herself to visit the shop,
explaining her reticence to Stan: 'I can't go; I just can't go. I
simply don't know what to say.'

Stan was a docker, and was capable of being as blunt as his
wife was sensitive. 'You don't know what to say? You don't
know what to say? I'll tell you what to say. Simply say "Fish and
chips three times please," and then bugger off home.'

Bearing his immortal advice in mind, I set off to the
Weightons' farm and simply asked Rebecca to translate some
prayers and part of my sermon into German. She gladly agreed,
promising to bring the completed text to the vicarage by the
next evening.

Prior to Rebecca's visit, I set about intensely tidying my
home. Although bewildered by it herself, Mrs Weighton had

kindly tipped me off about her daughter's 'obsession' with neatness. Carpets were hoovered, dust which had been neglected for days was flicked away, cushions were plumped up, sinks were polished until they shone. Dewi followed me around, trying his best to return things to their disorderly state, but this time, for once, he was no match for me. Without the slightest compunction, I picked him up and dumped him unceremoniously in the yard, oblivious to his pleading look which had melted my heart so many times before. I then returned to my labours, accompanied by an incessant barking which must have made his throat feel like sandpaper.

By the time Rebecca arrived I was physically exhausted, and gibbering like an idiot. Never mind about my German pronunciation; I couldn't even get my English words out.

'Do c-c-c-come in,' I stammered. 'You're brave cy-cy-cycling on such a cold night.' Rebecca simply gave me a warm, understanding smile as I babbled a load of nonsense about muscles freezing up in the cold and feet slipping off icy pedals. Having ushered her into the living room, I escaped into the kitchen to make a cup of tea.

I brought Dewi in from the yard to put a stop to his wretched barking, then I duly filled the teapot to the brim with cold water and switched the kettle on empty. There was a loud crash as the fail-safe mechanism came into operation and the plug sprang out of the kettle. I am sure Freud would have had a field day interpreting the significance of all this. For my part I decided to take a firm grip on myself and concentrate on what I was doing. It seemed like an age before I succeeded in resetting the kettle, and then a further age before the thing managed to boil, although eventually switching it back on at the socket helped. Having spread tea-leaves over the pristine kitchen floor like a profligate sower and tipped half a bottle of milk over the cooker, I succeeded in pouring two cups of tea. Leaving Dewi to lap up the fall-out, I carried the cups into the living room on a tray. This also contained a plate of rather nice chocolate biscuits, which I had sensibly put out earlier in the evening before my manual dexterity had gone totally to pot.

I congratulated myself on not spilling a drop of tea as I gingerly processed along the long corridor to the living room, deftly kicking open the door with my new-found confidence and kicking it to again when I had walked through. Unfortunately I managed to trap my jacket in the door, with the result that as I strode towards Rebecca with calculated aplomb, I came to an abrupt and startled halt. The tea tray, however, conversant as it was with Newton's laws of motion, continued with its velocity and direction unabated, shooting out of my hands and landing with a smash at Rebecca's feet, scattering biscuits en route.

'It's too cold for snow!' farmers often told me. In a similar vein, I felt that night's situation was too tragic for me to cry. Rebecca, however, was simply wonderful and saved the day. She burst out laughing, making light of the fact that she had been showered with tea (which at least had cooled by the time I delivered it). Her laughter was contagious and exorcised my awkwardness. She came back with me to the kitchen, and broke out laughing again as she encountered my rather novel floor covering, which Dewi's attempts as a tea-leaf harvester had considerably worsened. We made another cup of tea together with the conversation flowing as effortlessly as the water from the kettle.

Rebecca proved exceedingly kind. Not only did she deliver an impeccable translation, patiently coaching me to avoid too many gaffes in my pronunciation. But she also humanized the sermon, which I proposed to preach at Hans' funeral, by suggesting anecdotes and personal recollections which vividly caught the man. That sure pastoral touch impressed me as much as her linguistic ability. Not that she needed to impress me at all.

As we sat close beside each other on the settee, with my heart thumping, and my mind screaming, 'Kiss her, go on, kiss her!', something held me back. I was very, very conscious that she was a parishioner grieving for someone who had been around for the whole of her life, and that I was her parish priest. I felt it was improper and unprofessional to take the relationship beyond that for the moment, however much I might want to. To make a move now would be to take a gross advantage.

Rebecca sensed that things weren't taking their expected turn. Rather boldly, she put her arm around me and asked, 'David, what's the matter?'

I could only tell her the truth. How I had been fond of her since I first caught sight of her. How I had made countless visits to her parents' farm, only to be disappointed when she was not there. How I had wanted to ask her out as we met repeatedly at the church door, but was thwarted by the rest of the congregation eavesdropping. How my heart had raced as it had never raced before when she had sung so beautifully on Christmas Day. Which brought me to Hans: how it would be wrong even to presume to talk of love, when she was sorrowing for him.

Rebecca's eyes flashed as she interrupted my monologue. 'Well yes, of course, I'm sorrowing for him. How could I not be, when every word I speak in my second language I owe to him? But just because I'm sad doesn't mean I'm deranged. And what has happened to Hans doesn't somehow suspend all that happened beforehand. Don't you realize that my heart burned within me when I first saw you? Don't you realize how mad I felt when mum said you'd called and I'd gone and missed you yet again? I knew you wanted to say more at the church door; I wished, more than once, that the rest of the congregation would bugger off and leave us alone.' She halted her serious speech as she broke into laughter. 'You see, Hans has even influenced my English!'

But then she resumed the more serious vein. 'David, Hans would never have wanted his death to put a stop to us, when, when we've got so much going. I'm touched, so very touched by your courtesy and thoughtfulness. Absolutely typical of you. But I know what I'm doing. I'm in control. I'm not out of my mind.'

We kissed after that. Intense. Natural. Without shame. Private...

Kirkwith Church was so packed for the funeral that we had to clear a path down the aisle before we could get the coffin in; it would have been a novel funeral indeed without it. Hans' family sat on the front row beneath the pulpit and did their very best to sing hymns whose meaning they hadn't got a clue about. Mind you, even English people find a lot of hymns bewildering, so they were hardly in a minority. When I began my sermon in German several of our East German visitors wept spontaneously. It could well have been that my accent, still pretty hopeless even after Rebecca's painstaking tuition, brought tears to their eyes. I suspect, though, that they were moved to be addressed in their native tongue.

If a funeral can go well, it went well. I quoted the Bishop of Pocklington's words to Hans the night before he died about no one being unresurrectable or beyond God's love: 'If he can raise his Son to glory, when he had been so terribly mutilated on the cross, then he can raise us up too.' They were probably the last words he heard on this earth. In a very real way they were as good as the Last Rites, which because of the suddenness of his death, Hans never had.

Every funeral I take tears me apart with conflicting feelings. Each time I sense an agony, which is almost piercing in its intensity, as I focus on the person who has died and those who are left behind in deep sorrow. But this is coupled with an awareness that, though it hurts like hell, there is nowhere in the whole world I would rather be than here, that to be here is sheer, tremendous privilege.

Hans was buried in the graveyard with the floodwater from the Derwent lapping against the churchyard wall, the many geese calling to each other across the waves on this chilly day.

147

Hans adopted Kirkwith as his home because he loved its natural beauty; that day he became one with it.

I greeted everyone at the lychgate. The East German contingent assumed my German was fluent, so gabbled greetings and sentences that I could hardly get the gist of, let alone respond to. It seemed supremely right that Rebecca was at my side, kindly interpreting and responding for me. I just tried to look understanding, interspersing my smiles with '*danke*', rounding off each conversation with '*auf Wiedersehen*'. I checked my German dictionary afterwards, just in case it could be translated as 'Bugger off, then!'

It was two weeks later that thirteen people were sitting around a table in an upper room, food and drink arrayed before them. Any suspicion an observer might have that he had suddenly gate-crashed on Jesus and his Last Supper could be dissipated for several reasons. First, seven of the thirteen were women. Second, nearly all had pints of Guinness standing before them, not a common beverage in the Palestine of Jesus' day. Third, one of the thirteen sported a dog collar, hardly a fashion for even the most tediously pious of first-century individuals. Most conclusively, it was simply the wrong script. Of that just a few moments' eavesdropping would leave no doubt:

> 'Oh it's lovely to be in the Withs,
> because here, there's an absence of cliffs.
> The river is fine,
> better than the Tees and the Tyne,
> though the country air occasionally whiffs.'

The 1960s had been an age for radical scholars, books like John Robinson's *Honest to God* insisting that our old-fashioned images of God must go. Some denied that Jesus had said some things we'd always thought he'd said, others claimed that he had said peculiar things we'd never dreamt of him saying. But even the most anarchic of scholars would draw the line at putting that poem into his mouth.

Our venue was not Jerusalem but Beckwith, with the upper room of the Stack the meeting place for Dr Seaton's poetry group. The generous supply of liquid refreshment meant that the poetry flowed more easily as the evening progressed, with inhibitions and shyness soon put to rout.

It was Sam Harsley's turn to read next. He had brought along a poem Doris had written about a flower festival hosted by Kirkwith Church, mercifully before my time. Doris had been hoping to come along herself and read it, but had developed a spot of 'tummy trouble' following a visit to the Weightons' farm. We therefore had to endure Sam punctuating what otherwise would have been a breathless performance. Sam, smartly dressed in his verger's black suit, his hair greased down with a double application of Brylcreem to mark the occasion, was clearly very proud of his wife's offering. He stood erect, puffed his chest out, cleared his throat and began:

'All the flowers of the Vale
had been kept overnight in a pail,
all the colours of the rainbow
could be seen if you bent very low.
People from all the Withs thronged to the spot
in the dry summer that was so very hot.
Even the Archdeacon he did see
the flowers when he came to tea.'

Sam sat down, amidst loud cheers and clapping from the rest of the company. His moustache bristled with the thrill of it all. There were tears of pride in his eyes as he whispered to me, 'My Doris has a way with words, Vicar.' The truth of his statement was undeniable.

Dr Seaton had been urging me to come along to his monthly group ever since my arrival last autumn. It had taken me until now to pluck up the courage, which was bolstered when I saw Rebecca was there too. Apparently Dr Seaton had dropped by the farm shortly after Hans' death to see how the Weightons were coping and had encouraged her to join his poets' corner. Certainly Rebecca's bravery exceeded mine, for not only was she in attendance, but she had written a poem for the occasion. She read it with a lovely lilt to her voice:

An owl's cry pierces the dark.
I awake,
scrape a ring of frost from the window
and spy the night.
A flock of geese
fly across the moon,
full and high.
A fox's bark is echoed
by his vixen,
far away.
The stars smile down at me,
'Even now,
in the darkness,
you are not alone.'

No cheering this time; the appreciation was measured by a pregnant hush. All were quiet, save Sam, who whispered across to me, 'She's almost as good with words as my Doris. A pity she can't make them rhyme, though.'

Afterwards I cycled alongside Rebecca as we made our winding way back to the farm. After a short while, our conversation took a serious turn. 'I know it'll sound funny, this,' she gently began, 'but even though we were upstairs in a pub, there seemed to be a certain holiness there. You were the one with the dog collar on, David, but in a strange sort of way it was Dr Seaton, not you, who was the priest at that celebration. I hope that doesn't offend you.'

'Not at all,' I replied, wobbling my bicycle to avoid a rabbit that had shot across our path. 'But what do you mean?'

'Well,' she continued, 'it was he who called us together. It was he who gently encouraged each of us to make our offering. It was he who gave us the nerve to risk rejection, generous as he was with praise, measly only with criticism. However fragile and stunted the blossom, he made it his business to affirm it. All that strikes me as a very priestly activity.'

I was stunned into silence, loving her all the more for a perceptiveness which put mine to shame. Perhaps one could be forgiven for confusing the event with the Last Supper after all.

PART THREE

✠✠✠✠✠✠✠✠✠✠✠✠✠✠✠✠✠

CHAPTER TEN

It was just the worst time of year for a journey, a wintry March morning in the Vale of York, the fog thick, clammy and cold. It was the sort of morning to wake up, peep through the curtains and then retreat back to bed again, but I had no option other than to be up and off, my destination a monthly meeting with clergy in far away climes, to bolster each other's ministry. This seemed a curious way to bolster it, as I laboured to pedal my bicycle, seemingly getting nowhere, the mist impenetrable. I circled the aptly named village of Foggathorpe three times before finally discovering the road out of the place. The fog had such a timeless feel about it that I feared I was consigned to orbit the village for eternity.

The odd vehicle, its headlights dim, loomed out of the mist, roared for an instant and then was gone. Its engine was quickly muffled, so that the eerie silence soon returned. When the fog thinned slightly I was able to catch sight of the hedgerow, which was a mass of cobwebs highlighted by a million droplets. I felt empathy for the poor spider in its struggle to weave, water the only prey to be caught.

After seven very long miles I knew I was nearing my destination as the ground began its slight rise. A sparrow-hawk, as disorientated as I was, hovered alongside my bicycle for a few seconds. She then darted away to search elsewhere, her victims safely hidden in this cloak of damp darkness.

At last I reached the village of Charm-on-Spalding-Moor, in the foothills of the Wolds. I stood to give purchase to the pedals as I struggled to ascend the highest peak, on which the church was perched. My swaying cycle inched its way up the lane which snaked up the hillside, my heart pumping, my breathing heavy, until suddenly the gradient gave way and I was there. In an instant the mist swirling around the church vanished. It was replaced by a sky, which was a glorious deep blue, and by a sun which shone warmly, defrosting my frozen bones. It was an uncanny sight. The church and I were bathed in sunlight whilst beneath us was an unremitting carpet of cloud. Such a sight made the arduous struggle to get there all worthwhile.

I stayed outside, basking in it all, putting off going into the dank and dark church until the very last moment. The other clergy arrived, their cars destroying the silence, spewed out by the mist below. Hale and hearty greetings followed. 'What a pea-souper! Worse than the London fog of 1954!' and 'Good heavens, you haven't come on the bicycle, have you? You'll wear yourself out before you're 30 at this rate,' and 'My windscreen wiper packed up just outside Pocklington, but I managed to mend it with an elastic band and a paper clip.'

If it wasn't for their dress, no one would guess that this was a band of men who had immersed themselves in the things of God. And even their apparel gave conflicting signals. True enough, all sported a dog collar. But this one note of consistency was drowned out by a cacophony of ill-matched clothing. One had donned brown suede shoes, navy blue trousers, a maroon jacket, topped with a bright orange scarf. Another modelled trousers with a loud black and white check, a brown checked tweed jacket, beneath which was a blue and green checked jumper. I tried not to look at him directly, otherwise my eyes started doing strange things. Another wore fluorescent green socks, brown trousers, a pink and yellow sweater made for a man with another twelve inches around the chest, over which he wrapped around him a donkey jacket which had clearly served its time in the building yard. 'What do you think of this,' he proudly boasted, squeezing the cloth to show off its thickness. 'Good stuff, this. Only two and six from the Christian Aid shop.' I think he was done.

The best dressed of them all was not a clergyman but a lay reader, whose parsonical voice and unctuous manner betrayed a frustrated ambition to be a priest. He wore black shoes, a white polo neck jumper over which was a black sweater, finished off with a black gabardine. He was doubly frustrated that he had been going around like this for years, but not once had anyone mistaken him for a clergyman. I wasn't in the least surprised. People expected their vicars to be bizarrely dressed and to look the least holy of men, as a cursory glance at this motley collection revealed only too well.

Those clergy were dressed like that because they were desperately poor. I was lucky: I had no family to support. All the rest had quiverfuls of children, with their parishes expecting them to have the lifestyle of a squire on a ploughman's income. They were forced to live in draughty, dilapidated vicarages, with most of their salary consisting of glebe rents paid very much in arrears, if they were ever paid at all. Little wonder, then, that these men were driven to raid charity shops and jumble sales. Each year they waited in hope for the trunk from the Poor Clergy Relief Fund, as excited as children on Christmas morning when it arrived. They pored over its contents of oversized and under-sized and ill-matched musty clothing as eagerly as if they were spun with gold.

I did not despise this motley-clothed lot in the least. In fact I was immensely proud of them, humbly following their Lord, who died with soldiers gambling beneath him for his few rags, whose coming was heralded by a man in a coat of rough camel skin. It was me, and the rest of our well-dressed population, who they put to utter shame.

We shuffled into the church and sat huddled together in the choir stalls, awaiting the Communion service. At 8.35, five minutes after we should have started, Charm's vicar and my life-long friend, Stamford Chestnut, staggered out of the vestry. Even in his robes, he had the dishevelled look of the rest of his brother clergy. His alb was distinctly off-white, more unwashed grey. His chasuble, a garment much like a Mexican poncho, had a lop-sided look about it, one end draped off his left shoulder, the other end crumpled up around his right ear. His ruffled hair had clearly yet to see a comb that morning. Worst of all, as he processed in he was still smoking his pipe, clouds of ready-cut wafting into the air like a peculiar form of incense. Fortunately he realized his error when he got to the altar, nonchalantly tapping the contents of the pipe into a conveniently sited collection plate. Our lay reader and would-be priest tutted loudly.

Stamford took the service with great dignity, bathed in light as the sun's rays shone through the east window. He spoke rapidly, like a cross between a cattle market auctioneer and a horse racing commentator, rattling off the four hundred words of the lengthy Prayer for the Church in a record 45 seconds. The rest of the clergy hastily snapped in 'Amen' at the end before he sped on, without pause for breath, to the Invitation to Confession. He barked the versicles, the clergy barked back the responses, rising to a crescendo which managed to complete Our Lord's Prayer in eight seconds flat. The whole Communion, from start to finish, took just 12 minutes. Stamford Chestnut staggered out as he had staggered in, retrieving his pipe from the collection plate and relighting it with a taper which he had lit from one of the altar candles.

I was immensely fond of this man, who single-handedly had persuaded me to come to the area, against my better judgement. He had been proved right and I had been proved wrong, which exalted him even higher in my estimation. So I was particularly irked by the lay reader's loud complaints which were visited upon us all, as we waited for Stamford in the porch. 'That man's a disgrace to the profession, celebrating like that. He ought to be barred from office. Why, after I'd taken Evensong at Warter last Sunday, every person in the congregation made a point of taking me aside. "You've got such a clear, holy voice, Mr Molescroft," they all said. "It's a great loss to the Church that you're not a vicar." '

'If God could survive the utter tragedy of Good Friday, I guess He'll just about be able to get over your not being ordained,' I quipped. Herbert Molescroft went silent for a moment as he tried to gauge whether my comment was intended as an insult or was a piece of theological obscurity he had yet to fathom.

'But you could hear hardly a word of that service,' he eventually retaliated. 'What's the point of worship without any words? It's got no relevance.'

'That's not true, you could hear one or two words,' the vicar of Foggathorpe chipped in. 'We all know it off by heart, anyway. I only need one word to trigger off the whole service in my mind, like a spark, kindling a fireworks display.'

'But you've got to be relevant, worship can't be meaningless gabble,' Herbert Molescroft insisted. 'That's the trouble with the Church of today, it's so out of date, so irrelevant. It needs to be immediate, to have the right words to grab people's attention.'

'Ee, I'm not so sure, Herbert,' the Vicar of Warter now joined in the fray. His accent gave away the fact he had been born and bred in these parts. 'We're becoming too obsessed with relevance. Everything has to have instant meaning and instant impact these days. Instant coffee, instant soup. They're all immediate. But they taste foul, like something from bottom of t' Derwent. Never mind about words. I think t' best worship is silence. "God's in heaven, you're on earth, so let your words be few," as it says somewhere in t' Bible. What book is it, David? You're supposed to be a biblical scholar.'

'Ecclesiasticus,' I replied, letting my words be few. The argument continued on the road as we strolled to breakfast at Stamford's vicarage, at the base of the hill on which his church was set. It struck me as immensely sad, having to leave the sunshine behind and descend into the murky fog again. However, a meal which proved as sumptuous as it was hilarious, served in the vicarage's palatial dining room, helped dispel my melancholia. It got off to an unfortunate start with the porridge. Herbert Molescroft was the first to slurp a mouthful, only to spit it out immediately, treating us to some uncharacteristically impious language. 'What the hell?'

Before any of the rest of us followed our lay reader's good example, our host took the smallest pinch of the stuff and savoured it on his tongue. After pondering calmly for a moment he exclaimed, 'Ah, that's what happened!'

We all waited agog for further explanation. Stamford chewed on his ever-present pipe and continued, 'You all know how this place is so low-lying that we regularly get flooded. A couple of weeks ago, a box of groceries standing on the kitchen floor got soaked so much that the contents of the sodden boxes had to be decanted into biscuit tins. In the confusion we must have mistaken soap powder for oats.' Hence Herbert Molescroft being startled by a starter which matched his acerbity, which the rest of us mercifully avoided.

Stamford scratched his head commenting pensively, 'I thought that urn of porridge took a long time to thicken!' Clearly the reek of tobacco had prevented him noticing it also had rather a scented smell. He grinned, good-naturedly, before adding, 'That'll explain why the washing machine seized up the other day as well.' He had the contented look of a sleuth who suddenly finds a solution to a series of hitherto inexplicable events.

I knew that the repeated flooding had caused him a fair few problems in his 30 years as Vicar of Charm. The vicarage was such a massive place that his son was able to use the east wing as a farm, keeping chickens in the cellar. A flash flood had drowned the entire stock, and so incensed Stamford that he wrote to Archbishop Garbett to complain about the poor drainage around the vicarage. The Archbishop had replied by return, as succinct as he was prompt:

My dear Chestnut,

Sorry about the flooding and the chickens. Try ducks.

Yours,
Cyril Ebor.

Since then the cellars had remained unused, and Stamford's son had tried his hand at keeping pigs instead. The breakfast was a more than adequate testimony to his success. Home-cured ham, gammon, bacon, sausages, black pudding, liver, kidneys and even chitterlings were served in abundance, fresh from the Vicar's farm. It was a feast of medieval proportions which carried on late into the morning. It gave your whole being a well-sustained, warm feeling which set you up, and enabled you to be undaunted even by the fog which continued to swirl around outside.

Just after eleven o'clock Stamford, who was Rural Dean as well as Vicar of Charm, called the meeting to order. 'I'm sorry to spoil this feast by introducing Church business...'

'Then don't bother,' quipped the Vicar of Warter.

'...but there are two items we need to plan before they happen rather than after they happen.'

'Planning things after they happen sounds much more sensible. It stops them getting out of proportion,' the Vicar of Foggathorpe sagely commented.

Stamford ignored all these wisecracks and carried on. 'Now the Archdeacon wrote to me last week, informing me that he will be visiting every parish in the autumn to check that all is in order.'

'Oh, no!' the rest of the clergy shouted with one voice. I was relieved to find out his visitation was universally dreaded. 'I suppose I'll have to get up the ladders and clear the gutters. He's a devil for gutters,' the Vicar of Warter complained. ' "A constipated gutter makes for a constipated church," he's always saying. Pompous ass! Better than a church with diarrhoea.'

'Oh heck! I'll have to get the old registers back from my niece in Cambridge,' the Vicar of Foggathorpe said in a wearied way. 'She's borrowed them for her PhD thesis, "Incest and Burials in the Diocese of York". The Archdeacon's fussy about us letting the things out of our sight, insisting we keep them in a fire-proof and damp-proof and anything-else-proof container. He'd have a fit if he knew they'd been holed up in her student digs these last eighteen months.'

'I'll have to get the road done to Kirkwith Church,' I confessed. 'I don't want him dancing around in cow pats ever again.' Everyone laughed. They'd all heard about my first night, with the experience meaning that I won their sympathy and acceptance far more quickly than was usual with newcomers to their ranks. We were bonded like serfs together, suffering under the same baron.

Stamford was certain that the ingenious way he used the vicarage would once again come under the Archdeacon's attack. Not only was the east wing used as a farm by his son, but the west wing was used to house his daughter and her family, who ran a hairdressing salon on the premises. I had wondered about the succession of ladies, with hair slightly unkempt, who had kept passing the dining room windows all morning. I now realized they were coming for their fortnightly shampoo and set. I only hoped, that unlike David Harsley, they could tell their right from their left. Otherwise they might find themselves doused with pig-slurry rather than blue-rinse.

It was an interesting survey. Every priest harboured a different skeleton in his cupboard which he feared the Archdeacon would discover. Having named the ghosts which haunted us, we agreed that the Archdeacon might rant and rave about them but could do little else to hurt us. So we were comforted.

The other item of business to discuss was the campaign entitled 'Now's your chance!' This, so the ecclesiastical whiz kids from York claimed, was shortly to take the Church in the North by storm. There would be a galaxy of activities including teaching sessions, sermons, special services, advertising, posters and a roadshow touring each city and town north of the Trent. Every opportunity would be grasped, in season and out of season, to proclaim: 'Now's your chance to tell people about the Good News of Jesus!' Excitement was at fever pitch; or so we were told.

Unfortunately the proposals disgruntled rather than excited those clergy gathered that morning. 'Haven't I been telling people about the Good News of Jesus all my ministry? Yet this campaign presents the idea as if it were a novelty!' The venerable Vicar of Stamwith spoke for us all. Outright rebellion was avoided, however, as outrage gave way to laughter. To launch the initiative, every envelope of every letter posted from the Diocesan Office and the Archbishop's palace contained the logo, 'Now's your chance!'

'The problem is,' Stamford explained, 'letters posted in York are often franked with other messages. Only yesterday I received a missive from the Diocesan Secretary. The Post Office had overprinted "Now's your chance!" with the tempting words, "Don't miss the York races!" '

Though the fog still loomed on my slow cycle ride back to Kirkwith, it could not dispel the intense encouragement that meeting had given me. I was heartened that these old rural parsons seemed indestructible, would hold to their God and their faith come what may, resistant to trends and fashions and innovations. Their very clothes proclaimed that they had no desire whatsoever to be thought well of. They would truckle to no man, but would brave the severest unpopularity for what they believed. The Church in York's Vale could not be in safer hands.

I recalled a conversation between the Archdeacon and one such intransigent vicar. 'My good man, don't you think it's about time you moved with the times and risked a little change?'

'Nay, nay, Archdeacon,' the vicar had replied. 'Change might be alright for you townies, but you see, round 'ere it's our inertia which keeps us going.'

By the evening the fog had cleared. I cycled to the Weightons' farm by moonlight, the crispy heavens speckled with a radiant lattice-work of stars. I leant my bicycle by the farm gate and gazed at it all: in homage. Something within me was shouting: 'Forget all the doing and busyness; just stand here, watching, for ever.'

Sadly I ignored it, as always, and went on my way. My visit to the Weightons' farm for once was official and not contrived. Fond though I was of the inertia which was a local trademark, I felt that my parish ought to engage a bit with what was going on in the twentieth century. To this end I had taken the radical step of having a fortnightly housegroup, doing a roadshow of various homes around the parish, to discuss such exciting topics as arms for South Africa, banning the Bomb, uniting with other denominations, revising the Prayer Book, and had even blushed and stammered my way through sex before marriage.

In theory such meetings gave people the chance to exchange views and grow in how they applied their faith to the world. In practice, the discussions easily lapsed into the airing of prejudices or irrelevancies unless they were very tightly chaired indeed, which was hardly the intention of gathering informally.

The Weightons' five star entry in Doris Harsley's *The Withs' Guide to decrepit dwellings* had put off a fair few for tonight's session, with only eight folk eventually turning up. Miraculously there was a seat for everyone, since the sleeping sheepdogs had woken up and vacated the sofa, the ironing had been removed from the easy chairs and the menfolk had beaten a hasty retreat to the pub in Beckwith. Even then, those who dared to attend were a bit cautious about sitting on the settee. They had obviously been tipped off by Doris that it formerly housed a rats' nest.

We began with a few short prayers led by me. The rest of the group kept their eyes tightly shut, quite an eerie sight in the yellow light of the flickering oil lamps. Grandma ignored us all and kept her vigil by the fire, stirring the stewpot with her candle tilted. From time to time a veritable gush of hot liquid wax ran into the ingredients.

From our vantage points the two of us could see what the others certainly could not see. A rather scruffy cat had crept into the kitchen and had decided to amuse herself by leaping from chair back to chair back to sofa back, brushing against the head and shoulders of each avid prayer as she did so. This made for an electric atmosphere to say the least, ironic considering the Weightons hadn't been electrified. Geoff Goodmanham clenched his teeth and hunched his shoulders, Hannah Everingham had a grimace on her face which would have done justice to a gargoyle. The cat's progress was marked by a trail of pent and stiff people as each person tensed, fearing assault by some unidentified creature. The expectant air was ultimately broken when the cat leapt onto the lap of her final victim, Mrs Ludlow, Eastwith School's cook. She proved a model of moderation. 'Well goodness me, a cat,' she exclaimed in genuine surprise. Everyone opened their eyes and breathed a corporate sigh of relief. Further prayer was useless after that. When your fervent plea not to be devoured by a fierce rodent is heard and answered, then further intercession is superfluous.

Archbishop Michael Ramsey was to meet with the Pope next month, a historical first. I talked for a few minutes about the issues it raised and then invited questions. 'But Vicar, what do you think about the Black Sea Scrolls?' The questioner was Mrs Ludlow, who, to her credit, never missed a single housegroup session. Also to her credit, she always broke the ominous silence which followed whenever I invited comment. Unfortunately she always broke it with the same question, following which it was extremely difficult to return to the topic in hand.

Despite Mrs Ludlow's confused geography, something had clearly impressed her about the Dead Sea Scrolls. At one housegroup I had decided to draw her fire and devote that night's topic to the ancient scrolls discovered on the Dead Sea shore less than 20 years before. Infuriatingly, it was the only occasion on which she failed to ask her question.

Our discussion, as usual, degenerated into a general gossip, until the time came for the usual cup of tea and a light supper. It was clear that I was not the only one who had observed the Weightons' unconventional culinary methods, since one and all made their excuses and were off in an instant. Their sincerity was almost convincing with excuses delivered with the deepest remorse. 'Ee, I'm right sorry to miss t' cuppa and supper, Ivy, but there's somethin' else I've got to rush on to,' Hannah Everingham explained.

'I'd better go, Ivy. I was so rushed before I came out that I didn't have t' time to feed t' dog. He'll be ravishing by now.' Mrs Ludlow, who clearly had a way of getting not quite the right words, duly gave her excuse, followed by everyone else proffering theirs. It had up until then escaped my attention that there were so many conflicting things going on in the sleepy Withs at 9pm on a dark winter's evening.

I stayed, convincing myself that it was because of the deep and increasing respect in which I held the Weightons. It had nothing to do, of course, with the fact that Rebecca was due back from a parents' evening imminently. I even enjoyed the pork and wax sandwiches. It was a hitherto untried delicacy, but one which was likely to be repeated if my future visits to the Weightons were to be as frequent as I hoped. As I bit into a particularly tough bit of tallow, I closed my eyes and thought of Rebecca.

CHAPTER ELEVEN

There they sat on the front row of Beckwith Church, nervous, self-conscious, awaiting their confirmation, two boys, six girls and two women who had spent months preparing for this great day. The women were farmers' wives, proudly decked out in new outfits by courtesy of Marks and Spencer at the grudging reluctance of their husbands. 'My man wasn't best pleased, Vicar,' one of them reported to me beforehand. ' "What the hell do you need a new outfit for?" he fumed. "That so-and-so church is so cold you'll never take your overcoat off, so who's to see what's beneath it? I don't know what you're getting confirmed for, anyway. It doesn't do to take religion too seriously." ' That the women had turned up despite such 'encouragement' from their spouses made me immensely proud of them.

The girls, their faces pale, were decked in white, flimsy frocks and shivered in a building so chilly you could see your breath condense in front of your eyes. The boys were warmer, kitted out in their grammar school uniform, which had been carefully sponged down to remove mud, ink, mashed potato and other unmentionable stains for this great occasion.

I had been quite innovative with the children's confirmation preparation. We had sat under my large kitchen table, pretending we were in the Roman catacombs in which Christian worship was forged. Half the group had been blindfolded and led around by the other half to experience what trust and faith was all about. We had crammed into the telephone box, pretending it was Dr Who's Tardis, and travelled back in time to

AD 33 and watched Jesus being crucified. With the two adult candidates I had been more restrained. Given that their husbands were hardly enthusiastic to start with, I sensed that blindfolding their wives and crawling with them under my kitchen table would not be the surest way of winning them round. Even so, with the spectre of my own confirmation lessons haunting me, I was determined to make the lessons I took more fun and less boring.

The Archbishop had matched our well turned out candidates by bringing his own party best. Gorgeous robes, the weight of a couple of thick velvet curtains, were completed by a gaudily coloured mitre, his version of a party hat. Since Beckwith Church had no vestry, we had to billet him at a nearby cottage where he could get dressed in some privacy.

Mr Sancton, the highly honoured householder, attended him, and the two men fell naturally into conversation. 'And what do you do with your time, Mr Sancton?' the Archbishop inquired.

'I keep pigs, sir.'

The Archbishop looked at his watch and added, crisply and decisively, 'We've still got a good quarter of an hour before the service; let me see them.'

'Do you really think that's a good idea, Archbishop?' his chaplain asked anxiously. 'I'm sure the ladies of the York Minster Embroiderers' Guild would have a fit if you got the slightest mark on those robes.'

'Never mind those blessed women; I want to see this good man's pigs,' the Archbishop replied, determined not to be cowed by his chaplain.

Even if a cope and mitre is perhaps not the best outfit to tour a pigsty in, Archbishop and small-holder, vicar and chaplain trooped out into the muddy stackyard and peered into the pigsty. The Archbishop pointed things out with his crosier. 'Do you know, I've carried this crook around for ten years now, and I think this is the first time I've actually found a proper use for the thing.'

The chaplain whispered a story to me of how, following a confirmation at a school, one of the pupils had written home, 'I was able to sit near the Archbishop. I now know what a crook looks like!'

The Archbishop gave me a funny look as I burst into laughter, but kept up a rapid fire of questions to Mr Sancton. 'How old are they?' followed by 'Do you slaughter them yourself?' At this the Chaplain went pale. He clearly knew his master better than the rest of us and obviously feared the Archbishop would request a demonstration of pig-culling.

Fortunately he was put out of his misery by Mr Sancton's explanation. 'No sir, I don't have anything to do with that. I just wouldn't have it in me, having brought them up from tiny piglets. Mr Hinchcliffe, our local butcher of distinction, does the necessary when the time comes.' I liked his euphemistic 'does the necessary', whispered so as not to offend his porcine charges grunting before us.

Mr Sancton had an old sow he treated like a dog, in the best possible sense. Each night, without fail, he took her for a walk on a lead through the village. He even allowed her into the house. The Archbishop made a particular fuss of her. 'What a magnificent beast,' he cooed. 'Does she have a name?'

'Sophie, sir.' The sow grunted appreciatively; Mr Sancton beamed. The Archbishop's interest in his prize possession had warmed his heart all the more. Until his dying day, he would never forget the busy Archbishop who had taken time out to linger over his pigs. If an archbishop could do that, maybe even an immensely more busy almighty God could spare him a moment or two.

The congregation sniffed to a Mother's Union member as the Archbishop processed, beaming, into church, with the distinct odour of the pigsty. Given the Archdeacon's unfortunate accident prior to my being 'put in', the local folk would start wondering whether 'smelling a bit funny' was a qualification for high office in the Church. The service duly began, but half-way through the first hymn, the Archbishop bellowed the singing to a halt: 'Good people of Beckwith, this – will – not – do!' He shouted at the shocked congregation in clipped tones, which had a distinct guttural twang. 'Tonoight the church is very full. The sound we make should be very loud and very sweet.' He then launched into a line or two at the pitch and pace he wanted, before rounding on the organist, whom he addressed in a headmasterly tone: 'Miss Organist, I'll make a bargain with you. If you can play at twice the speed, I will sing at twice the speed. Otherwise the – hymn – will – be – grim.' I had noticed before that Donald Coggan used the word 'grim' rather a lot.

Doris Harsley speeded up her arthritic hands as best she could, also speeding up her feet to pump the pedals of the harmonium faster. It was a veritable race for her to keep up with the Archbishop. Whether her face was red with exertion or fury I did not find out until later. 'How dare he call me a Miss when I've been legally married to Sam nigh on 50 years,' Doris had protested to me, as breathless as ever. 'I'll tell you something Vicar I wouldn't welcome him into my front room like I welcomed you and t' Bishop of Pocklington.' She shook her head in fury. 'And I'll tell you something else even if he did visit me he wouldn't have a crumb of my cake or a sniff of my sherry.' I realized, not for the first time, the Archbishop was an immensely shrewd man.

Uncowed by hostile looks from her or the breathless choir, the Archbishop went on to preach: 'Good people of Beckwith. The confirmation which we are celebrating tonight to the best of our ability,' he broke off to give Doris a scathing glance before continuing, 'is the gateway to Holy Communion, the service in which God provides, week by week, perhaps even day by day if you are of a certain High Church persuasion, rations for His troops to fight his battles and transform this grim world into His glorious kingdom.' There went that word 'grim' again. His sermon was brief and to the point. He soon reached his conclusion. 'When you go home tonoight, I want you to wroite in the front of your Boibles the text "I am the Lord's man forever", so that you will never forget this day.'

The issue of inclusive language had yet to appear on the horizon, but even in 1966 I wondered what our two farmers' wives and six girls would think as they followed the good Archbishop's instructions to the letter. Sensitivities of a later age and disgruntled organists aside, the Archbishop had made a major impact. He was a master of sound-bites which would stay fixed with those confirmation candidates for the rest of their lives. And the pigs were quite impressed too.

As the bunfight which followed drew to its close, and the hall emptied, Rebecca and I were talking quite animatedly by the door. Almost the last to leave, the Archbishop came over to bid me farewell. 'And who is this young lady, David? Your sister?' he asked, as direct as ever.

'Er, no your Grace,' I replied, stumbling over my words. 'This is Rebecca Weighton who lives in the parish and teaches German in York.'

'Good to meet you, Rebecca,' the Archbishop responded. He made as if to go, but then turned round and added, 'I've been watching the two of you talking for some minutes now, and I can see there's more between the two of you than normally between a vicar and his parishioner.' Rebecca blushed; I felt the blood rushing to my head too, as he continued, 'All that may have little to do with me, but I hope you'll forgive me if I add two things. The first is that the loife of a woife of a discoiple of Chroist can, at toimes, be grim. Grim and hard. The second is that there is no greater privilege on earth than such a loife together in the service of our Lord. God bless you both in all that lies ahead.'

And with that he walked away. Tears filled my eyes. As I said, he was the shrewdest of men.

Rebecca came back with me to the vicarage. I made a cup of tea without hurling the contents across the living room and we settled down, eagerly watching my rather ancient television set. A strange Canadian with a pendulum which kept swinging from side to side seemed to know what the outcome of the general election would be, even before the first result was declared. Notwithstanding his forecast, the finish promised to be an exciting one. Would Harold Wilson and his white heat of technological revolution be returned with the majority he needed? Or would it be another hung parliament? Or would Tory patricians, led by a fresh-faced Ted Heath, once again hold sway?

Unfortunately, something had gone wrong with the TV's horizontal control, with the result that all the politicians were stretched out and looked like rather gangly giants. I thought about adjusting things so that they could revert to the midgets they were, but decided against. We didn't want to lose the picture altogether, since it provided a convenient excuse for Rebecca to be here. Self-sufficient though the Weightons were, a television had yet to be discovered which would run on candles, oil lamps or a Yorkshire range.

At 11pm the wretched phone rang. 'Beckwith 143,' I answered sharply. Telephone numbers had a cosy feel about them in those days. The neighbouring vicar was Beckwith 140, Bill Everingham was Beckwith 141, Sam Harsley was Beckwith 142, Ron of the Ron Ran Run bus service was Beckwith 144. The one-forties were obviously a holy line.

'Hello, is that the Vicar?' bellowed a faintly female voice. Once reassured of my identity, the caller continued, 'Can you come and see mother? She's dying and wants her Communion. We're at Thorntons' Farm.' And with that very matter of fact message, she rang off.

I left Rebecca to keep a lonely vigil and cycled off, back to Beckwith. After a long bumpy ride up a rutty farm track, I saw Thorntons' Farm lit up before me. Although this was my first visit, I'd heard about the place on the Beckwith grapevine. It was Hannah Everingham who had pointed the place out when she and Bill were giving me a lift to York one day. 'Now that's a rarity, Vicar,' she had announced. 'It's a woman-only farm. Apart from a couple of labourers hired at harvest time, all the work is done by mother and daughter, with grandma keeping the books. Grandma has been a widow these past forty years. Mother was abandoned by a no-good husband shortly after giving birth to a baby girl. The girl then grew up and married only to have her husband walk out on her too. What do you think of that?'

I was duly dumbfounded. Clearly, losing their menfolk seemed to be a genetic trait.

Hannah had continued, 'Not that they needed men. Mother Edna and daughter Doreen are so built that they can easily sling a bale; the muscular hired-men seem like weaklings beside those two.'

I could see Hannah's point as the bulbous Edna let me in to the ramshackle farmhouse, and, with barely a grunt of welcome, showed me immediately up to her mother's bedroom. I noticed the threadbare carpet on the stairs, the chill of the bedroom which would have made Beckwith Church seem positively balmy in comparison. Legend had it that in her prime, Grandma Thornton too had been of similar build to her daughter and grand-daughter, capable not just of lifting a bale, but also of hurling it onto a high wagon with one flick of her pitchfork. Such prowess regularly forced the sinewy Dubbins into second place in the Howden Show.

That legend seemed particularly incredible as I gazed on the frail, wizened figure that night. That the virtual skeleton between the sheets was even a relative of these two strapping women who attended her, let alone the giantess of folklore, was beyond belief.

Dr Seaton had called and warned that Grandma would not last the night, giving her an injection 'just to ease the pain'. Whilst I was there, Grandma drifted in and out of consciousness, not saying a word, in contrast to Edna, who never stopped talking.

I was a bit slow-witted, with half of my brain still back at the vicarage with Rebecca and the other half asleep, but eventually I pieced their story together. In her younger days, Grandma had attended church fiercely, one of the few who were besotted with Father Cornwall. He had been the vicar of Beckwith thirty years before, when the village had boasted its own parish priest, and had injected a whiff of Anglo-Catholicism which had been rejected by most of the xenophobic village folk as simply un-English. Yet Grandma Thornton adored him. Edna told me why he had proved so popular with mum. 'She used to say that t' church at Beckwith smelt as damp and musty as the Derwent before he came along. His incense made it smell sweet.'

It's funny what wins souls. When he left the village and had been replaced with a more middle-of-the-road vicar, who had all the Withs to look after, Grandma's church-going had lapsed. But the old faith still lurked deep within, hence this death-bed request.

As we kept watch over her mother, Edna told me in hushed tones how she had come to her daughter's rescue, some twenty-odd years before. 'Our Doreen was five at the time. Silly little thing had been playing with her friends on a haystack. She went and fell off and impaled herself on an irrigator.' Edna told her story in short, blunt sentences, leaving it to my imagination what sort of instrument of torture an irrigator was. 'Oh, she was a mess, right through her those prongs went. She yelled like blue murder. They say you could hear her screams at Eastwith and beyond. There was nothing we could do but get her in farm truck and drive to City Hospital over in York. She shrieked at every bump in the road.' I wasn't at all surprised; I found the long, drawn-out journey painful enough when well.

There both Edna and Grandma watched beside her bedside. Obviously the fact that we were similarly watching now had triggered Edna's memory to flashback. Septicaemia had set in and things began to look very bleak indeed. 'It was terrible, a grandmother watching her grand-daughter in the death-throes,' Edna recalled. 'But then, somehow her grief was overtaken by a resolve that the inevitable was not going to happen. She sought out the ward sister and asked to see the consultant. "He's off duty at present, Mrs Thornton, but he'll be back on Monday." '

Sensing that her ailing grand-daughter would not survive until then, Grandma had taken her cause to Matron and requested she disclose the consultant's home address. 'Ee, that Matron was a big, powerful woman. She was a bully, without a doubt. You had to be like that in them days to run a hospital. She wouldn't give her the address at first. But my mother kept on at her, she just wouldn't take no for an answer. After a while, Matron realized she was in the presence of twice the bully she was, and gave in.' Edna stared at her dying mother with a look of sheer pride.

Grandma Thornton had steamed off to the consultant's home with the momentum of a battleship, only to be greeted by disappointment. The maid loftily informed her that her master was at Bootham Park, watching the football. He would not be returning until late in the evening, since he was going out to dine with the directors.

'But she just would not be beaten,' Edna continued. 'She stormed off to the football ground and somehow bluffed her way into the directors' box. There she found the consultant, relishing the unusual experience of York being in a two goal lead. He wasn't over-fussed to be disturbed, I can tell you. "Madam," he said, sneering at her working clothes, looking down on her as beneath him, "I'm off duty now and I will not be returning to the hospital until Monday morning. I will see your child then and not before."

'But my mother didn't waver a fraction. Rather she employed the full force of her faith and strength into shaming him in the presence of his high and mighty friends. "Have you no conscience?" she boomed, "No decency? There's a little girl in that hospital ward, a little girl who you're supposed to be looking after, writhing in utter agony. You're going to watch football are you, while she slowly dies? Well, may God forgive you, because I won't, not until my dying day." And with that she turned to walk away.

'Suddenly she found the surgeon was walking beside her. He said not a word, but meekly followed her across the Scarborough railway bridge and back to the hospital. There he examined Doreen and made his diagnosis. "I'm going to put her on a new drug, Mrs Thornton, which has been recently developed. She's a very lucky little girl, because it's very expensive indeed." With that, he left to see the end of the game. It was far from the end of Doreen's game, for she recovered from that hour. Doreen owes her life to this woman.' Again, Edna looked down at her mother so fondly, so gratefully.

No one even spoke to consultants in those days, let alone dragged them from their football matches. Apparently, what had inspired Grandma to perform her feat of breathtaking cheek was the Gospel she had heard at Mass on the previous Sunday. It told of a Gentile woman, an outcast under Jewish law, who had begged the busy Jesus to come and heal her dying daughter. Despite Jesus' reluctance, she had persisted, throwing herself down at his feet. Grandma felt that if Jesus could be distracted from his mission to Israel, then the surgeon could abandon his football match. And so, nineteen hundred years later, the Gospel was replayed, with Grandma and the Gentile woman sharing a perseverance in common that spanned the centuries.

That tale alone made me feel it was immensely right for Grandma to make her Communion with her Saviour in her final moments. The only problem was she hadn't eaten anything for days and could hardly swallow. She could barely take a drink, let alone anything solid. How could she consume the Bread of heaven when she couldn't even take the bread of earth?

I suddenly had an idea. 'Edna, do me a favour and get me a cup of water and a teaspoon,' I asked. Although undoubtedly surprised by the request at such a high point in the service, Edna duly obliged. Breaking the smallest crumb of the consecrated bread, I placed it on the teaspoon which I had filled with water and gently placed the spoon into Grandma Thornton's mouth. The words, though familiar, never had a greater poignancy before or since:

'The body of our Lord Jesus Christ which was given for thee, preserve thy body and soul unto everlasting life.'

She swallowed and made as if she wanted to say something. I knelt beside the bed and bowed my head so as to be as close to her lips as possible. She was barely able to talk, in fact the voice seemed to come from deep within her, exhaled with each breath, 'Thank you.'

I ended the service with the words:

'Unto God's gracious mercy and protection we commit thee. The Lord bless thee and keep thee. The Lord make his face to shine upon thee and be gracious unto thee. The Lord lift up his countenance upon thee, and give thee peace, both now and evermore.'

A few moments later she breathed her last.

I stayed a while, consoling Edna and Doreen. Then I cycled home to Rebecca. She had already left, although a brief note on the coffee table lifted my spirits: 'Labour have won! All my love, R.'

Apparently in my absence the strange Canadian's pendulum had swung to the left and stuck there. I looked forward to a socialist dawn; Grandma Thornton basked in heaven. Undoubtedly she had the better deal.

CHAPTER TWELVE

'Fold t' short strut ov-er long strut, fold it a-gain and then fold long strut ov-er short strut and tuck it in round back and pull it as tight as you can. Then thread short strut through t' knot, thread it back a-gain and make it ev-en. Then thread long strut though t' knot and thread that back ag-ain to fin-ish top.' Bill Everingham beamed, rather proud of his explanation. He himself had only learnt how to make palm crosses that very afternoon, and now he was teaching the art.

His pupil, however, did not share her master's grasp of Origami-with-palm-leaves. To say Doris Harsley's brow was furrowed would be an understatement indeed. 'I followed you as far as long strut over short strut but you lost me with t' knot and all that threading left over right and right over left would you go through t' rest again?' Following the Bishop of Pocklington's visit, Doris had reverted to her punctuation-free speech. Making palm crosses was simplicity itself compared to making sense of what she said.

Her breathless pronouncement had certainly lost Bill: 'Come ag-ain, Dor-is, I don't quite fol-low what you're on ab-out.' I decided to leave the mono-syllabic to fight it out with the multi-syllabic and moved on to check on how the others were doing.

It was the Saturday before Palm Sunday and I had converted my sitting room into a palm cross factory, with Bill and Hannah Everingham, Sam and Doris Harsley, Mrs Weighton and Rebecca, Emma and George Broadhurst and Pam manning and womanning the production line. To say the least, it was a motley workforce. None had ever made a palm cross before, so I had given several careful demonstrations before splitting them up into pairs. Whilst I didn't delude myself that they'd all cotton on immediately, my hope was that each would iron out the other's deficiencies.

Some hope! Doris' perfectionist streak asserted itself and made her and Sam incompatible cross manufacturers. Frustrated with her own effort, she poured scorn on Sam's equally futile attempts. Sam went bright red, his moustache bristled and he looked fit to burst. To prevent a most unholy row prefacing this most holy of weeks, I intervened and imposed a reshuffle.

Putting Bill Everingham and Doris Harsley together proved a touch of genius. Bill had grasped the technique amazingly quickly, so there was nothing Doris could find fault with. And even had she been able to, she would have to temper any criticism with the courtesies from which married people all too often claimed immunity when dealing with each other.

Emma Broadhurst proved a natural, whereas her father proved all fingers and thumbs. It took him a considerable length of time to produce just one specimen, a sorry-looking sight if ever there was one, palm leaf bedraggled, cross beam askew. No more than breathing on the thing caused it to spring apart and scatter, with George ruffling his hair as he was forced to start yet again. That afternoon he looked more like a perplexed five-year-old trying to fathom how to tie his shoe-laces than the professor who had taken the academic world by storm.

One thing caught my eye. Pam and Mrs Weighton had proved an effective team and had all but finished their quota before George had even started. Pam was just putting the finishing touches to their efforts when, on one of its many leaps, George's heavily worked palm cross landed on their table. As George retrieved it, his hand lingered on Pam's hand for a fleeting moment. Mrs Weighton had turned around to chat to Hannah Everingham, so she missed what I alone saw. Perhaps I was putting too much significance into what might have been only an accidental touch in the first place. Or perhaps I was primed to notice such things. I had taken hold of everyone's hand that afternoon to guide their fingers through the palm cross motions. Only the fleeting touch of Rebecca harnessed the power of a thunderstorm.

By the end of the afternoon, we had made a cross for every man, woman and child in the Withs, with several to spare. Which was just as well, because half-way through the afternoon, Dewi tore into our palm cross factory, raced around the room for half a dozen orbits, and then leapt over one of the tables, deftly snatching a batch of palm crosses in his mouth as he did so. He then hurtled out as suddenly as he had hurtled in, and didn't bother us again. When I took him for a walk after tea, I noticed a trail of chewed up palm leaves marked his earlier outing.

The conversation over tea veered from the sublime to the ridiculous. Making so many crosses had driven Hannah Everingham to focus on Jesus' final days. 'Ee, the fickleness of that crowd, Vicar, hailing Him with their hosannas on Sunday only to shriek "Crucify Him" by Friday.'

'Ay, but we'd 'ave done no bet-ter, Han,' Bill sagely commented. It dawned on us that had we been there, we would have betrayed Him just as devastatingly.

The numinous hush was broken by Sam Harsley, who piped up, 'I must say this palm oil doesn't 'alf make your hands smooth.' Doris smiled at him. Inept though his comment may have been, at least they were friends again.

We then moved on to a spirited discussion as to what Jesus' Last Supper must have been like. 'It would have been a meag-re feast if stained-glass in t' church is an-y-thing to go by. There's hard-ly a mor-sel of food to be seen. More frug-al than t' tea I had that time in York, when they tried to fob me off with a tin-y bun in-stead of a prop-er cake.' Bill shook his head, although I was none too sure whether he was despairing of our stained glass or of York restaurants' dainty fare.

'I prefer Leonardo Da Vinci's painting of the Last Supper myself,' Hannah Everingham confessed. 'It's so simple. The trestle tables remind me of our harvest suppers – there's even a cloth that looks like your tea-towel, Ivy.' Mrs Weighton smiled proudly; I avoided catching Rebecca's laughing eyes. 'And Jesus, he looks so, so heart-broken,' Hannah continued. 'The other disciples look so, so lost, so bewildered. It says it all to me.'

This time it was Doris Harsley who brought us down from our Olympian heights: 'Yes we've got one just like that over t' fire-place in our living room.' She thought for a moment before adding, 'Only it's with ballet dancers.' Maundy Thursday was never quite the same for me again after that. Pirouetting disciples invariably loomed in my imagination and spoiled things.

The next week flew by. Before the service on Palm Sunday, Bill Everingham rode through Kirkwith on a donkey. He looked a fool, just as Jesus would have done. Having circumnavigated the village, even risking the ever treacherous church road, Bill tethered the donkey to the lychgate and the service began. Pauses in praying were punctuated by her braying, transporting us effortlessly back to AD 33.

The next day another animal performed the same trick at Eastwith Church. The sun had just been rising as I had cycled out of Kirkwith. It was a quarter past six on the Monday of Holy Week, a beautiful spring morning. A heavy dew made the grass glisten with clusters galore of tiny silver droplets. A myriad of daffodils and narcissi carpeted the verges, their heads bowed, still rather shy at this hour. The light early morning mist gave the whole scene a sepia effect. The magic was completed by the distinctive call of a pheasant, startled in her nest in the long grass, as my bicycle swished by. It seemed ironic that at this time of the year with all its pregnant promise of new beginnings, I was out to mark an end, a death. April is undoubtedly the cruellest month.

The dozen or so congregation yawned, rubbing their sleepy eyes as I read the Gospel: 7am is an early hour for worship.

'Peter broke into curses and declared with an oath, "I do not know the man." At that moment the cock crew.' And sure enough, it did. A cockerel in a nearby farmyard provided chilling sound effects. The dreamy congregation woke up with a start, all calling to mind what Jesus had said to Peter: 'Before the cock crows, you will deny me three times.'

Late Tuesday afternoon I found myself preparing for what I had been told was the greatest religious feast in the parish's calendar: the Kirkwith Church Garden Party. The date had been set for the end of July, so I still had a little time in hand. Doing a spot of gardening to escape the intensity of Holy Week, I had stumbled over some uneven stone steps. If I could fall over them, so could our veritable army of old ladies who ran the garden party stalls. Whilst 'Break your limbs here' might suggest a rather novel side-show, on reflection I decided to re-lay the steps to banish the nightmare of hurtling geriatrics suffering injuries manifold.

I determined to do a thorough job, and dug up all the stones. I carefully levelled the path, placed the stones in steps, but then, horror of horrors, they wobbled, making them twice as dangerous as before. So back to the drawing board. I levelled the path once more, positioned new stones and held my breath. Marvellous: no wobbling whatsoever. I had solved that problem, but as I gazed adoringly on my handiwork and considered an alternative career in landscape architecture, I realized I had merely replaced one hazard with another. For the stones weren't level, but sloped downwards. Anyone who was unwise enough to walk on their licheny surface would have their feet shoot from under them. So I had to begin yet again.

Originally there had been a Norman keep next to Kirkwith Church but at some stage in history most of its component parts had ended up in the vicarage grounds. Hitherto I hadn't realized that having so many stones scattered about my garden was such good fortune. I realized it that evening, however, as I tried nearly all of them on those steps. And as the night went on, the stones got a peculiar hold on me. Inanimate, worthless, useless stones suddenly started influencing me, rather than I them. I even began to have feelings for the wretched things. I became angry with a stone, even felt a migraine coming on if it didn't fit. I was pleased with a stone, flushed with delight, if it was right. I would never have thought that stones could have incited such emotion within me.

And as the job drew to its close and the light started to fade, the siting of the final stones became more and more crucial. I became more and more tense. After all, if the right stone couldn't be found, the whole project would be in jeopardy and my labour would be wasted. As I heaved the last stone into place, I was all too conscious that it could either breathe calamity or victory. Fortunately it breathed victory and I was left with a set of steps which even the most infirm of elderly ladies would be safe on.

My limbs and my back ached as I packed away my gardening tools. By now it was completely dark, and I did wonder what I would have done if that last stone had failed to fit. I also began to wonder whether my little gardening adventure had really been an escape from Holy Week after all.

A few minutes later Rebecca arrived, with our supper in her cycle-basket. This was the day the touring fish and chip van from Hull visited Kirkwith, and so Tuesday night was fish and chip night, my favourite meal of the week. I did wonder how such an enterprise coped, driving from village to village along the ever winding roads. I imagined boiling fat, slopping over the vat sides on a particularly tricky corner, the van's gangway running with grease, with patrons slipping and sliding over one another as they struggled with their fourpenny-worth of chips. In reality, though, the van was spotless, the only grease to be seen on its product, which was delicious.

We had supper sitting around the stove in the kitchen. Dewi begged Rebecca, with pleading eyes, for the occasional chip and scrap of batter. I had become resistant to his charms long since. In any case, nothing in all creation would persuade me to give fish and chips away.

'It's a funny feeling,' I explained to Rebecca, harking back to my gardening project, 'but at one point, I suddenly realized that I was actually doing no creating. Rather, stones, inanimate objects, were creating moods in me. I was literally at the stones' mercy so that both my despair and my happiness depended on them. The stones themselves could dictate either tragedy or triumph.'

'That all sounds very grand, but what does it mean?' Rebecca asked, a dark smile on her face. 'Surely you were the initiator? The project was your idea, you started it off, you moved the stones.'

'Yes, yes, I agree,' I interrupted. 'And yet, the more I got involved with the process, as it moved to its peak, I somehow had this funny feeling that the material I was using could either make or break the whole venture.'

'Like, like, we could make or break the whole of God's venture,' Rebecca said slowly, as the idea dawned on her.

'Yes, that's it, you've put it in a nutshell,' I replied, excited now by a whole flush of thoughts her comment had catalysed. 'Just like the stones had the potential to hurt and thwart me, we, who had only come into being because of God's say-so, could hurt Him, could thwart His Creation, could make Him bleed.'

We sat in silence for a few moments, chomping our meal, thinking things over. 'There's a difference, though, between me and my stones and God and us,' I eventually concluded. 'Had that last stone let me down, had it not been right, I know that I would have given up, I wouldn't have had the stamina to carry on, even if I had had the light. But on his darkest day, God never gave up, breathing Easter triumph into Good Friday tragedy.'

'Ee, Dav-id, if you weren't a gard-en-er, you'd make a reet good preach-er-man,' quipped Rebecca, showing her mother's talent for impersonating Bill Everingham. Even so, gardens can prompt some strange ideas. Perhaps hailing the garden party as the greatest of religious festivals wasn't so wide of the mark after all.

Clearly another great religious festival took place two evenings later, with Women's Institute members packed into Beckwith Hall like very large sardines in a very small can. I had to be elsewhere, in church with half a dozen others to mark the first Last Supper. But I had heard in advance about what the WI were planning. 'It shouldn't be allowed, Vicar. You ought to put a stop to it. At such a holy time of year, as well,' blurted out Mrs Cave, a farm-worker's wife from one of the hamlets, who'd bustled up to my front door in a high state of indignation last Monday night.

'I never thought the WI would allow such a thing,' she gabbled on, as I sat her in my study and tried to calm her down. 'It was that trip last year to Scarborough that did it. I'd paired off for the day with Vera Newbald – her husband works with my Alf, so we're quite close. Or at least we used to be. Because it was raining, Vera was keen to seek shelter in a booth on the South Shore. "Madame Estrange, Clairvoyant Extrordinaire", it said, over the door. "Palms read and fortunes told. Satisfaction guaranteed."

'Vera was as keen as mustard, dragging me in with her. "Come on, Doreen, let's get us fortunes told and have some fun." I wasn't that happy about it, myself, you understand, Vicar. But it was pouring down, and at least it stopped me getting my hair drenched any further. It was fair washing the perm out, it was.' I made the sort of sympathetic noises that indicated that any sin could be forgiven when a perm was on the line.

'I could tell she was bogus from the start,' Mrs Cave confided. 'Dyed black hair, made up to the nines, right down to a false tan to give her the look of a gypsy, she didn't fool me for a minute. "I can see you've got three children, three young children, that you live in the country and that you love animals," she cooed into her crystal ball. You didn't have to be psychic to know that. Vera was clutching three sticks of rock, her shoes were muddied from where she'd ran along the farm track to catch t' bus and her overcoat was covered with dog hairs. She was just stating the obvious. "Don't believe a word she said," I told Vera, once we'd got outside again.

'But she'd have none of it. "You're only jealous, Doreen, because she predicted my Bert wouldn't be stuck at t' farm for ever, and that I had a big surprise coming to me. That must be my Auntie Phyllis who's at death's door. They say she owns a small fortune, and what's more, I'm her favourite niece." '

Mrs Cave sniffed loudly as she continued her monologue. I just listened, meekly. ' "You're her only niece," I replied. "Anyway, you won't get a penny, once her three sons have carved it up between them." But she'd have none of it, and went on and on about this Madame Estrange for the rest of the day, and all the bus journey back. And she's been on about her ever since. I've kept my distance from then on. It's pathetic, a grown woman being taken in by such a fraud.

'And what's more, the whole Women's Institute committee have been taken in, because they've agreed to let her be the speaker at their meeting this Thursday. Vera had them all agog with expectation. "If she's in the mood," she promised, "she'll go into a trance and we can hold a seance." What do you think of that, then, Vicar, holding a seance on Maundy Thursday night. My mother would turn in her grave.'

'Do you normally go to church on Maundy Thursday, then, Mrs Cave?' I asked. The only time I had seen her in church so far was at the infamous Nativity play on Christmas Eve.

'Well no, Vicar, I don't have time, what with Alf's tea and the children to look after, and a thousand and one other things to do. If I had the time, I'd come, but some of us have got work to do. But I still don't think it's right.'

Though I felt she was bearing a personal grudge, I thoroughly agreed with her, feeling hurt that so many of my parishioners should opt for this charade rather than the real thing.

When I was seven, I attended a Christmas party and observed a rather nasty child inveigle another into swapping a prized toy for a cheap imitation. I wanted to weep in sorrow for that cheated child and I wanted to weep now. Even so, I tried to give a balanced response. 'It all seems a bit rum, Mrs Cave, but I'm afraid there's very little I can do to stop it. The WI are independent of the Church and I don't own the hall. But don't worry. If Madame Estrange is the fraud you suspect her to be, then she's hardly likely to be a spiritual danger. You're wise to stay away, though.'

'Stay away, stay away?!' Mrs Cave exploded. 'If you can't put a stop to it, I'm going. I want to see what she gets up to.' And with that she bustled out, bristling with disgust at my inability to halt the proceedings.

I heard afterwards that the evening didn't live up to its promise. No seance took place. Madame Estrange told a few fortunes, although they were no more focused than the astrological predictions in the local paper. One of her forecasts was spot on, however. After the meeting she stayed overnight with the Newbalds, with a taxi due to pick her up early the next morning. She wasn't the taxi's only fare. Bert accompanied her too, leaving his sleeping wife a note declaring that he had decided to run off with the woman of his dreams. Madame Estrange's prediction that Vera Newbald's husband wouldn't be stuck on the farm for ever had proved searingly accurate.

At 3am on Good Friday, a few hours before the two lovers had driven off into a golden sunrise, an owl screeching in the cedar outside my bedroom window had woken me up, and try as I might, I just couldn't get back to sleep. I decided to pad down to the kitchen, brave the chill of the tiled floor on my uncovered feet and make myself a cup of tea. Dewi licked around my toes, both pleased and puzzled by my presence at an unexpected hour. As I boiled the water, my thoughts inevitably turned to Rebecca and the utter mess I had made of simply making a cup of tea on her first visit to my home. I counted myself fortunate indeed that so much promise had come out of so much chaos. But then, as I sat in the kitchen drinking tea, my thoughts inexplicably turned to Him on that Friday. What was happening to Him at 3am? The chief priests in a frenzy, spitting out their insults at Him. The armed men, raining blows upon His poor bruised body. He, standing there, saying nothing, shivering: with the cold and for what lay ahead. His best friend, standing outside, keeping himself warm by the fire, shaking his head, denying he ever even knew Him. That was what was happening to Him. Having drunk my tea, I snuggled back, gratefully, into my warm bed and immediately slept.

I awoke again at just after six o'clock. No early service to take today, so instead I went out for a brisk cycle ride. Kirkwith's avenue of poplars, with promise of bursting into leaf, was soon behind me. I rode south for about half an hour, crossing the Derwent on the Selby Road before riding north again on its western bank. I viewed my parish from afar on that gloriously sunny morning, the sky clear, not a cloud in sight. I could see the three churches in one glance, Kirkwith's squat tower, Beckwith's steep pitched roof, Eastwith's red brick. Huddled around each was a cluster of homes and farms, with the odd isolated building, separated from the community like a sulking adolescent. I thought of all the day's activity just beginning, the doing, the hoping, the hurting, the arguing, the loving, perhaps the dying.

After a couple of miles I cycled past Thicket Priory, which housed an order of Carmelite nuns. To the east I could still see my three churches. The Derwent formed a natural divide between us Anglicans on the one side and those enclosed Roman Catholics on the other side, forming a particularly poignant reminder this Good Friday of the gulf between us.

As a detour I cycled down a little lane to the river bank, where there was a tiny inn with a few boats moored. I walked a little way upstream and came across a wooden bridge which had long since fallen into disrepair. The supports rotted, the nails rusted, the beams splintered: an apt place for a pilgrimage when thoughts of wood and nails and broken-ness and the One who tried to bridge heaven and earth were never far away.

Ever one for adventure, I wheeled my bicycle cautiously over the narrow planks that were still intact and managed to cross the river, arriving in Eastwith at noon. Fortunately I had taken the precaution of packing my cassock in my rucksack, so I was already prepared for the service I was to take there at 2pm. Unfortunately I hadn't taken the precaution of packing lunch; having wended my way for over five hours, I was distinctly peckish. I decided to call on the Goodmanhams in the hope of scrounging a meal. I gave in to hunger whilst He gave in to life.

June and Geoff gladly let me share their simple fare of soup and cheese. Baby Elizabeth proved an eloquent example of minority rule, interrupting the proceedings with her shrill screams, demanding that mum should feed her. Which she did. These were the days of 'bottle is best', with breast-feeding a rarity, unknown in public. Yet as June suckled her child, it all seemed so natural. I, who could not say 'circumcision' without blushing, felt no embarrassment. It all seemed such a homely source of new life to balance Good Friday's cloying tragedy: 'Mother, this is your daughter; daughter, this is your mother…'

CHAPTER THIRTEEN

Early in the morning, when it was yet dark, I walked the half mile to the Derwent to watch the sun rise over Kirkwith Church. The mist, which had clung to the water as dawn broke, was soon burned off by the sun's rays. The inevitable heaviness of Holy Week evaporated at that same moment, as it gave way to Easter joy.

For as long as I can remember, Easter Day has never failed to thrill me. What sticks in my memory from boyhood is the wireless being turned on for the eight o'clock news from the Home Service. The weather forecast drew to its close. The airwaves were still for a moment. And then their silence was broken by the announcer, using the same measured tones which day by day pronounced triumph or tragedy: 'Before the news, we have an Easter hymn.' As the strains of 'Jesus Christ is risen today,' rang out, my heart swelled with pride.

When I returned home that morning, out of habit I switched the radio on. A man, with an excessively churchy voice, pronounced, 'Are we not, dear friends, reminded of our Lord's Resurrection by pickles?' It was certainly an arresting statement. Although I was a devotee of piccalilli, I had never made the connection with the Easter story before. Perhaps he was going to link it with the spices the women brought to the tomb to anoint Jesus' body.

But I was entirely on the wrong tack. He was talking about Pickles the dog, whose picture featured in every newspaper after he had tracked down the stolen World Cup in a gutter in the East End of London. The cleric pointed out how the whole of Britain had been thrust into sorrow and shame when the World Cup originally went missing. Pickles' alertness had transformed that remorse into joy. 'And is that not,' he concluded, 'the same pattern found in Jesus' resurrection, where affliction is eclipsed by gladness?' His voice had the glee of a mathematician, rather tickled with his cleverness as he finds a solution to a complicated equation. I was not so tickled. 'God save me, and my parishioners, from boring, parsonical clergymen,' was my Easter Day's resolution.

Later, as I walked into Kirkwith Church I noticed Ivy Weighton and her husband, Rebecca and her two brothers, standing by Hans' grave in homage and in hope. As on Christmas Day, I ended my run of services by having dinner at their home, a rack of lamb to mark our Passover. As we sat around the table there was one chair left empty. Given the usual difficulty of finding anywhere to sit down in that kitchen, the vacant seat was doubly poignant. It hardly seemed a moment since our last feast, when Hans had regaled us with his tales of the land 'vere the vampires come vrom'. Now his absence was keenly felt.

Mrs Weighton had confided to me how she often laid a place for him at table, even miscounting the cups and pouring him a mug of tea. 'I must be getting absent-minded in my old age, Vicar.'

'Ivy,' I had reassured her, 'twenty years of care cannot grind to a halt in an instant. That place accidentally laid marks both a remembrance and an affection. You should see it as something sacred rather than as a lapse of memory.' You can never overestimate how long it takes to come to terms with loss, and I had encouraged Mrs Weighton to be gentle, rather than harsh, with herself in her grief.

A few hours later, as the light was slowly fading, the low evening sun shone through Kirkwith Church's west window and cast long sinister shadows which played on the dark pillars and walls. It was just the right atmosphere for one of my favourite lessons, set for this evening service on Easter Day. Describing how the risen Jesus came to his frightened band of disciples, huddled together behind closed doors, the account had great poignancy. I read it ponderously to maximize the dramatic effect:

'On the evening of that day, the first day of the week, the doors being shut where the disciples were, for fear of the Jews, Jesus came and stood among them and said...'

' 'Ere, one's got caught in my hair!' Doris Harsley's interruption undoubtedly gave the whole episode a novel turn. When I read or preach, I am all in favour of surprising people to grab their attention, but this surprise I could have done without. The pathos of the passage was lost for ever as Doris shrieked and ruffled her hair. The other women in the congregation quickly followed suit, crying hysterically, protecting their heads by covering them with their hands or pulling their hats down low. Eagle eyes scanned the rafters, like air-raid wardens scrutinizing the skies for enemy craft.

It was clear that something would have to be done about the bats. Their nesting in the roof of the nave had not bothered me until now. I often sat in the church at sunset and wondered at their darting and swooping. Any droppings were hard and easily cleared up, and I even welcomed them: when members of the congregation were careless and left a hymn book open on the pew ledge, tiny black dots of excreta could add interesting punctuation to otherwise turgid hymns.

The rest of the Withs were not as tolerant. In part it was to do with the legacy that Hans had left behind. Terrifying tales of vampires emerging at dusk to hunt their victims were not easily forgotten. Hans may have died, but his Transylvanian lilt still lingered on, haunting those who were brave enough to risk evening service in the half-light of Kirkwith Church.

Evensong congregations were dwindling, favourite lessons were being ruined by mass panic: without a doubt the bats would have to go. Bill Everingham knew a man who would do the deed: 'It's no good get-ting a lad-der and climb-ing up there to try and catch 'em, Vic-ar. They'd be off be-fore you were ev-en on t' sec-ond rung. What we need is for t' place to be fum-ig-at-ed in its ent-ir-it-y.'

I was very taken by Bill's ability to make eight words out of two. So taken in fact, that the drastic nature of his proposal didn't sink in until he called at the vicarage the day after next. He stood on my doorstep, as ruddy as ever, his eye with the gleam of the hunter about it. 'I've got Hen-ry Grim-ston 'ere, Vic-ar, to get rid o' bats. Could you come and give us a hand?'

I willingly agreed and climbed with Bill into the cab of Henry Grimston's lorry, which had pulled up outside my front door. On the side of the lorry were painted the ominous words, 'Grimston Bros, Pest Control and Fumigation Ltd'. It was packed with a cargo of heavy yellow canisters, a large skull and crossbones decorating each. I was only grateful that we'd had a dry spell of weather recently. Had it been October, the wagon with its lethal cargo would have sunk to its axles and would have poisoned my lawn into a wasteland before Bill's tractor had had the chance to tow it out.

As stalwart as ever, Doris and Sam Harsley had worked hard to clear linen, portable furniture and sundry ecclesiastical knick-knacks from the church building. All that remained was for Henry Grimston, Bill and me to unload the lorry, setting the two dozen canisters at various points in the church. Mr Grimston proved a rather dour and fussy foreman, agonizing about the precise siting of each drum. The wretched things were so heavy that I was quite happy to just plonk them down wherever and be done with it. But Mr Grimston tutted with dismay at this clerical incompetent, and with a 'Too draughty 'ere!' and 'Too still there!' he signified where he wanted them moving on to with a simple twist of his head. From the shrugs of his shoulders and grimaces he made it all too clear that anyone but an idiot would find such strategy obvious. He was like a general, arranging his crack troops and weaponry for battle, frustrated by having a substandard conscript.

By the time all the canisters were in place, I could feel my face red. My heart was pounding and I was panting with the exertion of it all. Although Bill was used to such manual labour, I noticed he was breathing heavily too. Worse was to follow. 'Got a handkerchief?' Mr Grimston barked.

'Use your own,' I felt like saying. Weak as ever, though, I nodded my head, as did Bill.

'Well fold 'em up and wrap 'em round your face. Then we'll light eight wicks each and get the hell out of here,' Mr Grimston ordered.

Bill and I meekly complied, and looking like bandits from a Wild West film, we put a match to the sulphur candles as directed. The deadly cocktail of hydrogen sulphide and sulphur dioxide which they gave off made my breathing even more heavy. By the time I had lit all eight, I was coughing uncontrollably and tears ran down my face from my stinging eyes. I plunged through the yellow fog, staggered through the church door and out into the welcome fresh air. Never mind about the bats; the wretched stuff had nearly made an end of me.

Mr Grimston sternly warned us not to go into the building until he returned to assess the situation three days later, when he would dispose of the burnt out canisters. Early in the morning on the day of his return, Bill and I opened all the church doors to disperse the fumes. By the time Mr Grimston arrived only a few wisps of yellow smoke remained. Some were absolutely still and seemed suspended in the sunlight. Others were caught in the draught and produced strange three-dimensional shapes which were constantly changing, like laser holograms before their time. The atmosphere was extremely pungent, acidic permeated with the smell of bad eggs. When I was in East Hull, my boss had an argument with a lady who strongly objected to the use of incense in Church. 'Madam,' he retorted, 'there are only two smells mentioned in the Bible.

One is incense, a fragrant offering to God. The other is fire and brimstone. I know which smell I prefer!' As I inhaled the sulphurous stench that morning, I knew which smell I preferred too.

As we picked up the considerably lighter canisters and carried them out of church, it struck me that a crucial ingredient was missing. After a few minutes I summoned up the courage and voiced my concerns to the ever-sullen Mr Grimston: 'I know this might seem a stupid question, but shouldn't there be a few dead bats around?' It was noticeable that not only was there a lack of corpses, but also I couldn't see a single bat dropping.

Mr Grimston put down the canister he was carrying, a sharp and noisy intake of breath advertising his exasperation. He squared his shoulders, rising to his full height of five foot six and gave me a pitying look, which he clearly reserved for idiot clergy. 'You don't think for one moment that they'd die in full flight, do you? The gas 'ould get to them up there in their nests. You just wait for a week or two for gravity to take its course. Bodies will be dropping down all over t' show.' Duly put in my place, I said no more. I was glad to see the last of this poisonous man and his poisonous cargo.

The obnoxious smell hadn't really cleared by Evensong the following Sunday night. It was another of my favourite lessons, Jesus raising Lazarus from the dead. I have quite a loud voice, but even that was nearly drowned out by the coughing of the congregation. As last week, the drama rose to its crescendo, with Jesus standing before the tomb where the decomposing body of his friend lay. 'Jesus called out with a loud voice...'

' 'Ere one's got caught in my hair again!' As on the previous Sunday, mass hysteria broke out in response to Doris' exclamation. The incessant coughing was now supplemented by arms thrashing about, frantically clawing the air. Once again the poignancy of a cherished reading had been destroyed. I decided to call it a day and ended the lesson there, with Lazarus condemned to remain entombed.

Instead I sat down in my stall and gazed at the scene. The bats were back in force, scudding about in the twilight, terrifying the congregation, apparently unaffected by the stench which had wrecked everyone else's respiratory system. Despite the worst that Mr Grimston could throw at them, they had survived miraculously. This point only served to fuel local folklore, so tenderly nurtured by Hans, that bats 'vere ve undead...'

Ridiculous though Hans' claims were, the bats did provide a striking symbol of life out of death. In that evening hour, as the rest of the world was winding down for slumber, they spoke of vitality, darting about here and there, unstoppable, disturbing the apparently undisturbable. Twice in one week their intervention had stopped me pronouncing Jesus' words of life. I had the funniest feeling, though, that God had still managed to breathe a picture of resurrection into the gloom.

Thirty years on, bats are a protected species, and we would have faced the severest penalty for merely attempting to rout them. Even so, when they were at their most vulnerable they managed to survive quite well. Just like God, I suppose.

Back on Easter Day evening I arrived home from my final Easter service feeling absolutely shattered. Lots of services; a favourite lesson ruined; mass hysteria at Evensong; a bat cull to plan: all had contributed to my exhaustion. I firmly shut the doors on the world, collapsed onto my settee and listened to Handel's *Messiah* on the Third Programme. Too tired to provide a meal, I guzzled the Easter egg Rebecca had given me, with Dewi chewing chocolate crumbs at my feet.

My drifting in and out of sleep gave the performance even more mystique than usual. Dreams impinged on the oratorio to give the performance a surreal quality, with tenors and sopranos abandoning their score and giving voice to my thoughts instead. Even granted that funny things happen in dreams, the choir's hammering in the middle of the 'Hallelujah Chorus' seemed so out of place that I woke up. It was then I realized that someone was battering hard on my front door.

Clearly the bats were not to be my only surprise visitors that night.

I roused myself and, as I staggered to the porch, I tried to flatten down my hair which had been ruffled as I slept. There on the doorstep stood George Broadhurst and Pam. 'Sorry to bother you, David, when you must be absolutely whacked,' George began.

I stretched my eyes open wide to give the pretence of alertness. 'No, not at all, it's great to see you. I was just meditating whilst listening to Handel's *Messiah* on the radio. Come on in.' I suppose I hadn't actually lied, although the depressed cushions against the arm of the settee gave the game away. The two of them must have concluded that my meditation had been very deep indeed.

'Hasn't it been a beautiful day?' George began, rather hesitantly.

'Yes,' I replied, 'beautiful from sunrise to sunset.' A pregnant pause followed.

'I'm sorry to say I missed the sunrise,' Pam broke in, speaking very quickly, 'and I'm afraid those bats spoilt the sunset for me. I was terrified of them. How on earth can you go into that church on your own, David?'

'I have this funny idea that God's around too,' I quipped. 'Although I sometimes find Him more frightening than the bats.'

After another awkward pause, George blurted out the reason for their visit. 'David, Pam and I haven't come to disturb your well-earned rest to talk about the weather and those wretched bats. We have decided we would like to get married. We felt you should be the first to hear our good news.'

I suppose I should have seen it coming. Every time I had visited the Manor since Christmas, Pam had fitted in so well, she and George had seemed so natural together. And yet the possibility of their marrying simply hadn't dawned on me. The touch of their hands at the palm cross party had surprised me, had been my first inkling. Even then, during a hectic Holy Week, I hadn't given it a second thought. Which was unfortunate, since my sleepy brain had to think fast now.

They were clearly compatible. They were both totally committed to the children and their well-being. As Jennifer's closest friend, Pam carried her posthumous approval. She was not in competition with her, in the way that so many second wives live in the first wife's shadow. In such fertile soil, love had grown.

But had it grown too soon, like those tender early shoots that are withered by an April frost? Maybe, maybe not. Only time would tell. Undoubtedly, George and the children would need further time to mourn: grief suppressed would wreak havoc elsewhere. But they wouldn't have to put on a brave face with Pam. She would respect that need because she too was missing Jennifer. In a real sense, her death had brought them together; love had blossomed as they reached out to help each other. I thought of Geoff and June Goodmanham, how their union had actually been strengthened as they coped with the tragedy of repeated miscarriage. If it could happen there, it could happen here. And the alternative of George and the children struggling alone with all the space in the world to air their grief was hardly an attractive one.

All these thoughts flashed through my mind in a fraction of a second, as I took in George and Pam's news. A broad smile came to my face as I exclaimed, 'I'm so, so very pleased for you. I wish you all the joy you deserve.' I meant it with all my heart. I didn't think resurrection had come too early.

George rushed out to his car and returned with a large bottle of champagne. 'I thought if I brought this in to start with, it might let the cat out of the bag. But now it is out of the bag, and we have the Vicar's approval…' he furrowed his brow as he intoned the last few words with mock seriousness. Then he lightened again, '…let's celebrate in style!' I got out the wine glasses. The cork popped and hit the ceiling, sending Dewi into a frenzy. He tore around the room, sending furniture rocking, a wild orbit of victory which caught the mood of us all.

'To you both!' I raised my voice above the spontaneous laughter which had broken out, raising my glass as a toast at the same time.

'To you, as well, David,' Pam responded. 'And all that the next few months holds for you.' She had the same twinkle in those blue eyes as she'd had the first time we had met. That twinkle not only had brought resurrection to the Manor this Eastertide, but hinted that it would break out elsewhere too.

CHAPTER FOURTEEN

The broad river tumbled through Kirkwith, foaming as its flood waters forced their way past the rocks in the middle of its stream. On each side of the river, after no more than a dozen yards, the ground rose steeply, soaring to form majestic green-sided mountains that made the Wolds look like molehills. The rugged terrain was teeming with rabbits who darted in and out of their burrows, their movement making the hillside seem to pulsate with life.

I was not dreaming, nor had the San Andreas Fault suddenly been reallocated to the Vale of York, forcing hills to appear overnight. The squire whose son bequeathed our church tower had also owned land in Swaledale and had been squire of the village there, which also bore the name Kirkwith. Given that connection, our twin village seemed an ideal venue for the parish's Easter Monday trip. We'd even managed to get one of the few farms which still made Wensleydale cheese to host a visit from us.

It was just after seven in the morning, that Ron, of the Ron Ran Run bus service, had driven his elder coach around the Withs, gathering people from various collection points. I stood outside the Everinghams' farm with a crowd consisting of Bill and Hannah, Sam and Doris Harsley, Ivy and Rebecca Weighton, and George and Pam (soon to be) Broadhurst and all four little Broadhursts. 'Oh hell, he's tak-ing us out in cronk-y one,' Bill commented, as the aged bus spluttered towards us.

'Now then, Bill, watch your language in front of t' Vicar,' Hannah chided, before turning to me and adding, 'He's in a bad mood because he had to get up too early.'

'I thought you always got up early, Bill,' I commented.

'Ay, I do,' he explained. 'But this morn-ing I had to get up two hours ear-li-er than us-u-al to milk t' cows. They're stub-born lit-tle beg-gars. They would-n't keep their milk 'til I came back from Swale-dale. It would have turned in-to cheese by then, most prob-ab-ly. With Cheese; now there's an idea! More mark-et-ab-le than Wen-sley-dale I fancy. Eas-ier to del-iv-er, at an-y rate.' Bill chuckled to himself as he mounted the bus steps.

Despite our early start, we still had to queue for half an hour at Selby, where the rickety toll bridge straddles the Ouse. The Swale is one of the Ouse's tributaries, so in effect we were saluting the grandson in passing, before pressing on to meet the grandfather. Pressing on in one of Ron's coaches is perhaps a contradiction in terms, but the little bus gamely chugged up the Great North Road before turning through Bedale and gently climbing towards Leyburn.

Excitement mounted as Wensleydale's hills rose above us, the flat top of Ingleborough in the distance, startling in its own right, doubly startling when compared to the Withs' intensely flat climes. There was both amusement and amazement as we snaked through Patrick Brompton and Constable Burton. It was not long before even the slowest wit latched on to any anthropomorphic connotations. Mrs Weighton's comment was the first, 'Ee, I'm leaving Constable Burton. It sounds like a line from a Victorian melodrama, the ill-done-to police-man's wife deciding she's had enough.' The young farm-hands, sprawled on the back seat, started reeling with raucous laughter when one of their number shouted, 'Let's go into Patrick Brompton.' I pretended not to notice. After all, nor-mal men may think about sex twenty times an hour; priests never.

Once through Leyburn we started the serious ascent up to Redmire Moor. The dust from the limestone quarry had settled on the road and verges, carpeting everything white. 'There's been a heavy frost, Bill!' Hannah Everingham ribbed her husband.

Bill, back to his usual humble self, took the joke. 'Ay, ay, but it'll soon blow a-way, though.' We kept our heads low as we sneaked through the Army rifle range, with red flags flapping a menacing warning, miles of moor violated by men playing soldiers. The young farm-hands got quite excited as a tank ground over a hill towards us. The tank driver, however, thought better of toying with Ron's ancient vehicle's affections and skulked off, like a cowardly lion in the presence of the leader of the pride.

Impressive though our solid bus was in seeing off potential assailants, whenever we dropped down a hill, Ron had the disconcerting habit of turning off the ignition. In response to my quizzical look, he shouted out, over his wife who was sitting beside him, 'She's overheating a bit. I need to turn her off as much as possible to cool her down.' The lads on the back seat started guffawing again; at that age you see double entendres in everything.

However, as we rounded the next corner, the guffawing came to a sudden halt and everyone fell silent as they drank in an amazing view. Swaledale was arrayed before us in all its breathtaking glory. Ron pulled the coach up, and we sat there and simply stared. The April-shower clouds scudded by, enhancing the scene by casting their shadow on the hills, emphasizing their contours.

'Ee, I could sit 'ere for ev-er.' Bill Everingham spoke for us all, his ponderous, booming voice catching the timelessness. Eternity however was interrupted by an impatient driver behind us tooting his horn. Ron let the handbrake out and we moved off, adding a roller-coaster ride to the other treats of the day as we free-wheeled down the steepest of descents into

Grinton. We careered around corner after corner, with passengers first being thrown one way and then another, frequently ending up on each other's laps. I was fortunate enough to have Rebecca sitting beside me, so I quite enjoyed the experience. Lean old men, perching next to twenty stone matrons, had that I-wish-I-was-somewhere-else look about them.

As we crossed over from Grinton into Reeth, we encountered the Swale for the first time. 'I was with your grandson, the Ouse this morning. He sends his regards,' I addressed the river in a mock-serious tone. Rebecca was loyal enough to laugh at my bizarre humour.

Others, who overheard the comment, were less sympathetic and furrowed their brows. 'What's he doing, talking to a river?' someone whispered to their neighbour.

'Oh, I've heard he was a bit shy,' the neighbour explained. 'It's easier talking to things that can't answer back when you're like that.'

'So you think he's shy do you?' the first speaker replied. 'He doesn't seem very shy to me. He's not too shy to be keen enough on that Weighton lass, any road. They say he's always round at that farm. It can't be he's attracted to Grandma's waxy cooking.' This intriguing conversation about my love life came to a premature end as the bus came to a halt in the market square. Which was a pity, since I for one was rather looking forward to the outcome. Rebecca's laughing eyes indicated that she too had enjoyed the story so far.

Immediately the bus parked, its passengers scurried off and scattered. Most headed for the lavatories with a determined and rather desperate look – it had been over three hours since we set off. They then wandered around at a more leisurely pace before homing in on a most wonderful baker's, which sold, amongst other things, a lush local delicacy called a Reeth Cake. I had been the second to discover the place, following hot on the heels of Doris Harsley. Fortunately I was able to come to the rescue of the highly perplexed shop assistant, whom Doris was shouting at in her usual breathless way, 'Are you deaf or something I asked for a couple of those rich looking cakes and 'ave you any Cornish pasties left?'

'I think she must be foreign,' the assistant confided to her colleague. 'Sprachen Sie Deutsch?' she bellowed. I guessed from her hopeless pronunciation that she would have been dumbfounded had Doris replied in German. I felt things had gone far enough and intervened:

'The lady would like two Reeth cakes and two Cornish pasties please.' The assistant gave me a queer look before packing up Doris' order.

'I said exactly what you said,' Doris commented as we came out of the shop. 'Why didn't they pay attention to me?'

I was anxious not to hurt her feelings on what was proving such a happy day. 'I think in these primitive parts the men tend to do the shopping, so they're not used to dealing with women,' I said, tongue in cheek.

My white lie satisfied Doris, whose final verdict was, 'Well fancy that Vicar aren't there some funny folk about?' Indeed there are.

Having purchased our provisions we clambered back into the bus and chugged down the Dale. The road stayed close to the Swale, precariously overhanging it in parts, until we took a right fork at Gunnerside and rose up into the hills. The lane was even narrower than our single tracks in the Withs. With a rock face climbing to the right of us and a sheer drop to the left of us, a strained quiet prevailed. Ron, however, took it all in his stride. Suddenly the lane widened for a few yards, and he pulled over and parked on a grassy verge before giving us the briefest of instructions: 'I'll leave it here until we set off at two, sharp. Door'll be open if you want to sit in out o' rain.'

Immediately the young farm-hands got off and scampered up the sheer hillside like mountain goats. Those who had neither the footwear nor the energy chose a more level walk along the road, before returning to dodge the shower and eat their rations of Cornish pasty and Reeth cake, a culinary combination which managed to marry England's extremities.

I ambled along the road with Rebecca and her mother and Hannah and Bill Everingham. After about a hundred yards, Mrs Weighton chirped up, 'Now you two young uns don't want to be saddled with us old uns, pottering about as if you were on a promenade at Scarborough. Have a scramble up t' hillside to see what you can see, and leave Han, Bill and me to have a good gossip. You be our eyes and legs for us and describe t' view to us later. Now go on, now, be off with you.' There we were, two young people well on in our twenties, well established in our respective careers, being chided like two unadventurous children, too timid to leave mum's skirts. We took it all meekly, duly climbing the mountainside and leaving our seniors at the base camp, two people under orders. The meekness was feigned on my part, since I had been plotting for most of the journey how to separate Rebecca from the rest of the crowd without raising any suspicions. Although, to judge by the conversation I had overheard on the bus, suspicions were already roused.

Once we had arrived breathless at the peak, we sat on a wall to eat our lunch, with mackintoshes over our heads as shelter from the frequent showers. From our Olympian heights we viewed the other Kirkwith, a few stone houses huddled round a stone church, a stone bridge over the Swale. White smoke curled from a dozen chimneys and made it look the homeliest of scenes, all cast in miniature by our lofty perch.

Curiously, though we were less than half a mile away, the weather down by the river was clearly far worse than it was up at the top, with the rain driving down in sheets. In one of the fields I noticed a man, crouched against a very wet dry-stone wall. Though he had his coat wrapped around him, it was affording him minimal protection against the penetrating squall. Given such adverse conditions, I wondered why he stayed there. Yet stay there he did, alert, watching intently. It was lambing time, and a few new-born lambs staggered about uncertainly on the wet closely cropped grass.

It was clear from their bulk that some of the sheep had yet to give birth. One such animal buckled over; birth pangs were clearly beginning. Immediately the man by the wall sprang up and ran over, kneeling down beside her on the damp ground, stroking her, easing the birth. Clearly he was a good shepherd.

We watched intently, moved by his natural care, sitting in silence. That I was able to chat away to Rebecca without being tongue-tied signified her specialness. That I was able to share a silence with her on that hilltop, without feeling the need to fill the quiet with words, signified her uniqueness in my eyes. 'Rebecca, will you marry me?' I softly asked.

A further silence followed which seemed to last an age. 'Only if you promise me one thing,' Rebecca eventually replied.

'What?' I asked, eager and anxious simultaneously. What Herculean feat was she about to propose to win her hand? A mammoth feast consisting of 57 varieties of wax? A lifetime condemned to using the same tea-towel? A scale model of York Minster, constructed entirely of past copies of Farmers Gazette? All these and many more flashed through my mind as Rebecca bided her time.

'I'd love to marry you,' she declared. 'Just as long as you don't announce our engagement on that cronky old bus!'

I was in a dream for the rest of the day, only partially engaging with the marvellous things around me because of being engaged to someone more marvellous. The sky, though still unsettled, seemed twice as bright, the closely cropped grass seemed twice as green, the water of the raging Swale seemed twice as white, whiter than fuller's bleach. We clambered a little over the ridge before descending to walk along the lane by the side of the Swale. A Land-Rover drove past us, with bales of straw in the back. About fifty yards ahead of us it started tooting its horn. Literally hundreds of sheep, from miles around, suddenly converged on the vehicle which drew to a halt. The driver got out, tossed a couple of bales into a manger, and left the sheep to feed. Another good shepherd. Since one had prompted my proposal, I was getting quite fond of them.

We drove to Hawes over the Buttertubs Pass. You can't use 'breathtaking' too often in this magic land, but if you were only allowed to use it once, this Pass would win the accolade. With views sweeping down the length of Swaledale and then over into Wensleydale, it presents a most glorious panorama. The limestone formation of the Pass itself is a sheer wonder, with streams tumbling down its sides, glistening like veins of silver. We stopped to examine the Buttertubs, pillars of limestone which sank deep into the ground. Apparently they were so named because local farmers would store butter in their cool depths prior to taking it to market in Hawes.

Rebecca and I climbed the precipitous path down the Buttertubs, accompanied by Pam and George, who had baby Simon strapped safely to his back. The other three children scuttled down ahead of us, as carefree as we were cautious, oblivious to any danger. As we stood stunned once again into silence by sheer wonder, Pam took advantage of the four of us being alone. 'George and I would be delighted if you would join us for an engagement dinner on Wednesday night,' she said, looking directly at the two of us.

'How on earth do you know?' Rebecca blurted out, before I had the chance to signal whose engagement Pam was talking about.

'George and Pam came to see me last night, to tell me they're getting married,' I explained to my bewildered fiancee. 'Snap!' I added. I could tell from Pam's look that she had twigged already; George, with his mind on other things as always, was only just cottoning on.

'Oh, I'm so pleased for you both. Congratulations,' Pam said, with a genuine thrill in her voice. 'Wednesday night will be an engagement dinner twice over.'

'Could I ask one favour,' I added, 'I'd be grateful if you kept it to yourselves; we still have to tell Rebecca's parents and my parents.'

'Of course. Your secret's safe with me,' Pam assured us. 'In fact, it's been safe for weeks, so it can stay safe just a wee bit longer,' she laughed, that twinkle there again in her blue eyes. George still had that puzzled look. 'I'll explain it all to you later, darling,' she added, hugging him affectionately.

As we drove down into Hawes, I got Ron to attempt the same trick that the shepherd had played in his Land-Rover. Gamely, he tooted his horn repeatedly. Even though it made a sound like a severely dyspeptic cow, it sufficiently resembled the Land-Rover's horn to have the desired effect. Or so I thought. Yet not a single sheep stepped a single step towards us. One or two lifted their heads up and looked us up and down, as if to say, 'What do those idiots think they're up to?' But other than that, nothing.

A couple of weeks later, Jesus' words from John's Gospel sprang out of the page at me: 'I am the good shepherd. The good shepherd lays down his life for the sheep ... the good shepherd knows his own and his own know him.' Those words were such a vivid reminder of what we had encountered in Swaledale, that I seriously began to wonder if Christ had paid the area a visit too. If so, paradise would come as a bit of a disappointment.

'We're just about to come into Hawes,' Ron commented, causing guffaws from the back of the bus once again. We wandered around the busy little market town for a while before driving on to see Hardraw Force. We first had to buy a ticket at the Green Dragon Inn – locals enjoying an Easter Monday drink seemed oblivious to this procession of trippers of sundry sizes – and then we gained access to the steep-sided gully. We scrambled along for half a mile whilst a continuous thunderous roar rose to a crescendo. Then as we rounded a corner, there it was, a waterfall, spouting from a cliff 90 feet above our heads, crashing down onto the dark lichened rocks below. Another sight which was utterly breathtaking in its immensity, in a day already saturated with wonder.

'It is dangerous to walk behind the waterfall', a rather dishevelled sign informed us. 'Come on, let's go,' I urged Rebecca. Our perilous journey was watched by a crowd of parishioners who were clearly in two minds about whether they should be amazed by their vicar's adventurousness or by his choice of companion. When I slipped on a mossy stone and nearly ended up in the dark, cold pool hollowed out by the Force, 'Oooh,' shrieked the crowd, as one, their anxiety audible above the waterfall's noise. When Rebecca caught my hand and steadied me, 'Ah,' the same crowd gasped, in sympathy. I looked back at them all, through a filter provided by the teeming cascade; the sepia-like effect casting them in a kindly, flattering light. Less than a year ago I had known none of them; now I looked on them fondly from my watery perch, each one special, almost family to me.

We scrambled safely out at the other side, to wild applause from our delighted audience. It had all been a bit of an adventure, a bit of a risk. Even on my greatest day, it was right to be reminded that the sword of Damocles hung over my head.

'You're a game one, you are, Vicar,' Sam Harsley commented as we trudged back to the bus. 'I was thinking of that time when we had our own waterfall in Kirkwith Church, and you fair shot up that ladder to clear t' snow. My impetigo would have made an end of me even before I began if I'd tried to scuttle behind that Force. I'm right proud of you, I am. And that Weighton girl's as brave as you. You'll make a good team.'

'There's another one who knows already,' I thought to myself.

We returned to Hawes for a fish and chip tea before making our slow way down Wensleydale's twisting, turning road. Halfway down the dale we turned off the main road, with the bus juddering and jolting along the track to a farm half-way up the hillside. We all spilled out of the coach as the farmer and his wife rushed out to welcome us, four sheepdogs circling us, giving us a wary eye, less sure of us than their master and mistress.

Jack and Edna Spennymoor, distant cousins of the Everinghams, kindly showed us their cheeses and explained how they were produced. The whole party turned a shade of green when Jack showed us rennet, one very essential ingredient: 'Now we take this from t' cow's stomach and t' acid is mixed with t' milk to curdle it in this vat 'ere.'

Normal colour returned to us all as we were shown the traves, the shelves on which the individual cheeses, bandaged in linen, dried out. As we got to the back of the dairy, Jack pointed to one shelf. 'If you'd all like to 'elp yourselves, me and t' missus have made forty little Wensleydale cheeses for you to take home as a memento.'

Most of us couldn't resist having a taste of Jack's generosity as our little bus chugged back down the Great North Road. The cheese was far moister than any shop-bought Wensleydale cheese, far creamier. A delicious end to a truly delicious day. As it got later into the evening, Rebecca fell asleep beside me, breathing rhythmically, her head on my shoulder. I felt immensely proud, as all eyes in the omnibus were fixed on us. Or at least those that were still awake.

The chugging of the tired engine resonated with the rhythmic breathing of those in slumber. As I too dozed off, the background noise beat out an hexameter in my floating mind, 'This-is-where-you-belong … the-best-is-yet-to-come.' Sweet dreams indeed.